a writer of penny dreadfuls

a prima ballerina

a coffin maker's daughter

a physician

"For I have all the instincts of . . ."

a secret agent

a stockbroker

a trapped miner

a postmaster's daughter

a caterpillar

a princess in a tower

a prized stallion

a junior Sherlock Holmes

a prima ballerina

a Buddhist monk

"For I have all the instincts of . . ."

a princess in a tower

a writer of penny dreadfuls

a stockbroker

a five-star general

a coffin maker's daughter

an assistant librarian

a physician

a sedated cow

a caterpillar

a postmaster's daughter

a highland hermit

a secret agent

a startled rabbit

a lion

a trapped miner

a cheese-maker's niece

·ANYONE BUT·
Ivy Pocket

By CALEB KRISP

Illustrations by
BARBARA CANTINI

ANYONE BUT

Ivy Pocket

By CALEB KRISP

GREENWILLOW BOOKS
An Imprint of HarperCollins Publishers

Text copyright © 2015 by Caleb Krisp.
Illustrations copyright © 2015 by Barbara Cantini
First published in 2015 in Great Britain by Bloomsbury Childrens under the title
Anyone But Ivy Pocket. First published in 2015 in the United States by Greenwillow Books.
The right of Caleb Krisp to be identified as the author of this work has been asserted by
him in accordance with the Copyright, Designs and Patents Act, 1988.

The text of this book is set in Spectrum MT Std. Book design by Sylvie Le Floc'h

∞∞∞

Library of Congress Cataloging-in-Publication Data.
Krisp, Caleb. Anyone but Ivy Pocket / by Caleb Krisp ; illustrations by Barbara Cantini.
"Greenwillow Books."   pages cm
Summary: "Fate intervenes when Ivy is called to the sickbed of a dying duchess and
is charged with delivering a mystical (and possibly cursed) diamond necklace
to the utterly revolting Matilda Butterfield for her twelfth birthday"—
Provided by publisher. ISBN 978-0-06-236434-0 (hardback)
[1. Adventure and adventurers—Fiction. 2. Orphans—Fiction.
3. Necklaces—Fiction. 4. Blessing and cursing—Fiction. 5. Aristocracy
(Social class)—Fiction.] I. Cantini, Barbara, illustrator. II. Title.
PZ7.1.K75An 2015
[Fic]—dc23   2014044994
15 16 17 18 19 CG/RRDH 10 9 8 7 6 5 4 3 2 1
Greenwillow Books

For my housekeeper Mrs. Cuttlefish,
who I buried in the garden

1

I found the note upon my lady's bed.

It read as follows:

Dear Miss Pocket,

As you can see, I have gone. Do not follow me. I repeat, DO NOT follow me!

I am sailing for South America for no other reason than it is far enough away from Paris to ensure that I never see you again. The hotel bill has been paid. As for your wages, after taking into account my pain and suffering, I have left you the sum of one pound. Which is generous, given your conduct. You are now on your own.

Good riddance,

Countess Carbunkle

I was stunned. Shocked. Appalled. Hadn't I been a loyal and kind maid to the Countess? *Hadn't I?* I thought long and hard about my conduct, and I could find nothing wanting in it. If I needed further proof that Countess Carbunkle was unhinged, I now had it. The woman was bonkers.

Things had begun so promisingly. Countess Carbunkle had lured me away from a wonderful family in London. The Midwinters were delightfully eccentric and I had been very happy with them—until the Countess came to stay at Midwinter Hall. She spent a month at the mansion and saw me performing my duties, bringing order and cheer wherever I went. On the eve of her return to Paris, she practically *begged* me to come and work for her. In truth, I was reluctant to leave Lady Prudence and her six children. I admit they were an ugly bunch (Master Tobias had a head like a piglet and Miss Lucy was surely part bullfrog), but Midwinter Hall was the first real home I'd ever known.

Despite that, the chance to travel and see the world was impossible to resist.

Paris. We had gone to Paris. It was glorious, and I was

glorious in it. I was taller in Paris. Prettier too. And as I was a twelve-year-old lady's maid of the highest quality, Countess Carbunkle came to depend on me in all matters. I was always by her side, day and night, ready to be of service.

At times she was very difficult to find. One morning I found her crouching behind a chest of drawers with a sheet over her head. Another time she saw me coming and pretended to be a lamp. Only once did my lady manage to escape me—she used a side door in her dressing room to steal away and visit an old friend who was staying in the hotel. I put all of this odd behavior down to the fact that Countess Carbunkle was an aristocrat and therefore barking mad.

Just how unhinged she was didn't become clear until the great disaster.

It was at the end of our first week in that magical city. Countess Carbunkle had been invited to a grand dinner party at our hotel. The cream of French society was to be in attendance. At first, Countess Carbunkle had been reluctant to let me accompany her.

"I don't want you at this dinner, do you hear?" she spat,

trying to push me out of the elevator. "Good lord, how did I ever let Lady Prudence talk me into taking you? She knew I needed a new maid and seized the chance to be rid of you. Anyone, that's what I told her, *anyone* but Ivy Pocket. But she swore you weren't nearly as insufferable as you look. What a fool I am!"

"Well, of course you are," I said, weaving around her and slipping back into the elevator. "But you must think clearly, Countess. This dinner party is a very great affair and you are as blind as a bat. Face it, dear—you *need* me."

Countess Carbunkle huffed, but I could see the fight had gone out of her. "Do not embarrass me, or I will have your head."

The dining room was aglow with silver candelabras and hundreds of fresh orchids. Dinner began in earnest. Countess Carbunkle was seated between the president of France (fat, utterly bald) and a princess from Romania (short; hairy chin). But I was troubled. It was all on account of the turtle soup. The Countess did not handle soup well. She tended to dribble.

I stepped forward as my lady took her first spoonful. She slurped majestically; a trail of soup tracked its way down her chin. With heartbreaking discretion, I hurried to Countess

Carbunkle's side, gently tilted back her head, and used the hem of my apron to wipe her chin.

"Are you all right, Countess?" asked the president, with a mocking grin. "You seem to be having some trouble with your maid."

"All is well, Mr. President," cried the Countess, smiling wildly. Then she turned to me, slapping my hands away. "Go!" she whispered. "Leave this instant!"

"Calm yourself, dear," I said. "Dribbling is no crime. I'm sure your mother was a dribbler and your father too."

While Countess Carbunkle's watery green eyes glistened with rage, I could see the anguish behind them. My lady was in desperate need of help. "Attention please," I said, placing a supportive arm around my mistress. "Like many true aristocrats, the Countess has a drooping bottom lip and no real chin to speak of. This makes eating soup both difficult to achieve and unpleasant to behold."

The Countess gasped. Her teeth clenched. Her nostrils flared like a charging bull. Then she started to growl at me. Surely not a good sign. "I have had a great many maids in my long life, Ivy Pocket, but until now I have never wanted to stuff one in a cannon, point it toward the ocean, and light the fuse! In short, I loathe you!"

The poor dear had lost her mind. Urgent action was required. With lightning speed—for I have all the natural instincts of a physician—I grabbed the Countess by the back of her neck and plunged her face into the fruit punch. It was the only remedy to relieve her brain fever. As Countess Carbunkle came up for air, she shrieked like a donkey and started to sob. I took that as a good sign. Not wishing to make a spectacle of the Countess, I threw a napkin over her head and began to dry her face. In response, my lady called me a variety of unpleasant names and begged the Princess of Romania to fetch a musket and shoot me.

In no time, the entire dining room was ringing with mocking laughter. It was really rather awkward. The moment was saved by Countess Carbunkle, who decided that it was the perfect time to run screaming from the room. Which allowed me to make a dignified exit, following swiftly after her.

When I got back to our suite, I found the door locked.

I knocked, of course. Called out. Banged rather loudly. But nothing. I slept out in the corridor. It was perfectly comfortable. So comfortable, in fact, that I did not wake until well after sunrise the next morning. Worse still, I awoke to find that Countess Carbunkle had fled the hotel in the early hours. The suite was empty. All that remained was the note upon my lady's bed.

I collected my carpetbag from the wardrobe and sat down by the window. I needed time to think. The situation was rather serious. My options, rather limited. I had one pound to my name. No job. No ticket back to England. No prospects. What to do?

I am remarkably good in a crisis—for I have all the natural instincts of a five-star general—so in no time at all, I had formed a plan. I picked up my carpetbag and headed down to the lobby, replacing my anxiety with the flickering flame of hope. The streets of Paris were sure to lead to adventure and opportunity. No doubt I would stumble upon something utterly thrilling. Or I might end up a beggar, friendless and

starving. Which would be terribly inconvenient. But on the bright side—how wonderfully tragic!

The lobby was a hive of activity. People coming and going and rushing about. I stopped for a moment to drink it all in. Which is when it hit me—the answer to my problem. It was staring me in the face. A hotel like this was full of travelers from England—and who better to wait upon them than a genuine English maid? I would speak to the manager and apply for a position.

He was sure to love me.

"We have no vacancies," said Mr. Gateau firmly, scratching at his thin mustache. "Besides, you are too young to work at the Grand."

"I am twelve," I declared with considerable pride, "and you will not find a better maid in all of Paris. My talents are legendary."

Mr. Gateau smiled thinly. "Yes, I have heard all about your *talents*. Countess Carbunkle had much to say about you before she departed the hotel."

"Well, there you go," I said, slapping Mr. Gateau on the

shoulder to cement our budding friendship. "So, when can I start?"

"Out!" he bellowed.

A rather ill-mannered doorman was escorting me from the hotel when a bellboy raced across the lobby and called my name. The poor chap was rather breathless. "Are you Ivy Pocket?"

"Of course I am, dear."

"The maid who was traveling with Countess Carbunkle?"

I was thrilled that he had heard of me. But not surprised. A good maid gets a reputation. "That's right," I said.

"She wants to see you," said the boy gravely.

I gasped. "Countess Carbunkle? Is she still here?"

The bellboy shook his head. "The Duchess of Trinity. You've heard of her?"

Well, of *course* I had. My lady had called on the Duchess just the day before—slipping away from me rather sneakily, and paying a visit to her private apartment on the top floor. Countess Carbunkle said her old friend was the richest woman in England, though she had lived abroad for the past sixty years. Not sure why exactly. Something about a broken heart.

"What on earth does she want with me?" I said.

The bellboy looked alarmingly pale. "She is dying. Please, just come."

The next thing I knew we were hurrying up the grand staircase.

When I first set eyes on the Duchess of Trinity, two things were immediately clear. One, she was gravely ill. Two, she was monumentally fat. A great big slug of a woman—part goddess, part hippopotamus. She was as magnificent as she was terrifying. The poor creature was lying in the center of a large brass bed, her face a sickly shade of yellow, her enormous body spreading out on every side like an avalanche. The Duchess's eyes were shut, her head sunk deep into a pile of silk cushions. I might have thought her dead if it hadn't been for the wheezing breaths escaping from her gray lips.

I shivered. Which was shameful. Why was I feeling so spooked by a sick old lady? I was no coward. In fact, my bravery was legendary. Hadn't I saved that blind man from a runaway carriage by pushing him to safety—and wasn't I crushed

11

under the wheels in the process, horrifically injured, yet when I woke up in hospital my first thought was not about myself, but rather, the blind man I had saved? And wasn't I awarded a medal for bravery by Queen Victoria herself? Yes indeed! Well . . . no. Not exactly. Some of the particulars may be exaggerated. But I had certainly *thought* about doing such things. Which was practically the same thing.

The suite was enormous, filled with plump sofas, fine carpets, a grand piano, and assorted antiques. But what did I care for any of that, when England's richest—and possibly fattest—woman was lying right in front of me?

All right, I must admit to a tiny pinch of fear—like icy water in my veins—as I stood there by the bed. Just the two of us. Me and the Duchess of Trinity. No witnesses. Nobody to help should the Duchess wake up, roll me in some sugar, and have me for lunch.

The Duchess's heavy eyelids suddenly shot open. "Close your mouth, child, you look like a bucket."

I gulped. Like a frightened infant on a stormy night. Which was infuriating!

"You're a plain little thing, aren't you?" she said next.

"You poor deluded creature," I replied, finding my voice. "Dying has sapped the strength from your eyes. I'm remarkably pretty, and that's a genuine fact."

The old woman shrugged. "As you wish."

A cool breeze blew through the balcony doors, fluttering the Duchess's halo of white hair. For some reason it made me rather sad. I felt it was probably the right time to say something kind and reassuring. I am skilled in such small talk.

"Your eyes are a fine shade of green," I said softly. "The rest of you is a nightmare, but your eyes are lovely."

She smiled faintly. "Are you hungry?"

I had helped myself to some crispy bacon from the silver breakfast tray sitting outside the Duchess's apartment door, so I wasn't at all hungry. "No thank you," I said.

"Well then, down to business," announced the Duchess. "You've been traveling as Countess Carbunkle's maid?"

"More a companion than a maid," I said. "That half-blind fossil loves me like a granddaughter. Or, at very least, a second cousin twice removed. In fact—"

"Hush!" The Duchess's green eyes fixed on mine. "I know you have been abandoned. Left high and dry in this ghastly city. Did you *really* plunge the Countess's head into the fruit punch?"

"How else was I to relieve her brain fever?" I said crossly.

The Duchess looked rather pleased. "Countess Carbunkle told me you were abandoned at the Harrington Home for Unwanted Children, aged five. Is that correct?"

"Highly doubtful," I said. "I'm certain I grew up in a stupendously loving family."

"Claptrap," muttered the old woman, though she appeared to smile faintly. "Before you came to Paris you worked for the Midwinters of London?"

"Oh, yes," I said. "I was with them for nearly a year. Delightful family. Monstrously unattractive, but delightful."

"Then you are familiar with Lady Prudence's cousin, Lady Amelia Butterfield?"

"I met her once or twice," I said, utterly baffled as to why she was asking me such things.

The Duchess of Trinity lifted her head from the pillow, her double chin swelling like a balloon. "And her daughter, Matilda?"

"Never met the girl," I said. "Why?"

"Go to the piano," instructed the Duchess of Trinity, "and open the lid."

I did as she said.

"You know how to play?"

"Very well," I said. "Miss Lucy hated having to practice, but her mother insisted—Miss Lucy would give me a toffee apple if I would go into the music room and pretend to be her. Turns out, I'm a natural."

"You are familiar with "'Row, Row, Row Your Boat'?" asked the Duchess.

I laughed. "Everyone knows *that* one, dear."

"Excellent. Play it."

"Duchess, if you wish to hear a tune, let me play some Beethoven. You will be moved to tears." I smiled proudly. "Everyone cries when I play the piano."

"Do as I ask," she demanded. "'Row, Row, Row Your Boat.'" Just once. From start to finish."

The old bat was clearly off her rocker. But as I had nowhere else to go, and homelessness awaited me out on the streets of Paris, I sat down and played the tune. As I hit the last note, I could feel the piano begin to vibrate beneath my fingers. Softly at first. Then more urgently. It was as if the ground was shaking. Then I heard a mechanism cranking from deep inside the instrument. *Click. Click. Click.* Without warning, a panel at the front of the keyboard began to move. It slid back. *Click. Click. Click.* It only took a few moments, then there it was. A hidden chamber. A small cavity, cast in darkness.

"Reach inside," instructed the Duchess of Trinity.

Now I'm a brave girl by nature. Plucky. The courage of a lion. But the thought of sliding my hand into that dark recess— gaping at me like an open mouth—filled me with a small amount of trepidation. Still, I wasn't about to let that stop me. Carefully, I reached into the blackness. My fingers quickly hit upon an object. It felt soft and firm, all at the same time.

"Pull it out," the Duchess said.

It was a box. Roughly the size of a book. Covered in plush black velvet. An intricate silver keyhole carved in the top.

"Bring it to me."

I set the box in the Duchess's puffy hands. She held it like it was a sacred offering, her green eyes glistening in wonder as she stared at it. Then she set it down on her lap, and her plump hand vanished into the bedcoverings and came out again holding a brass key.

She dropped it on the bed, her gaze never leaving the box. "The key, child," she whispered. "Quickly!"

2

I slid the key into the lock and turned it. A crisp, heavy *snap* broke the silence. The velvet lid flew open. I felt a rush of anticipation. What on earth was I going to see? Perhaps a severed finger with a signet ring still upon it. Or an eyeball, frozen by the terror of a violent death. Or a human heart, still beating.

"Look," cried the Duchess as she pulled out a perfectly ordinary necklace with a perfectly ordinary (if rather large) diamond hanging from it.

I was crushed. "Is that it? Is that *all*?"

The old woman smiled grimly. "You are not impressed?"

"Oh, I'm sure it's lovely," I told her, sitting down on the bed.

"No doubt it's worth a fortune."

"Priceless, in fact," said the Duchess. She looked at it hungrily. "I haven't had the stone long, but I will be sad to part with it—though it has tormented me so."

Tormented her? The old bat was bonkers. Dying does that to people, I supposed.

The Duchess huffed. "You look at the necklace, and all you see is a pretty jewel. But the Clock Diamond is so much more than that. It is a thing of withering power."

I frowned. I may have even snorted (but in a dainty fashion).

"You doubt me?" said the Duchess, and now she looked rather delighted. "Well, I don't blame you. But the fact remains, this diamond has several *fascinating* qualities. It keeps time, for one thing." She thrust the necklace towards me and hissed, "Look!"

If only to soothe this excitable creature, I did as she asked. The diamond was large, roughly the size and shape of an egg, but flatter. Above it, a tiny clock was set into the elegant silver mounting that connected the chain to the stone.

"Day or night, sunrise or starlight—you can set your watch by that necklace," said the Duchess. "And you will find no mechanism within the clock, nor can it be wound. Yet it has run for centuries."

I frowned. "But how?"

"The clock is powered by the stone," said the Duchess with eager delight. "No matter where you are in the world, the clock will adjust itself, right to the last second—as if by an unseen hand."

I'd never heard of a diamond that could do such a thing. But I simply refused to lose my head over a silly clock. Beneath it, the stone sparkled and flared in the candlelight of the Duchess's dim bedroom, which was probably why I didn't see it. The *next* thing about the stone that made it different.

Inside, in the center of the diamond, a gray mist billowed and churned. Then, without warning, it parted, and I could see the sun high over Paris—its shimmering glow bathing the rooftops in honey-colored light. The whole city seemed to be captive inside that stone. It was remarkable, I suppose. Remarkable, but nothing more than a clever trick.

"There is even more," said the Duchess eagerly. "When the stone chooses, it can give the one who holds it a glimpse of the past, the present, or the future. Not just their own, but others' too. These visions can delight." Her eyes clouded over. "And they can horrify." Now *that* was interesting. I didn't believe it, of course. But still, it was a delicious thought. "Does the stone do anything else?" I asked.

The Duchess closed her eyes. "Nothing that concerns you, child."

I stared at the stone and began to sense an opportunity. The old woman was dying. She had sent for me. Showed me this precious necklace. Entrusted me with the key. There was only one possible explanation. "You dear, sweet, sickly old windbag!" I cried, flinging myself at her. "You are giving me the Clock Diamond! Passing this mystical legacy from one generation to the next. Bless you, dear!"

Her laughter was weak and dry, but it filled the room. "Don't be a fool. You are right in assuming I have business with you in connection with the stone. But as a messenger and nothing more."

"Oh." I cleared my throat and stood up. "Of course I didn't really think—"

"Your task is a simple one," interrupted the Duchess of Trinity. "I mentioned the Butterfields. I wish you to take the Clock Diamond to their estate in Suffolk—it is called Butterfield Park and will be easy enough to find—and present the necklace as a gift from me."

"A gift?" I said.

The Duchess nodded. "For Matilda Butterfield. She is about to turn twelve. You are to present the stone as a present for her birthday. There is going to be a ball in her honor—give it to her then, in front of all of her guests, and not a moment before. Do you think you're equal to the task?"

I shrugged. "I'm sure I can manage to deliver a silly old diamond to Butterfield Park."

"I am not finished," snapped the Duchess. "If you accept this commission, you must understand that it comes with conditions. Strict, unbreakable conditions." She lifted a plump finger and beckoned me closer. "You are not to try on the necklace. Not once. Nobody is to see it before the ball. And absolutely no one is to wear the diamond except for Matilda Butterfield. Do you understand?"

Frankly, I was insulted. Did this half-crazed fatso *really* think that I was some sort of unprincipled street urchin who would try on her precious diamond the second I was alone? The nerve!

"You must present the stone to Matilda come what may." The old woman's voice hissed like a rattlesnake. "In front of her guests. Do you understand, child?"

"Yes, yes, I understand. No offense, dear, but you seem rather overexcited by this whole business. That can't be good for your health. You know, being at death's door and whatnot."

"Do not worry about my health," snapped the Duchess of Trinity. She took a shallow breath. "There is a ship sailing for England this afternoon. You will be on it."

"That's a lovely idea," I said, going to the window and staring out at the morning sun, "but I haven't any money. A girl can't sail if she can't afford a ticket."

"Stuff and nonsense," said the Duchess with a wave of her hand. "Do this thing for me, and I will pay for your passage back to England and more besides." She nodded at the table by the window. "You will find everything you need over there."

"Duchess," I said casually, plonking myself back down on the bed, "when you say 'and more besides'—exactly how much more? I only ask because my savings are rather low at present."

"Five hundred pounds," said the Duchess. "Fifty now. The rest payable through my lawyer, Horatio Banks, the day after the birthday ball." She reached out and grabbed my hand (hers was astoundingly cold to the touch). "Will you do it, Ivy? Will you give me your solemn word?"

"You have it," I declared, looking grim as an undertaker. "I will hang the Clock Diamond around Miss Matilda's neck myself."

"You won't try it on, no matter how strong the temptation?" she asked sternly.

"Never," I promised. Then a frown creased my glorious forehead. "Forgive me for asking, dear; I'm normally not one to stick my nose where it doesn't belong—having all the natural instincts of a highland hermit—but what is your connection to the Butterfields?"

The Duchess groaned softly, her eyelids fluttering.

"Matilda's grandmother, Lady Elizabeth, is an old friend. We grew up together as girls. I'm ashamed to say we had a falling-out over a young gentleman many years ago. It seemed terribly important then, but rather foolish now. The necklace is a peace offering, I suppose. There is a letter inside the box for Lady Elizabeth—give it to her when you first arrive at the house."

"It is a monstrously generous gift, dear," I said with just a pinch of envy.

"Lady Elizabeth adores Matilda—all of her hopes and wishes reside in that child. You have no idea how it soothes me, as death draws near, just knowing that I can bestow this gift on her." The old woman pointed to the box. "Come, it is time to lock the necklace away."

I was about to hand the stone back to the Duchess when it began to pulse in my hand. Faintly, to begin with. Then with great intensity. Silvery light, soft and rippling, seemed to spill out from it, illuminating every corner of the chamber. The necklace felt warm against my skin.

"It is happening!" hissed the Duchess, trying to lift her head from the pillow. "Tell me, child, what can you see?"

At first I saw nothing; the light was too bright. But soon it dimmed and, as before, a billowing gray mist churned and swirled, then parted. I stared closely. What I saw as the mist cleared was a wide hallway. Lit by gaslight, but dim—the corridor was long, paneled in dark wood, with red carpet upon the floor. A door was revealed. A silver tray stood on a trolley beside it. I recognized it immediately. It was the door to the very apartment I was sitting in. I was about to tell the Duchess what I could see, when something moved. No, *someone* moved. Emerging from the shadows and stopping before the Duchess's door was a woman, though her face was shrouded in darkness. She wore a gray dress. Dark gloves. The woman dropped down, crouching outside the door. She pressed her face to the keyhole. She was peering inside!

"What is it, child?" snapped the Duchess impatiently. "What do you see?"

I dropped the stone and raced from the bedroom. Bolting as fast as my legs would carry me—which was frightfully fast—I charged across the drawing room and threw open the door. My heart hammered in my chest as I prepared to confront the spy (for I have all the natural instincts of a secret agent). But the hallway was empty. The silver tray was there. The half-eaten bacon. But no sign of the devious woman. It was a crushing disappointment.

When I returned to the Duchess's bedroom, the vision in the Clock Diamond had vanished. It now looked like a perfectly ordinary necklace. I told the Duchess what I had seen.

The blubbery old bat shivered, her eyes shifting about the room.

"I was warned . . . but I didn't believe it," she whispered.

"Warned about what?" I said.

"The Clock Diamond has its fierce admirers—and its enemies too. They have been after the stone since its discovery in the jungles of Budatta. I was told they would come for it before I die, but I didn't believe it. Superstitious claptrap, that's what I said." She fixed her eyes upon me. "It is possible someone may try to grab the stone before you reach Butterfield Park. That is why you are the perfect person to deliver the necklace. Who on earth would suspect a humble maid, orphaned and all alone in the world?"

That sounded vaguely insulting. Then I remembered the five hundred pounds, and my desire to hit the Duchess in the head with a pillow fell away.

"Perhaps it was just a nosy maid," I said helpfully. "Or perhaps the vision was wrong."

The old woman shook her head, and when she spoke, her voice trembled. "The stone does not deal in fantasy, child—only facts: what was, what is, and what will be." The fear in her eyes seemed to fade. "But perhaps you are right, and it was merely a maid peering through the keyhole." She chuckled. "They are always spying on me—hoping I will drop dead so they can steal my jewels."

I looked at the necklace, and for the briefest moment I felt a kind of longing. A mad desire to stare into its heart again and see what it might reveal. Before I could, the Duchess had pulled it from my fingers, placed it in the velvet box, and snapped the lid shut.

"Where on earth did you get such a diamond?" I said.

She paused. Licked her lips. "An acquaintance."

"Do you wish to write a note or a card for Matilda?" I asked.

"Give her the necklace at the ball," she wheezed, "and tell her it is sent with the kind regards of Winifred Farris. Her grandmother will understand. Now, lock it back up."

I took the key from my pocket and did as she instructed. "Place it in your bag," the Duchess said. "Never let it leave your side until you reach Butterfield Park. My lawyer, Mr. Banks, will meet you in London and see you on your way." She looked me up and down. "You can't go on board the ship looking like *that*. There is a dress for you in the wardrobe. You will find a dozen others in your cabin on the *Britannia*."

I clapped my hands in delight. "Duchess, you are barking mad, but wonderful!"

She huffed, yet seemed pleased.

The dress was lovely—a simple gown of white muslin with a pale blue sash—and I was lovely in it. Not like a maid at all. Like a princess. Or, at the very least, a postmaster's daughter.

With the box safely packed in my carpetbag and the envelope with my ticket and the fifty pounds in my pocket, the Duchess of Trinity appeared to have no further use for me. Her eyes were closed again. I assumed she was sleeping.

"Good-bye, Duchess," I whispered, watching her plump cheeks billow with every labored breath. "Enjoy the journey which awaits you. It will be thrilling, I'm sure."

As I closed the door to her suite, I heard her voice one last time, brittle and grim. "Good-bye, child," she whispered, "and thank you."

I hoped the ghastly manager would see me taking my leave of the hotel in a private carriage with two horses. But he was nowhere to be seen. The carriage took me to Le Havre, and I quickly found myself among a great swell of people clamoring towards the *Britannia*. She was a fine ship, and I was delighted to find that the Duchess had booked me passage in first class.

As the ship wasn't ready for boarding, I took a seat in the waiting area of the first-class lounge. The place was positively swarming with aristocrats—gentlemen in frock coats and top hats, and ladies luxuriating in furs, feathered hats, and jewels.

I had just checked my bag (I found myself checking on the jewel every five minutes), when a short man wearing a white suit sat down beside me. He looked rather crotchety and was muttering to himself with alarming frequency. Something about Paris going to the dogs.

"It's a crying shame," he said, to no one in particular. "I remember when you could sleep in this city with your window open. Your door unlocked. Now *this*. A crying shame, it is."

"Is it?" I said, unable to resist. I have a fondness for lunatics.

"Yes indeed," he said, shaking his head. "Just be grateful you and your family are getting out of Paris, little miss."

"I'm traveling alone," I said proudly.

"A girl your age? Outrageous!" He was frowning. "Main thing is, you're getting out of this place. Shameful, it is. And at a fine hotel like the Grand."

Suddenly I was very interested in the man's mad ravings. "I was just there," I said. "What about the Grand?"

"That's where it happened. Terrible thing. Shameful!"

"Stop babbling, you nitwit," I snapped. "Tell me what happened."

"Murder, that's what. The body was found this morning," said the man. "A maid found her there, dead and all. A dagger plunged in her heart."

A sliver of fear seemed to wake inside of me, coiling its way up towards my chest. It slithered and curled. Twisting ever higher. Ever tighter. It was heavy and cold and hungry. What I felt wasn't easy to explain. The only way to describe it is this—I knew before I *knew*.

"Who?" I said faintly. "Who was murdered?"

"Nobody you'd have heard of," said the man. "She was old, she was."

"Who?" I repeated, this time with more urgency.

The man smiled sadly. "Very well. 'Twas the Duchess of Trinity."

My heart began to pound.

"She was once a very great lady," muttered the man. "But I don't suppose a girl like you would have ever heard her name."

"I knew her," I said. "I mean . . . I knew her name."

"Don't look so grave, little miss," said the man. "You're not to trouble your mind with murder and mischief. Leave that to the grown-ups, you hear?"

He was right, of course. I was a junior lady's maid. Brilliant and beautiful. But still just a child. What did I know of murder and mischief? Of daggers plunged into hearts? Nothing, that's what. Until now. Until right now.

"Promise me you won't worry about this awful business."

He patted my arm, his eyes filled with fatherly concern. "Do you promise, little miss?"

I tried my best to smile. "I promise," I said.

3

The ship had just set sail. I sat on a deck chair overlooking the sea and tried to think. Which I normally did stupendously well—for I have all the natural instincts of a philosophy professor. Or, at very least, an assistant librarian. But not now. I was terribly anxious. My hands were trembling. They *never* trembled. My mind was a tangle. People were gathered like lemmings at the railing, watching the final glimpses of the coast. Yet all I saw was the Duchess of Trinity lying in her bed with a knife in her chest. And while stabbing was a marvelously interesting cause of death, it was no way for a genuine duchess to kick the bucket. She deserved something far more dignified. Like choking on a lobster claw. Or being crushed beneath a falling chandelier.

The facts were as follows. A woman near death—she hardly expected to live out the week—had been killed in her bed. Why? And by whom? I thought of the vision in the stone—the woman crouched at the Duchess's door, peering through the keyhole. Was she the killer? A shiver rattled my bones. There *must* be some connection between the Clock Diamond and the Countess's gruesome death. Hadn't the old bat warned me that nefarious fatheads were after the one-of-a-kind stone?

"Did you hear about the Duchess?" shrieked a woman with a glorious overbite and a neck like a giraffe, as she and her lump of a husband stopped at the railing in front of me. "It's utterly shocking!"

"Too much money," said the husband. "Rich folks like that always meet a grisly end."

The wife gasped (she sounded like a horse with a nail in its hoof). "Don't be beastly, Angus! It's terrifying, that's what it is. I only pray they've caught the killer by now."

"The murderer's still at large," came the reply.

The wife gasped again. "Angus, you don't suppose he's here on the ship?"

"Highly likely, I should think," said Angus.

His wife clutched her chest. "I'm going to faint! I'm sure of it! Oh Angus, I won't sleep a wink knowing there's a killer on—"

"Don't be absurd, you abominable nitwits," I said, getting out of my chair. "The killer is probably miles away by now. Of course, if he didn't find what he was looking for, he may be searching elsewhere, but as for him being on this ship—it's a violently stupid thought."

The wife looked relieved. The husband frowned.

"You seem to know an awful lot about it," he said, looking at me with interest. "Where are your mother and father, young lady?"

"My parents fell into a volcano," I said. "My mother was blown deep into the Congo, where she now lives with a tribe of vegetarian pygmies, and my father had the good sense to explode on impact."

The silly creatures looked positively bug-eyed. Which was the perfect moment for me to pick up my carpetbag and set off in search of my cabin.

I found it in no time. The room was small but perfectly comfortable. Though, to be honest, first class wasn't nearly as luxurious as I had expected. I lay down on the narrow bed, my mind a jumble of thoughts.

"Well, Ivy," I said, "what on earth are you going to do?"

I could abort the mission. In the envelope the Duchess had given me was the business card of her lawyer in London. Mr. Horatio Banks. I could take the necklace to him. Wash my hands of this murderous mess, and walk away. Nobody would think me a coward. Of course, there were other options. I could throw the Clock Diamond overboard and pretend I'd never had it to begin with. Or hand it over to the police when we docked in London. But then I thought of the Duchess— and the five hundred pounds. I had accepted the mission, hadn't I? Sworn an oath and whatnot. It was probably the last promise anyone had ever made to the Duchess. Surely that meant something. To me. To her.

In the end, it was an easy decision. I would fulfill my promise. Come what may (including dagger-wielding nincompoops), I would see the Clock Diamond hanging around Matilda Butterfield's neck.

I awoke a few hours later feeling remarkably fresh. Of course, the Duchess's grisly death still troubled me. But it would not deflate my spirits. After all, I had taken the necessary precautions to protect the Clock Diamond before I went to sleep. I had pulled a small writing desk in front of my cabin door, thus blocking any intruders. And I slept with the precious stone under my pillow. I had dispensed with the black velvet box and the old key—they were cumbersome and unnecessary and they practically shouted "Please rob me!" Which wasn't helpful.

The second I woke up, I felt beneath my pillow for the stone. My sleepy body flooded with relief to find it still there. I quickly decided to keep the stone in my pocket at all times during the day and to sew the pocket shut to eliminate the possibility of loss or theft.

Before I slipped the diamond into my pocket and stitched it in, I held the stone up to the light. Through the porthole, I could see the shimmering sun high above the rippling blue horizon. It cast the cabin in a bronze haze. In the heart of the diamond, the sun hung in miniature above the ship. The entire stone glowed like an iridescent egg yolk. It was beautiful. And all I know is, I got lost in it. Lost in its wonder.

A longing bloomed inside of me again, just as it had in the Duchess's bedroom chamber. A mad desire. I needed to wear the necklace. To put it on. To see myself with the Clock Diamond around my neck. Yes, yes, I had promised the Duchess I wouldn't. But how could it possibly hurt her now? I could try the necklace on—just for a second. A minute or two. Then take it off. No one would know.

I walked to the mirror. The silver necklace pooled in the palm of my hand like a puddle. I looked splendid in my new dress. My dark hair was tied back in a braid and was very fetching. I held both ends of the clasp behind my neck. I glanced in the mirror. The Clock Diamond hung in the air, the heavy stone swinging like a pendulum. My hands trembled. My mouth was dry. A feeling of lightness rushed through my head.

With new determination, I steadied my fingers and fixed the clasp together. The necklace dropped to my chest and hung there, its warmth radiating through my dress.

The Clock Diamond glowed a silvery white. Then the stone began to pulse. I could feel it beat against my chest. At first it was irregular, throbbing out of rhythm. Then the pulse steadied. I cannot say for sure, but it seemed to have synchronized with the beating of my heart.

The stone dimmed. *Thump. Thump. Thump.* It felt awfully hot in the cabin. Stuffy. I took a breath. It took more effort than usual. My head was positively spinning. Or was it the cabin? The stone throbbed and filled with a billowing black mist.

The dark fog churned like a thunderstorm, then cleared.

In its place I saw something move.

A baby. Looking up and laughing.

In an instant the infant was older. A girl now. Dark hair in two braids. Gorgeous blue eyes. But pale. Plain. She was crying. Sitting by a window. Wondering why she had been left in that awful place. Then older. Eleven or twelve. Dressed as a maid. Serving tea. In a fine house.

Then a glittering white mist filled the stone. And the girl was gone.

The girl who was me.

A glow burst from the diamond like a searchlight. It seemed to reach for me.

It filled my eyes, pouring into me. It swallowed me up.

Then the world fell away.

All was black.

Tap. Tap. Tap.

The door.

Someone was knocking at the door. I opened my eyes and blinked. My head ached. I was lying on the floor of my cabin. Bright sun filled the tiny room. I squinted, shielded my eyes, and slowly got to my feet.

Tap. Tap. Tap.

"Just a moment!" I called out.

My brain felt like it had been taken out of my head, kicked around like a football, then shoved back in. I had overexcited myself. Such things were always happening to girls in novels.

Tap. Tap. Tap.

I quickly straightened my dress and took a deep breath. My hand was gripping the door handle when I remembered. The necklace! I was still wearing it. I unfastened the clasp and slipped the necklace into my pocket.

Then opened the door.

"I'm Geraldine Always," said a rather prim-looking woman in a brown dress and matching gloves. "My cabin is right next to yours. I heard a thump and I was concerned. Are you all right?"

She had unremarkable brown hair pulled back from her face. Round spectacles. Excellent teeth. And I liked her from the start.

"I'm perfectly fine," I said. "I dropped . . . my bag. Yes, my bag. That must have been the noise you heard."

Geraldine Always sprung up on her tiptoes (she was short, but not shockingly so) and looked over my shoulder. "You are traveling with family?"

"Heavens no," I said. "My parents are currently on an expedition in Mongolia. Hunting aardvarks. I am traveling back to England to spend the summer with my grandmother. She's beastly."

"You must think me awfully nosy, knocking on your door and interrogating you," said Miss Always rather meekly.

"Yes, dear, that is *just* what I was thinking."

Miss Always laughed. Which was odd. She said, "You see,

like you, I am traveling alone—which is very dull. What is your name?"

"Ivy Pocket."

"Well, Ivy Pocket, we shall have to be companions for the length of our voyage. There is no other option."

And so we were.

The poor woman was a writer. Her first book—*Famous Ghosts of Scotland and Wales*—had sold just sixty-three copies. For the last year she had been traveling the world writing a new book on lost myths and legends—cursed relics, hidden worlds, vengeful gods, that sort of thing. Now Miss Always was heading back home to England to care for her sick mother. My new friend was sweet natured and monstrously dull. But being a generous sort of girl—for I have all the natural instincts of a stockbroker—I did my best to ensure she had a jolly good time.

Over the two days and nights of our voyage, I was never parted from the Clock Diamond. It stayed sewn in my pocket by day, and safely beneath my pillow by night. I was still troubled by the Duchess's murder, but despite this, my spirits remained high. In fact, following my ridiculous fainting spell, I'd never looked better. And I had the appetite of a small army.

That first evening, Miss Always and I took a moonlight walk along the upper deck after supper. We discussed my parents' many adventures. They were mapmakers by profession. Traveling to the darkest corners of the globe, mapping its uncharted valleys and gorges and mountains. They had been everywhere. Done everything. Dug up mummies in Egypt. Carved tracks through the Amazon. Miss Always was utterly fascinated by their adventures. As was I. After all, I was hearing them for the first time.

Yes, yes, it is wrong to tell lies and whatnot. But I couldn't help it. I knew nothing of my real parents. The only information I had was that someone—a lady of grim countenance—had brought me to the Harrington Home for Unwanted Children in London. And left me there. I was five. My memories don't really begin until after I arrived at the orphanage—the years before it are a blur. But I am certain my early life was filled with amazing adventures.

"You must treasure your parents, Ivy," said Miss Always gravely. "That is why I am so keen to get back to England, to see my poor mother. She is terribly ill." She came to a stop, resting her hands on the railing. Beyond us, the milky moonlight played upon the black sea. "Shall I tell you a secret, Ivy?"

"I insist that you do," I said.

"In Paris, I bought a very special gift for my mother," she whispered. "A diamond ring. My father couldn't afford one when they first married. But Mummy has always wanted one."

"Was it stupendously expensive?" I asked.

"Shockingly," said Miss Always. She leaned close to me. "Perhaps you could help me, Ivy. For I haven't been able to think of a place to hide the diamond while we are at sea. You know, somewhere no one would ever think to look. I'm *terrible* at such things."

I looked around to make sure we were quite alone. "I shouldn't be telling you this, Miss Always," I said softly, "but I'm traveling with a diamond myself. Very rare. One of a kind."

"You are?" She looked stunned.

"Nobody knows about it," I said. "Not even the captain."

Now perhaps it was unwise of me to speak of the stone. But I am an excellent judge of character, and I knew I could trust Miss Always. She wrote *books*, how dangerous could she be?

"Where did you get it?" asked my new friend eagerly.

"From a fat old duchess," I said brightly. "We were monstrously close. It was her dying wish that I deliver the diamond *personally* to Matilda Butterfield of Butterfield Park. The Duchess trusted no one but me with the mission."

"Then you know how nervous I feel about carrying something so valuable myself," said Miss Always. She licked her lips. "How on earth did you figure out where to hide the Duchess's necklace?"

"It was easy, dear," I said. "I always carry it with me."

Miss Always's eyes widened. "You have the Cl—" She coughed all of a sudden, undoubtedly choking on a wasp or some beastly sea bug. "You have the diamond on you right now?"

"I do."

She looked at me eagerly. "May I ask where?"

What a simpleminded nincompoop she was.

I giggled. "I keep it in my pocket," I explained. "I sew the pocket shut—so you see, it's perfectly safe. Nobody could take the stone without my knowing about it."

"And at night?" asked Miss Always. "What do you do at night?"

"Under my pillow, dear," I answered. "I'm a very light sleeper. If anyone tried to steal it, I would wake up and thrash them brutally. Plus, I barricade the door."

I thought Miss Always looked slightly disappointed. But I'm sure I was mistaken. She swiftly took me further into her confidence (that dear, trusting, dimwitted creature). "My mother's ring," she whispered. "Would you like to see it?"

Now I must confess, apart from the Clock Diamond, I have little interest in jewels as a general rule. But the bonds of friendship demanded that I at least try to look interested.

"I would love to," I said.

Miss Always's cabin was just like my own. Only darker, and lit by a single candle on the bedside table. With the door safely locked, my friend patted down her mousy brown hair, pushed up her spectacles, and took a deep breath. Then she opened her travel bag and removed a large book on ancient Greece. For a moment I feared she was going to read to me. Fortunately, the book had a far more interesting function, for carved inside was a chamber, and in it, a small red box. Miss Always pulled it out and with great care opened the lid.

"Here it is," she said dreamily.

"Oh, it's beautiful!" I cried.

It wasn't. It was small. And dull. A thin gold band. A tiny diamond. I'd seen dust with more sparkle. Still, it was my job as a bosom friend to lie. I *ooh*ed and *ahh*ed. Was suitably complimentary. Declared that her mother would be so delighted she would probably die of shock. Which was an unfortunate choice of words given the poor woman's perilous health. But Miss Always seemed pleased by my reaction.

The smile soon faded from her lips. "The ring must appear very insignificant when compared to *your* diamond, Ivy. Could I—?" She shook her head. "No, I shouldn't ask. It's terribly rude of me."

"What is?" I said.

"I was going to ask if I might take a look at it," she said shyly.

"The necklace, I mean. But please forgive me. I shouldn't ask such a thing."

Now of course I had vowed to show no one the stone. Not until the birthday ball. But Miss Always was a sweet-natured blockhead. What could be the harm in giving her a glimpse of the Clock Diamond? "Come closer and I will show you," I said quietly.

Miss Always edged towards me, hands behind her back. "Only if you are sure," she said with heartbreaking intensity. She was close to me now. I turned, searching the bedside table for something to cut open the stitching on my pocket. I could feel her breath on the back of my neck.

"You don't know how much this means to me, Ivy," I heard her say. "You will never know how much."

"Calm yourself, dear," I said, opening a series of drawers, looking for a pair of scissors or a small knife. "It's only a silly diamond. Though I will admit, it *did* look rather glorious when I tried it on."

I turned to face her just as her arm was swinging towards me. Something in her hand flared in the candlelight, blinding me for a moment. It sliced through the air, coming right at me. I didn't have time to flinch. Just as quickly, Miss Always froze. Her hand was steady. She had the scissors poised right in front of my chest. Which was rather troubling.

"Miss Always?"

The poor creature looked horribly bewildered. A small gasped escaped her lips. "What . . . what did you say?"

"Be careful with those scissors, dear," I said with a furrowed brow.

Miss Always blushed. Looked down at the scissors. "Goodness. Yes, of course. I found them on the desk and was so eager to hand them to you, I nearly . . . oh, Ivy, I'm awfully sorry. It's all the excitement, I suppose."

I took the scissors from her hand. "Yes, dear, you're monstrously excitable."

"Ivy, did you say you tried on the necklace?"

I nodded and began to snip the stitching on my pocket. "Only for a moment. I didn't see any harm in it. Of course, then I fainted—and the next thing I knew, you were knocking at my door."

"I . . . I don't believe it," she muttered.

"Oh, it's perfectly all right," I said brightly. "The stone wasn't damaged, and as I said, it was only for a minute or two."

Miss Always smiled tightly. "You really are full of surprises, Ivy."

With the stitching cut away, I slipped my hand into my pocket to retrieve the necklace. Suddenly Miss Always's fingers snaked around my wrist. Her grip was rather tight. "Stop," she commanded.

"Whatever's the matter, dear?" I said.

"I hear voices outside," said Miss Always, glancing towards the door.

"I'm sure it's just someone passing by." I was now rather eager to show Miss Always the stone, hopeful she might actually explode with excitement (which would be frightfully tragic, but violently entertaining). "Don't worry, dear. We are perfectly safe."

But Miss Always did not seem to believe it. Only moments ago, she had been drooling with anticipation at seeing the stone, and now she refused to even look at it. She said she would see it some other time. Then she hurried me from her cabin, suggesting I get a good night's sleep.

"Oh, and Ivy," she said, pushing me out into the hallway, "do be sure to lock your door. With a diamond so rare and valuable, you must be terribly careful. There are thieves around every corner. You will be careful, won't you, Ivy?"

Before I could answer, Miss Always had closed her cabin door.

The next evening, before dinner, I went hunting for food. I was hungrier than I had ever been in my entire life. Some of my cravings were really very odd. I had a newfound appetite for potatoes. Raw ones. Also, cabbages. Unfortunately, all I found in the empty tea room was half a strawberry cream cake and two stale scones. Still, they were rather scrumptious.

When I returned below deck to freshen up, a peculiar thing happened, and it stopped me in my tracks. As I rounded the narrow corridor leading to my cabin, I spotted Miss Always at the far end. She had her back to me. Her head bowed. She appeared to be talking. And in front of her was a small hooded figure, dressed in some sort of brown robe. The figure was partly obscured by Miss Always, but from where I stood, it looked as if the two of them were deep in conversation.

"Miss Always?" I called out.

She lifted her head, then turned around with a rather sweeping gesture—and as she did, the hooded figure seemed to vanish with the swish of her skirt. As if into thin air. Which was frightfully odd.

Miss Always hurried towards me. "You look pale, Ivy," she said. "Whatever is the matter?"

"Who were you talking to, dear?"

"Talking to?" Miss Always smiled and waved her hand. "Oh, *that*. Just some passenger who had lost his way. I was telling him how to get back to his cabin."

"He was dressed very strangely," I said next.

"Was he?" Miss Always looped her arm through mine and began to walk with me. "One passenger is much the same as the next to me, Ivy."

"But his robes were positively medieval," I said, "and he was terribly short."

Miss Always stopped. Put her hand on my forehead.

Frowned a great deal. "You don't look well at all, and you are making very little sense. The gentleman I spoke with was dressed in a dinner suit." She nodded grimly. "I'm afraid you have a bad case of seasickness, Ivy. The most common symptoms are hallucinations—which you are clearly suffering from—and sudden changes in appetite. Have you noticed anything unusual about your eating habits?"

Well, of course I had. Ravenous hunger and whatnot. "Not really."

"You look flushed, and your forehead is terribly hot," said Miss Always.

Was it? It seemed all the signs were there. I was monstrously hungry *and* I had conjured up a hooded dwarf from thin air! "Perhaps you are right," I said as we mounted the stairs towards the dining room. "After supper, I will pay a visit to the ship's doctor."

Miss Always stopped suddenly. "There's no need for that, is there?" She looked positively alarmed. Then she burst into merry laugher and prodded me playfully on the arm. "I didn't think a little seasickness would send you scurrying to the doctor,

Ivy. Who knew you were so fragile?'

Me, *fragile*? I suppressed a sudden urge to push Miss Always over the railing and into the ocean. Instead, I declared that I was feeling perfectly fine and had no intention of visiting the doctor. My friend seemed rather pleased.

At dinner, Miss Always's interest in my plans knew no bounds. Not just about my mission to deliver the Clock Diamond to Matilda Butterfield. But about where my grandmother lived in London (I had told Miss Always I would be staying with Grandma Pocket until I left for Butterfield Park). It was all rather difficult to explain, as I didn't exactly have a granny.

So naturally I made one up.

"Grandma has several homes in town," I said helpfully. "One never knows *exactly* where she will choose to sleep. Grandma is something of a halfwit, but we love her dearly."

Miss Always looked bothered. Just for a moment. She said, "I only ask because I will be staying in London briefly to meet with my publisher. I would love to pay you a visit."

"Sounds delightful, dear," I said, "but quite impossible. Grandma hates company."

Miss Always insisted on giving me the address of her publisher. She practically begged me to write to her the moment I was settled with the address where I would be staying. Naturally I promised that I would.

The *Britannia* anchored at the Royal Albert Pier the next morning, sailing in through a blanket of heavy fog. Miss Always seemed to dread our parting. She looked smart in her best scarlet dress, but her face looked gaunt and her expression terribly depressed. To my surprise, she said *I* looked tired, and she urged me to stay in London for a few days to rest.

We stood together on the deck of the great ship and watched the city drift into view.

"Perhaps we could take tea in the saloon before we disembark?" I said, certain that Miss Always would leap at the chance. To my surprise, she declined.

"I am meeting my publisher the moment we berth," she explained. "He is anxious to hear all about my new manuscript."

We parted then and there. Miss Always cried. I pretended to. It was touching. An hour later I had my carpetbag in my hand, the Clock Diamond in my pocket, and London in my sights. Just before I departed, I glanced around for one final look at the *Britannia*. She was splendid. There was a line of passengers mounting the gangway. I took my place, but it was a painfully slow business. Glancing down, I noticed a black carriage with four horses carving a path through the bustling crowd. It turned sharply, pulling up around the side of the terminal. The windows were covered in dark drapes. The driver wore a hat, pulled low. All very interesting. I waited for a moment to see who would get out. No one did.

When the line started to move again, I followed the stream of chattering passengers. I would never have given the black carriage a second thought, were it not for the streak of scarlet that caught my eye. A dress. A scarlet dress. Moving swiftly towards the large black carriage. It wasn't one person, but two. I stopped and stared at them. Utterly captivated. When they reached the carriage, the door swung open. The tiny hooded figure I had seen on the ship was the first to climb in. Followed swiftly by Miss Always.

4

London was just as I had left it. Grim. Filthy. Miserable.
But my mind was elsewhere. What on earth was Miss Always
doing getting into a carriage with that strange little man? A
strange little man Miss Always claimed I had hallucinated
due to seasickness! It made no sense. None at all. And hadn't
she said that her publisher would be meeting her at the pier?
I stopped outside the terminal and put down my carpetbag,
a cyclone of thoughts spinning through my mind. That
hooded dwarf had forced Miss Always into the carriage at
knifepoint. Yes, that must be it! No, wait. Miss Always had

climbed into the carriage *after* the strange little fellow.

"Think, Ivy," I said aloud. "You're a brilliant girl. Just *think*."

For a fleeting moment, the Clock Diamond popped into my mind. Instinctively, my hand flew to the pocket of my new royal-blue dress. I felt for the precious jewel. It was there. Safely sewn in. How stupid of me! Yes, Miss Always had taken an interest in the Countess's one-of-a-kind diamond. But only because I had told her about it. And in the end, she hadn't wished to see it at all.

I thought a little harder. It only took a moment. Perhaps two. Using my natural instincts (which would rival a writer of penny dreadfuls), I quickly solved the puzzle of Miss Always and the hooded stranger. The black carriage did indeed belong to Miss Always's publisher. And her mysterious traveling companion was the publisher's long-lost *son*. I was certain the young man was a pitiful creature—monstrously short, face like a chimpanzee, heartbreakingly stupid—banished from England after a scandal and forced to live in France with a brutish uncle. The poor chap had snuck onto the ship, desperate to return to his family, but terrified of being rejected. The kindhearted Miss

Always had befriended the stowaway and learned his tragic tale. Delighted to be of help, she had arranged the ship-side reunion I had just witnessed. A father and son, separated by an ocean, now reunited. It made perfect sense!

Nothing gets past Ivy Pocket.

It was late afternoon. Eager to get on with my adventure, I took a rickshaw into the city, intending to spend the night in a suitably fancy hotel. I had ten pounds left from the voyage, and as I was soon to deliver the Clock Diamond to Matilda Butterfield and collect the bulk of my reward, I figured I could certainly afford a little luxury.

Unfortunately there was some trouble at the hotel. The Grosvenor was suitably grand, but *apparently* twelve-year-old girls aren't supposed to stay in deluxe suites all on their own. Ridiculous! I told the manager (who had teeth like a walrus), that I was in London to meet my neglectful parents—self-absorbed mathematicians helping the British government decode a Russian cable concealed in a circus elephant's left hoof. All very top secret. Thousands of lives at stake and whatnot. The manager didn't believe a word and I was just about to tell him what I thought of him when—

"Miss Pocket?"

I turned around to find a tall man standing right behind me. Gray hair. Stern eyes. Long face. Dark suit. Top hat. He regarded me coolly. "Miss Pocket?" he said again.

I nodded. "Who are you?"

"That can wait," he said firmly. "Come, let us take a walk."

Now I am not one to go strolling with strange men. But the remarkable thing was, I felt I didn't have a choice. Top Hat walked out of the hotel without another word, and like a lemming I followed after him. Extraordinary!

We walked to St. James's Park and took a seat under a maple tree. He told me his name was Horatio Banks, the Duchess of Trinity's lawyer. How he had tracked me down was a mystery that he was unwilling to shed any light upon. But on other matters, he had much to say.

"Tell me about your voyage," he said, looking at me with his fierce green eyes. "Any strange occurrences? Anything unusual?"

"Nothing. I was on my guard," I said.

"Did anyone befriend you?" he asked.

"Hundreds of people, dear. I'm the sort of maid who attracts a crowd."

Horatio Banks cleared his throat. "Did anyone show an interest in the Clock Diamond? Did anyone know you were traveling with it?"

"Mr. Banks, do I look like someone who would go blabbing to strangers about the Clock Diamond?" I *could* have told him about Miss Always, but what was the use? She was a penniless writer. An innocent spinster. Terribly fascinated by me. But delightfully clueless.

He got up from the bench and began to pace back and forth in front of me. He pressed his finger to his lips and frowned a great deal. Then he stopped and turned to face me.

"You've heard about the Duchess of Trinity's murder?"

"Oh, yes. Terribly sad. Monstrously tragic. I can't imagine who would do such a thing."

"I can," said Mr. Banks grimly. "Miss Pocket, did you see anything suspicious, *anything* at all, when you were in the Duchess's apartment in Paris?"

"Nothing." I didn't see the point in telling Mr. Banks about the mysterious woman at the keyhole. The vision proved nothing. And besides, I suspected he would gladly try and separate me from the diamond. And without the diamond, there would be no five hundred pounds.

"What did the Duchess tell you about the stone?" he asked.

"Only that it's rare and valuable, and it was her dying wish that I present it to Miss Matilda at her birthday ball."

"I don't like it," muttered Mr. Banks. "The Duchess refused to tell me how she came to possess this mysterious diamond—I just know that it cost a sizable chunk of her fortune. When are you leaving for Suffolk?"

"Tomorrow morning," I said, tightening the bow on my braid (it seemed the right moment).

"Very good," he said. "There is a deeper mystery at play, Miss Pocket, and I intend to find out what it is. I am still baffled as to why the Duchess would wish to give such a priceless jewel to Matilda Butterfield—a girl she had never met before."

"There is no great mystery there, dear," I said matter-of-factly. "The Duchess had a falling-out with Matilda's grandmother decades ago. The necklace is a peace offering. Old people are awfully keen on such things."

"Miss Pocket, I believe there is a direct connection between the Duchess's murder and the Clock Diamond. I also believe you were probably followed from Paris."

Poor man. He was shockingly melodramatic. I suspected he had a fondness for the theater. "Mr. Banks, wake up. If someone was stalking me on the boat, they would certainly have struck by now."

Horatio Banks looked stumped, which I found rather thrilling.

"There's a bigger picture here," he said at last. "But I cannot see it as yet."

"Well, I can," I told him. "I will leave in the morning, stay a few days at Butterfield Park, and give the necklace to Matilda at her party. Then you will pay me my money, and this whole thing will be at an end. Agreed?"

He did not.

"The Duchess has a town house in Belgravia. I've arranged for the housekeeper to open a few of the rooms for your use." He handed me a card. "Here is the address. Collect your things and be at the house by three o'clock. I will meet you there."

I protested. Stomped my feet. Stuck out my tongue. Nothing worked. Which was infuriating!

"If you want your payment, Miss Pocket," said Mr. Banks, "you will do as I say. I have an important meeting across town; otherwise, I would escort you myself. Talk to no one. Do not tell a soul where you will be staying. Are we clear?"

"Perfectly," I said in my most sullen voice (which is astoundingly sullen).

Then the beastly man spun on his heel and stalked away without so much as a good-bye. He stopped suddenly and turned back. "I worked for the Duchess of Trinity for forty years, and in all that time, I never knew her to trust a single person," he said. His eyes narrowed and fixed on me. "Why did she pick you to deliver the Clock Diamond? Why *you*, Miss Pocket?"

I smiled sweetly. "Oh, I just assumed you knew, dear— I'm one of a kind."

Mr. Banks may have smiled then. Just for an instant. Then he tipped his hat and walked away.

My journey to Belgravia was unremarkable. Except for one thing. I bumped into Miss Always. Quite by accident, of course. She was taking a walk in the park just as I was leaving. The poor creature was thrilled to see me. Hugged me several times. I was curious why she was still in London. She explained that her publisher had asked her to stay on and discuss her new manuscript. Apparently it was shockingly dull and needed more "color" and "excitement." Miss Always seemed bitterly disappointed. She talked a great deal about the changes she had in mind. But I stopped her. For I had questions.

"Miss Always," I said gravely, "I saw you leaving the ship. You got into a carriage with that little hooded man. The one you said I had *imagined*. Care to explain?"

Poor Miss Always looked stunned. Her mouth dropped open. Her eyelids blinked rapidly. She adjusted her glasses. "Well, Ivy, that is a very good question." She looked at me keenly. "Nothing escapes your notice, does it? Tell me—what do *you* think I was doing with that little man?"

What a clever woman! She knew that I was full of startling insights. I told her my theory. About her publisher and the hooded dwarf being long-lost father and son. About the poor little man being exiled to France following a scandal. About her role in reuniting them.

My friend gasped. "Ivy Pocket," she cried, "you are a wonder! Everything you have said is true. How do you do it?"

I spent the next several minutes explaining my brilliance to the baffled writer.

"Where are you staying?" asked Miss Always casually. "On the ship, you were not sure which one of your grandmother's *many* houses you would be lodging at. I am sure the matter is now settled."

"Oh, yes, thoroughly settled," I said, pushing a lock of hair behind my ear. "Grandma has a fine house in Belgravia. I am staying there."

"How grand." Miss Always leaned closer. "Where exactly? I only ask because I am leaving London after my meeting and I would like to write to you."

Of course I remembered Mr. Banks's warning—"Do not tell a soul where you will be staying." But that hardly applied to dear Miss Always. Besides, the Duchess's London home was sure to be terrifically impressive. Just the place for Grandma Pocket to live. I gave Miss Always the address. She wrote it down rather furiously in her notebook. Closed the notebook. Opened it again. Read the address out to me so as to confirm it. Questioned me again about my plans. Was I *sure* I would stay in Belgravia tonight?

Poor Miss Always. I was touched that she found me so fascinating. But I was anxious to get going. We parted with a hug. Miss Always promised to write to me that very night, and I promised to read her letters when I could find the time.

I reached the Duchess's town house in Belgravia just before three o'clock and was ushered inside by Mrs. Vans, the housekeeper, a toothless, red-faced butterball of no importance, who quickly vanished into the kitchen to smoke her pipe. Horatio Banks was waiting for me in the drawing room, still in his dark suit and top hat. He quizzed me about my activities and seemed rather fixated on my meeting with Miss Always.

"I would like to meet this friend of yours," he said sternly. Then he forbade me from leaving the house. Said it was much too dangerous. So dangerous, in fact, that he had decided to chaperone me until I was safely on the train to Suffolk.

Even worse, the crusty old lawyer insisted I write a note to Lady Amelia Butterfield (Matilda's mother), informing her that I had a birthday gift for her daughter from the Duchess of Trinity. He said it was the *proper* thing to do. As if I needed a lesson in manners! With the note written, Mr. Banks vanished into the Duchess's study to attend to some legal matters, issuing me strict instructions to stay in the drawing room and read a book. Naturally, I promised to do just that.

Alone at last, I set about exploring the Duchess's house.

It was old. Dusty. Full of outdated furniture. Faded carpets. Vulgar antiques. Even the paintings on the walls were dull and lifeless. The Duchess had appalling taste.

I wandered through a series of tragic rooms on the upper floors. The furniture was covered by sheets, and the windows were shuttered up. There was only one chamber of interest among the dozen I explored. The music room. It was as stuffy and dark as the rest, but a sliver of light from the late afternoon sun washed in between the shutters, illuminating the grand piano like a spotlight. I sat at it. Opened the lid. My mind immediately flew back to the Duchess's hotel suite in Paris. Something stirred in me. A kind of fluttering in my stomach. Which is probably why I played "Row, Row, Row Your Boat." Or perhaps I had a hunch. Either way, I wasn't completely shocked when I played the final note and a cranking sound sprang to life deep within the piano. A panel drew back. A darkened cavity. I reached in. Felt around.

Nothing there.

I admit, I was rather disappointed. I suppose I was secretly hoping that the Duchess might have other hidden treasures. I tore at the thread of my pocket, pulled out the Clock Diamond, and placed it inside the hidden chamber. It would be much safer here than in my pocket. There was another reason. I'd become rather preoccupied with the stone. I was thinking about it a great deal. Remembering how it felt to wear it. Picturing what I saw when I looked into it. The girl who was me. And the glorious, blinding light. And the darkness.

"Stuff and nonsense," I said aloud. I closed the piano lid. The panel slid back, vanishing into the woodwork. Then I went off in search of food.

The evening was devastatingly dull. Horatio Banks was buried in his papers. Mrs. Vans stayed holed up in the kitchen smoking her pipe. I read a little. Wandered about looking at the Duchess's odd collection of art—she had a fondness for marble statues of animals dressed in evening wear.

It was almost a relief when Mr. Banks ordered me to bed.

The mattress was gloriously soft. The pillow, a delight. Sleep came quickly.

I'm not sure what woke me. The snap of a floorboard? The low murmur of a window being pushed up? Something, anyway. My eyes shot open. My nerves afire. The bedroom was a patchwork of shadows—a splash of moonlight slipped in through the parted curtains. Then something else. On either side of my bed. Two small figures scurrying away. I leaped up. At least, I tried to. But I couldn't move. Not an inch. I was strapped down—the bedsheets pulled tightly across my body with the sort of enthusiasm usually reserved for mummified pharaohs. I struggled to free myself. Wiggled and kicked. But it did little good. I was utterly trapped!

A pair of shadows flew across the room and out the door.

A current, urgent and hot, surged through my body. The Clock Diamond! I gritted my teeth and pushed hard against the impossibly tight bedsheets. I pushed and kicked with all my strength. Did a large amount of grunting. Wiggled my shoulders. At last the restraints began to give a little. Showing heartbreaking strength and perseverance, I managed to loosen the sheets enough to wriggle my way up and out. Not unlike a caterpillar.

Once on my feet, I could see that my bedroom chamber had been ransacked—drawers opened, clothes scattered. Had they come for the Clock Diamond, just as Mr. Banks had predicted? I was sure they had. Luckily the stone was hidden away in the Duchess's piano. It would be impossible to find.

Flying out of my room, I crossed the landing and hurried down the curved staircase. I wasn't afraid. Not a bit. In fact, I was monstrously calm—having all the natural instincts of a sedated cow.

"*Shhhh!*" A woman's voice. Coming from the drawing room. Then hurried footsteps. They grew louder. Indeed, they seemed to be coming right towards me! I stepped back against the wall, vanishing into the shadows. Two figures dashed across the darkened entrance hall and disappeared into the kitchen. As villains went, they were remarkably short. A cauldron of anger bubbled up in me. Monstrous thieves! I stepped out of the shadows and raced after them, fully prepared for battle.

The kitchen was gloomy and still. A candle flicked on a bench. Copper pots and pans hung from an iron rack above the table. Mrs. Vans was sound asleep in a rocking chair, a spent pipe dangling from her lips. A fire still burned in the large open hearth. No sign of the intruders.

I walked around the table. Looked under it. Nobody there. Perhaps they had fled out the back door? I was about to check when a plucked chicken came flying out of the larder. Followed by a side of beef. Then a sack of potatoes. I ducked behind the table just as the two little intruders came scurrying out. They wore dark robes, their faces concealed by hoods. I thought immediately of the strange little man getting into the carriage with Miss Always. The resemblance was striking. Which was odd. One of the devious dwarfs had a large bag of flour in his hand—he tore it open as if it were made of wrapping paper, and emptied the contents onto the floor.

Filthy beast!

The villains stopped suddenly. Then turned their heads in perfect unison. They appeared to be staring straight at me! Then the blackguards split up, taking rapid little steps as they rounded the kitchen table from either side. In moments they would be upon me. I jumped up and grabbed a pot from the rack above. I felt something coil around my left wrist. With no time to spare, I swung the pot as forcefully as I could—hitting one hooded cretin in the head. He tumbled to the floor.

The second intruder made a beastly hissing sound. His face was hidden by the hood, but I was certain he was an ugly little wretch! I reached for another pot, but too late. The four-foot fathead grabbed my arm and flung me across the table as if I were a rag doll. The nerve! I slid across the table, flew off the other side, and rolled over the stone floor. Remarkably, I was unhurt and jumped quickly to my feet. In seconds both my attackers were upon me again. The one to my left struck first, his hideous talons reaching for my throat. With no suitable weapon in sight,

I grabbed a handful of flour from the pile at my feet and threw it in his face. The tiny brute hissed. Shook his head. Stumbled back.

His accomplice lunged for me. I bolted across the kitchen, jumped on a chair, and leaped onto the table. A shadow flew past me. I felt a hand from behind grasping for my ankle. My options were rather limited. They had me surrounded. The only way to go was up. With momentum on my side, I reached for a hook hanging from the iron pot rack above my head. I swung at great speed just as the hooded thief appeared before me. I let go of the rack. Flew through the air. My foot connected wonderfully with the villain's head, knocking the stuffing out of him. I felt like whooping with delight. Unfortunately, there was no time. For I was still rocketing through the air. With no way of stopping myself, I flew over Mrs. Vans's head with gusto.

Then crashed right into the fireplace.

Which wasn't at all good.

My body landed in a tangle. A burning log crumbled beneath me. The flames raged—licking my legs and my arms. Smoke billowed. I heard Mrs. Vans scream. And then . . . darkness.

The housekeeper pulled me out. She was hollering a great deal. Crying and praying and whatnot. It only took a moment or two, and I was wide awake. I blinked several times. The fire in the hearth had been doused. My arms and legs (and no doubt my face) were covered in soot and ash. But I was unhurt. Not even a slight burn or red mark, Mrs. Vans informed me. She looked thoroughly befuddled. Said the flames had swarmed around me. Said it was a miracle. I very much doubted that. I was certain my nightdress had snuffed out the fire.

Then I remembered.

"The intruders," I said, getting to my feet. "Where did they go, Mrs. Vans?"

The housekeeper had no idea what I was talking about. Indeed, she seemed to doubt my story. Then we heard it. A crash—probably a vase breaking. It came from the drawing room. Mrs. Vans looked terrified.

"You must wake Mr. Banks," she whispered frantically. "And I will call for the constable!"

"No time, dear," I said.

Mrs. Vans tried to stop me as I ran from the kitchen—but she was no match for Ivy Pocket.

I charged majestically into the drawing room, and I was met with a scene of utter destruction. The whole room had been turned upside down. Moonlight pooled in the middle of the floor like a milky pond, while shadows clung to the corners and walls. I saw movement in the darkness. One of the tiny hoodlums was riffling through a bookcase by the window. The other was busy pulling out drawers at a writing table. Both had their backs to me. I searched among the wreckage for a suitable weapon.

To my right was a marble statue of a bear dressed like a footman in a frock coat and bow tie. Perfect. I picked it up and lunged at the nearest villain. He seemed to sense me, turning around as I swung the statue at his head. But "turning" is not really the correct word. The tiny blackguard spun on the spot! At great speed. Rather like a spinning top. So fast and so furiously that it created a violent gust of wind. It lifted me off my feet and sent me flying back. Which was shameful. I wasn't the kind of girl to blow away in a breeze!

I landed with a thump against the wall—my head and back bearing most of the impact. The statue broke in my hand, gouging a large hole in the wall. I fully expected to have broken a bone or two. Perhaps a crack in the skull. But no. I felt slightly sore, but everything else seemed to be in full working order as I got to my feet.

My quick recovery seemed to fascinate the intruders. They looked at me, heads tilting in unison. Then I heard a dry laugh from the shadows.

"Remarkable," hissed a voice. It belonged to a woman. It was faint. But cold as ice.

"Who are you?" I shouted, unable to see this third intruder. "Show your face!'

I reached for the closest weapon—which, unfortunately, was a bowl of fruit. With a pear grasped in each hand, I walked toward the curtain of shadows. The villains stepped forward in unison, blocking my path.

"I must warn you," I said firmly. "At Midwinter Hall I once felled a runaway chimney sweep with only half an apple. So just imagine how lethal I could be with two pears!"

At that moment Mr. Banks thundered into the room, brandishing a pistol and making all sorts of declarations about policemen and putting hands into the air and whatnot. There was sudden movement in the gloomy half-light. I saw a shadow bolting along the wall. The edge of a dark shirt flaring in the moonlight. The woman jumped through the open window, followed by the two hooded henchmen— who seemed to dive into the thick swarm of dusk right behind her.

5

"Miss Pocket, explain yourself!"

Horatio Banks was not at all happy. He was pacing back and forth in the drawing room as the police scurried about. His endless forehead bulged with purple veins. His steely eyes looked me over as if I were a regular halfwit. The nerve!

"Why would you attempt to take on these thieves by yourself?" he barked. "Have you any idea what might have happened to you?'

I was magnificently composed. "I am perfectly capable of dealing with a few hooded dwarfs, dear. As you can see, I had the situation under control."

Mr. Banks pointed to the hole in the wall. Which was terribly unfair. "It doesn't look like it, Miss Pocket!" he thundered. "And from what Mrs. Vans has told me, you very nearly burned to death."

"And not even a mark on her," said Mrs. Vans, clutching her rosary beads.

"Miss Pocket, the deal is off," said Mr. Banks gravely. "The situation is far too dangerous. As the executor of the Duchess's estate, I am empowered to make decisions concerning her property. That is the law."

I was stunned. I hadn't expected this. Call off the deal? Could he *do* that? I could see the five hundred pounds slipping from my grasp. But I hadn't just fallen off the turnip truck. I knew precisely what was needed. Which is why I began to sob. Rather hysterically.

"I've had an awful night!" I wailed. "Horrible! Treacherous!"

Mr. Banks regarded me coolly. Before he had a chance to speak again, I launched my offensive. Sparing no detail, I recounted the events of the evening. Being strapped to my bed.

Attacked in the kitchen. Flung about the drawing room. Mr. Banks listened to every word. He said nothing for a moment or two. And then . . . "This woman, the one who stayed in the shadows, did she speak at all?"

"Only once," I said, rather disappointed that of all the questions he might have asked me, *that* was the one he chose. "She said, 'Remarkable.'"

"What do you think she meant?"

I shrugged. "Perhaps she noticed my naturally silky hair."

"Thieves in the night!" cried Mrs. Vans. "Roaming about looking for treasure!"

Mr. Banks huffed. "This was no random robbery, Mrs. Vans. They came for Miss Pocket as much as for the necklace."

"Stuff and nonsense!" I said with a frown.

"Do not be foolish, Miss Pocket," he said. "Why did the intruders seek to immobilize you in your bed, but not Mrs. Vans or myself?"

I hadn't an answer for that.

Mr. Banks continued, "I believe they intended to find the Clock Diamond, then come back and take you."

"But why?" I said. "For what purpose?"

Now it was Mr. Banks who had no answer. He looked about at the wreckage. "All I know is this—you are in grave danger."

I shook my head. "Fear not, Mr. Banks. I'm terribly good in a fight. Stupendously brave. But your concern is understandable—as I possess all the delicate beauty of a princess in a tower."

Mrs. Vans snorted. "*You*, a princess."

"You're not the first to notice, dear." I smiled regally at the bloated dingbat. "My mother is from a noble family. *Tragically* noble. Enchanted castles, wicked stepsisters, poisoned apples, and whatnot."

"Enough of this foolishness, Miss Pocket," said Mr. Banks gruffly. "The necklace, is it safe?"

"I think so."

His voice softened. "It might be an idea if you checked."

"I will." It was curious he never asked me where the diamond was hidden.

Mrs. Vans went out into the hall and began berating the night constable. Mr. Banks followed her, trying his best to calm her down. He urged me to go back to bed. I did. But not before visiting the music room and making sure that the Clock Diamond was still there. It was.

They searched the house. The police and Mr. Banks. Looked everywhere. It was no great shock to find a window broken in Mrs. Vans's bedroom. Clearly that had been the thieves' point of entry.

By lunchtime the next day, a letter had arrived from Lady Amelia Butterfield. I read it with interest, Mr. Banks looking on.

"Well?" he said at last.

"It's as I expected," I said, folding the note. "Lady Amelia was delighted to hear from me. I'm invited to bring the necklace down to Butterfield Park on this afternoon's train. She claims not to remember me from her visit to Midwinter Hall—which I put down to a slight case of stupidity—but she says I am very welcome. So you see, Mr. Banks, our business is nearly at an end."

The grumpy lawyer didn't look at all happy. "I think you should wait before making the journey to Butterfield Park—

see if the police have any luck locating the thieves. Then we can decide what to do next."

"Wait for what?" I demanded.

"Miss Pocket, I am worried about you." He looked at me with something like tenderness. "I had a sister, once upon a time. She was a force of nature, rather like you, I suppose. I was very fond of her and . . . well, you remind me of her." He cleared his throat. "We must keep you safe, Miss Pocket, that is all there is to it."

This caught me off guard. Just a little. While people loved me as a general rule, I haven't much experience of them *worrying* about me. That's the sort of thing a parent might do. Or so I am told.

I smiled brightly. "I have a job to do, Mr. Banks, and I intend to do it. I shall catch the train to Suffolk at four o'clock."

"Then I am coming with you," he said quickly. "You can't do this on your own. It's too dangerous."

"I won't be on my own," I said, feeling rather pleased with myself. "Lady Amelia writes that her niece Rebecca is in London and will be traveling down on the same train. We will make the journey together."

Mr. Banks had no answer to this. But he had a stipulation.

"I will take you to the station and see you safely on board."

I sniffed. "As you wish. Silly man."

Mrs. Vans had packed me a hamper for the train, but I confess I ate most of it on the carriage ride to the station. Mr. Banks barked at me the whole way there—giving me a list of do's and don'ts that stretched on for days. I nodded in most of the right places.

While Mr. Banks was seeing to my ticket, I busied myself at the newsstand, selecting a penny dreadful or two for the journey ahead. Imagine my surprise when I ran into Miss Always—who was due to catch a train to her mother's village in the north. The pitiful creature explained that she had been delayed in London overnight due to the monstrous demands of her publisher. The brute loathed her new manuscript—said it had all the excitement of watching tomatoes grow—and was demanding a great many changes. But dear Miss Always was far more troubled by the events of last night in Belgravia.

"When I read of the break-in in the newspaper, and I

saw that it was the *very* house where you were staying . . ." Miss Always was overcome with the sort of emotion only a terrified spinster can summon. "I was filled with horror! Ivy, are you all right? Are you hurt?"

"Monstrously hurt, dear," I said bravely. "The whole ordeal was thrillingly dangerous. I came close to death on at least two occasions. Flung about. Burned to a crisp. I won't go into detail about how greatly I suffered—it's plain bad manners—but rest assured, it would make even a hardened pirate shudder in agony."

"You poor girl!" cried Miss Always, pushing her spectacles up her nose. "I trust the police have caught the villains who harmed you?"

I shook my head. "Still at large, dear. Probably planning their next attack."

Miss Always gasped. "Heavens!"

Which seemed like the perfect moment for me to mention the startling similarities between my pint-sized attackers and the hooded stranger I had seen talking to Miss Always on the ship. "It was uncanny," I said as I paid a shilling for two novels.

"How *peculiar*," said Miss Always. She looked terribly grave. "Goodness, Ivy, you cannot suspect my acquaintance from the boat? Walter was reunited with his father and is now in Bristol for a family reunion—so you see, it simply *couldn't* be him."

Which made perfect sense. Not that I ever suspected him. Well, not *really*. It was just that, well, how many hooded dwarfs does one usually come across in two days?

"Of course if you have any doubts, then you must report poor Walter to the authorities," said Miss Always, watching me carefully. "Unless . . . unless you already have?"

I assured her I had not. Which seemed to please her. What a kind soul she was!

"I'm dreadfully worried for you, Ivy," she said, linking her arm in mine as we began to walk. Her voice dropped to a whisper. "Traveling with the Clock Diamond and keeping it safe until Matilda Butterfield's birthday ball is a grave responsibility for a young girl. I wish . . . I wish I could come with you to Suffolk—so you wouldn't be all alone." Miss Always was suddenly bug-eyed. "Oh, Ivy, I've just had the most wonderful idea! What if I change my ticket and come with you to Butterfield Park? Wouldn't that be thrilling?"

"How can you, dear?" I said, rather startled. "Your mother being at death's door and whatnot."

Miss Always looked slightly vexed. But it quickly passed. "Yes, of course. Poor Mummy."

I saw Mr. Banks coming towards us from across the platform. I pointed him out to Miss Always—keen to make an introduction. Unfortunately, it was at that *exact* moment that Miss Always realized she was going to miss her train if she didn't hurry away. Which she did. At great speed.

Mr. Banks was terrifically interested in my friend. Asked a dozen questions. Looked about, this way and that. Then he walked me to my carriage (I had a first-class ticket, as you would expect) and waited on the platform until the train had left the station. He looked as if he expected an attack at any moment, poor man. I waved, but he didn't wave back.

I was glad to be leaving London and all its calamities behind. I had the Clock Diamond sewn into the pocket of my dress and my carpetbag at my feet. I looked breathtaking. Just like a banker's daughter. Or at very least a cheese-maker's niece.

I met Rebecca Butterfield on the train. Dear Mr. Banks arranged for me to have the seat next to hers (in first class!). Rebecca was thirteen and pretty, in a plain sort of way—though her freckles were deeply unfortunate. She had wavy blond hair worn loose around her shoulders, dull brown eyes, and unremarkable lips. She seemed rather glum—which caused her to stoop, giving her the posture of a washerwoman. A small box wrapped in brown paper and tied with string sat on her lap. She seemed rather fixated by it.

"Is this your first visit to Suffolk?" she asked not long into our journey.

"Well . . ." I looked out the window, then back at Rebecca. "I was recently in Paris. You see, I travel the world a great deal. I've been so many places, it's hard to keep track."

"How lucky you are, Ivy." She looked positively dazzled. "I would love to see the world and travel across exotic lands. To go far away."

"Oh, yes, it's terribly interesting." I sighed. "Though sometimes I wish my life was slightly less thrilling, a little less astounding. It might be rather nice to be a perfectly ordinary, utterly unremarkable lump—like yourself, dear."

Rebecca looked slightly stunned. Clearly she hadn't expected a junior lady's maid to have such fine manners!

"Do you live at Butterfield Park?" I asked.

She nodded her head gravely. "I have nowhere else to go."

"You mustn't look so glum," I said. "I've only known you a short time, but already I can tell your skin gets awfully blotchy when you're glum."

She gasped. "What did you say?"

The poor creature was obviously hard of hearing.

"Blotchy, dear," I said, this time louder. "When you think gloomy thoughts, which I imagine is terribly often, your cheeks flare up like you've been hit in the face with a cricket ball."

Remarkably, this seemed to please the strange girl. For she grinned for the first time and said, "Where are you from, Ivy?" She shifted in her seat to face me, her hands clasped around the box in her lap. "Who are your parents?"

"My parents?" I retied the ribbon in my hair, which gave me a moment to think. "My father is Polish. A painter. Mainly fruit. Occasionally flowers. Poor, but hauntingly gifted. My mother is defective. Has an obsession with the pan flute. She ran away to join an orchestra in Berlin when I was eight. She sends money when she can and writes every week. Her letters are in German, so I have no idea what she's saying—but I'm certain they're full of longing and heartbreak."

Rebecca Butterfield looked at me with a mixture of shock and envy. "But who takes care of you?"

"I do," I said brightly. "I've been in service for a year and a half, and it suits me very well. And just between you and me, I'm soon to come into a small fortune—on account of the diamond necklace I'm delivering to your cousin, Matilda."

"Oh." Rebecca seemed to pale at the name. "Yes, of course. I suppose it is a gift for her birthday?"

I nodded. "A special, one-of-a-kind present from the Duchess of Trinity. The Duchess is dead—stabbed through the heart, poor dear—but it was her dying wish that Matilda should have the necklace."

"Matilda has a great many jewels." Rebecca was smiling but looked rather like she had swallowed a dung beetle. "Too many to count. Do you know why I was in London, Ivy?"

"I think so, dear. London has the finest madhouses in all of England."

Rebecca shook her head. "I was in the city to be fitted for a new dress. Do I *need* a new dress? Do I want one? It doesn't matter. Grandmother said I must have one for the birthday ball. No one will be looking at me, but everything must be perfect for Matilda."

"Is she a horrid sort of girl?" I asked.

"Matilda is very pretty," came the meek reply. And then she said no more.

A lengthy silence settled in, and I had nearly been lulled to sleep by the train's gentle rhythm when Rebecca offered me a slice of cherry cake. Which I took gladly. I asked if she was traveling with any potatoes. Or perhaps a pumpkin. Unfortunately, she wasn't.

"I'm the eldest," she said between mouthfuls. "A full three hundred and seventy-six days older than Matilda." She looked intently at me. "That's nine thousand and twenty-four hours. You understand, Ivy?"

I had no clue. "Perfectly, dear."

"Butterfield Park should go to me, being the eldest. But Grandmother says Matilda will be her heir." Rebecca looked down at the parcel in her lap. "Mother wanted the estate to be mine—she loved it dearly, the gardens best of all. If she were here, she would never let Grandmother do such a thing."

"Your mother is dead?"

Rebecca nodded her head. "Last year. Her heart."

"I'm awfully sorry, dear."

"Father has a new family in Italy," she said faintly. "So it was just us—Mother and I."

"Now that she is gone, is the rest of your family shockingly cruel?" I said rather hopefully. "Do they beat you and starve you and lock you in the cellar?"

She didn't answer for a long while. Then she glanced out of the window and said, "They do not notice me most of the time. And when they do, it makes them uncomfortable. They think that I am strange." She looked at me earnestly. "What do *you* think, Ivy?"

"You're not the prettiest of girls," I said with heartbreaking tact, "and you seem slightly odd—but I like you very much. Besides, you seem awfully tortured, which is *terribly* interesting."

Rebecca was looking down again at the box she was clutching.

As such, I pointed to it. "What's inside?"

The question seemed to stun her. She gulped. "Nothing. What I mean is—nothing special."

"Why don't you let me be the judge of that? Come now, dear, I am *dying* to know."

Rebecca frowned. Looked slightly terrified. "Honestly, Ivy," she said, "you would be very disappointed. It's just a little something I picked up in London. It's really very boring."

I sighed. "I won't stop asking. I will drive you batty."

A great wave of defeat washed over her freckly face. She placed her hands around the package, holding it tenderly. "Very well, Ivy," she said. "It is a present for Matilda's birthday. Yes, that's all it is, just a little present. Nothing more than a few ribbons for her hair and a sash. Matilda will think it terribly dull. So you see—it's really not very interesting at all."

I didn't believe her for a moment.

6

We stood outside the station, bags at our feet, and waited for the carriage to come and whisk us away to Butterfield Park. I'm usually an excellent waiter. I once waited for a miracle. It took seven and a half weeks. Yet I never gave up.

But right now I was tired. And it was getting late.

"Lady Amelia didn't say she would send a carriage in her letter," I said, swatting away an insufferable moth. "I just assumed on account of me being a *welcomed* guest. . . ."

"Don't be shocked, Ivy," said Rebecca, still gazing with alarming fondness at the mysterious box in her hands. "I'm sure my aunt *meant* to send the carriage, but it's easy to be forgotten at Butterfield Park—unless your name happens to be Matilda."

"Do you have any more cake, dear? I'm positively starving."

"You ate the last piece twenty minutes ago." Rebecca sighed. "We'll have to go on foot. I hope you're a good walker, Ivy."

"Stupendous," I said, picking up my bag. "When I was four, I walked across India with my father. He wanted to paint ashrams and elephants and whatnot. I hardly broke a sweat."

Rebecca frowned. "You're lying."

"Who can say?" I pointed at the suitcase. "Shall we get started?"

We mounted the crest of a small hill and headed down an avenue bordered by elm trees, through which Butterfield Park was revealed in all its glory. It was a fine building with marble columns and magnificent turrets and chimneys reaching towards the heavens. A clock tower crowned the east wing. Surrounding the main house was a tapestry of formal gardens full of roses and tulips, a wildflower meadow, an apple orchard, and a pretty summerhouse. The entire estate was circled by woodlands.

"It's perfectly lovely," I declared.

"Wickam took care of the gardens," said Rebecca softly. "He loved them so. I think he was the only person around here Grandmother actually *liked*—well, apart from Matilda."

"Has he been gone long?"

"He died last winter. We have a new gardener now." Rebecca scratched her nose. "He's young and clever and full of new ideas for the wildflower meadow. Everybody hates him."

"Quite right too," I said.

Rebecca giggled.

We ambled up the gravel drive. "They are probably still packing up from the theatrical last night," Rebecca said glumly. "My aunt fancies herself a writer. She loves to put on plays and recitals." She must have noticed the ravishing smile upon my face because she said, "Do you act, Ivy?"

"Brilliantly," I said. "I toured America in a production of *The Secret Garden*. I played Mary Lennox, of course. The critics raved about me. Said I lit up the stage like a mid-sized house fire."

Rebecca was frowning. "You did no such thing."

"Of course I did." I shrugged. "I'm practically positive."

We reached the large oak doors and were ushered into a great hall. I spun around, taking in my surroundings. The hall had dark paneled walls, a massive carved staircase, a large coat of arms above a marble fireplace, and a stupendous chandelier suspended from the vaulted ceiling. Rebecca told me the house had more than ninety rooms. A west wing and east wing. Servants' quarters. A majestic library. Staircases everywhere you looked. Banks of stained-glass windows. More hallways and corridors than a hospital.

"Where is my aunt?" Rebecca asked the butler.

"She's in the library, waiting for little Miss Pocket," came a voice from behind us.

"Blast!" hissed Rebecca. She pushed her mysterious box into my arms. "Pretend it's yours," she whispered. *"Please."*

Of course I played along—for I have all the natural instincts of a professional trickster. I turned and was rewarded with my first glimpse of Matilda Butterfield. She was a contrast to her fair cousin—dark hair, hazel eyes, the reddest lips I'd ever seen, and an olive complexion. She looked like a doll. Lovely, but somehow unreal.

Rebecca introduced us and we exchanged a polite greeting, but the whole time Matilda's eyes were fixed on the package I was holding.

"Is that it?" she said eagerly. "Is that my diamond?"

I looked down. "This? Of course not, dear."

"Then what is it?" asked Matilda.

Rebecca gulped and looked at me with pleading eyes. I had no idea what was going on. But I knew she needed me. "Nothing," I said. "Just something I picked up in London."

Matilda smiled coolly. "Is it nothing or something?" she said. "You seem confused, Pocket."

I sighed. "It is really rather personal, dear. My aunt Agnes is a fruitcake. Barking mad. She's been locked away for years on account of her blowing up Mrs. Digby's prize-winning dairy cow. Naturally, Aunt Agnes spends most of her time in a straitjacket. But once a week, for one precious hour, she is freed from her restraints. And in that one hour, my insane aunt likes to bake. Cupcakes. She's very talented." I looked down at the box with suitable affection. "I receive a package like this every week, containing a single vanilla cream cupcake. It's really very sweet, don't you think?"

Matilda Butterfield didn't say anything at first, her eyes moving back and forth between Rebecca and me. At last she said, "Can I try it?"

"Try what, dear?" I said.

"Your insane aunt's cupcake, of course," said Matilda, flicking her dark locks.

Before I could answer, she snatched the box from my grasp. Then she did the strangest thing—she put the box up to her ear. I looked to Rebecca, but she just groaned wearily and stared at her feet.

"I knew it!" Matilda declared. "You've done it again, haven't you, cousin?"

"Done what?" I asked.

Now it was Rebecca's turn to snatch the box away. "Mind your own business!" she hissed. Then she hurried away, practically running up the staircase.

I looked back to Matilda for some sort of explanation.

"Come on, Pocket," she said, turning on her heel and striding from the hall. "My grandmother wants to see you."

"Where is Rebecca?" That was Lady Amelia's first question after I set down my carpetbag and introduced myself with a breathtaking curtsy.

"She's gone to her room, Mother," said Matilda sweetly. "Same as always."

Lady Amelia was a regal and slightly pudgy creature, in a yellow gown of the finest silk, perched before a writing table, a black cat at her feet. She had Matilda's dark hair and features (apparently she descended from Italian royalty).

"Did she . . . did she do it again?" she asked, looking anxiously at Matilda.

"I'm afraid so, Mother."

"I don't know what to do," said Lady Amelia wearily. "We have tried everything to make her stop—but she will not."

I could only assume they were referring to the mysterious box. Now, while I had no idea what *that* was about, I was certain I could help. "Forgive me, Lady Amelia," I said, pushing a bowl of grapes out of the way and sitting down on the edge of her writing table, "but I got to know Rebecca rather well on our train journey from London. It's clear the poor girl is unhappy. *Why* is she unhappy? Well, I can't say for sure, but I'm almost certain it's all your fault. Not just you, dear. The whole family."

Lady Amelia was smiling now (strange woman). "I see. Go on . . ."

I jumped off the writing table and plucked a grape from the bowl. "Well, if melancholia is her problem, I have an excellent remedy. All I need is a glass of cranberry juice and a hammer. It's remarkably effective."

Lady Amelia's laugh was rather musical. *Why* she was laughing, I hadn't a clue.

"She's mental," said Matilda with a huff. "She makes no sense at all."

I was outraged that she was talking about her cousin in that way. It was *very* rude. But before I could slap some sense into her, Rebecca appeared in the doorway. Rather sheepishly, she entered the library.

"Welcome home, Rebecca," said Lady Amelia. "Was London a success?"

"If you mean did I get fitted for the dress, the answer is yes," said Rebecca.

Lady Amelia regarded her niece carefully. "And did you keep your promise?"

Rebecca immediately looked at Matilda, who was smiling wickedly.

"Of course she didn't keep her promise," came a brittle voice from somewhere across the room. I turned but could see no one. That corner of the library overlooked the rose garden, and in front of the windows stood a single winged back chair. An elderly woman dressed all in black began to rise up from behind it. She moved slowly, with the aid of a cane.

"Foolish girl," she hissed at Rebecca.

"Lady Elizabeth, do not be too harsh," said Lady Amelia. "I am sure Rebecca tried her very hardest. This is a complicated matter."

"Claptrap!" spat the old geezer. "She must stop, and she will. Or *else*. Is it any wonder I will not make her my heir?"

Lady Elizabeth was not at all what I had expected. While she spoke with all the regality of Queen Victoria, she had a head like a walnut. Hands like claws. A body withered and thin as a rake. Her skin had seen more bad weather than a lighthouse. She was also rather mean.

Rebecca mumbled something about being sorry and promising to try harder and whatnot. I was on the point of asking for a snack when Lady Elizabeth turned her wrinkled gaze on me.

"Where is the necklace?" she said coldly. "That is why you are in this house, is it not?"

"The diamond is somewhere safe," I said, smiling at the old woman. "Now be a dear, and fetch me a dozen uncooked potatoes."

"Fetch you *what*?" she barked.

"You must be famished after your journey, Ivy," said Lady Amelia, hastily ringing the bell.

"Starving," I said. "Haven't eaten in days."

"The necklace, Miss Pocket," said old Walnut Head, eyeing me fiercely. "Bring it here this instant!"

"Not possible, dear," I said, shaking my head. "The Duchess of Trinity gave me very strict instructions about the Clock Diamond. No one can see it until the birthday ball."

Just then, a pale woman with startling red hair pulled back in a tight bun entered the library.

"Please excuse the interruption," she said crisply. The poor creature had an accent. American, I think. "I am after a book of French poetry for my next lesson."

"Where are the smelling salts?" muttered Matilda. "I

won't survive another of her *dreary* lessons!"

"Matilda, what an awful thing to say," whispered Lady Amelia. "Miss Frost has only been here a few days. You must give your new governess a chance."

Miss Frost hurried over to the shelves by the spiral stairs and busied herself sorting through the books. All the while, she kept stealing glances at me. There was something vaguely familiar about her, but I couldn't think what. Which was odd.

"I demand you show me the diamond, Pocket," snarled Matilda. "I have a right to see it! How else can I be certain it will complement my dress for the birthday ball?"

"Fear not, Matilda," I said brightly. "You are blessed with such a naturally weather-beaten complexion, I am certain the necklace will do wonders for your appearance."

A bitter smile creased the awful girl's face as she glared at me. "I pity you, Pocket. You'll never know what it's like to wear a priceless jewel. To have every girl in England just *wishing* she was you."

"Don't be so sure," I said, unable to help myself. "Not the part about having every girl in England wishing she was me, of course. Although I *was* voted Girl Most Likely to Burn at the Stake two years running. But as for the Clock Diamond—I hate to burst your balloon, dear, but I've already worn it, and I looked heartbreakingly pretty."

A loud *bang* echoed through the great library. All eyes snapped to Miss Frost, whose book had tumbled to the floor. She looked frightfully pale as she bent down to pick it up.

"You had no right to wear what doesn't belong to you," bellowed Matilda.

"The Duchess of Trinity said that I could," I told her, feeling the moment was right for some serious lying. "In fact, that dear, sweet, potbellied dingbat positively insisted. She was very particular when it came to the Clock Diamond."

"I am rather stunned that she wished to give Matilda such a valuable gift," said Lady Elizabeth shrewdly. "We were not exactly *friends* these past sixty years. It is most unexpected."

I retrieved the Duchess's letter from my bag and handed it to Lady Elizabeth. "I have a feeling she wished to make peace with you."

"Hush," snapped Walnut Head. She read the note, and I

saw the fire in her eyes dim just slightly. She muttered softly, "Well, well, old friend . . ."

"It's just so tragic," said Lady Amelia gravely, "what happened to the Duchess."

Matilda's face clouded over. "I'm not sure I want a necklace from a dead woman."

"Claptrap!" barked Lady Elizabeth. "The Duchess was rich and friendless, it's no wonder someone put a knife in her chest."

"Do you have any idea who killed her, Miss Pocket?" said Miss Frost rather suddenly. She had the book of poetry open in front of her. "She was murdered very soon after giving you the necklace, was she not?"

"Yes, dear," I said. "The whole business is terribly mysterious. Lunatics left, right, and center. And as the Duchess's messenger, I feel a great sense of responsibility to her memory." I sighed mournfully. "I was the last person to see her alive."

Miss Frost slammed the book shut. "I would imagine the *killer* was the last person to see her alive."

Then she excused herself and stalked from the library.

"Well, I don't think it's fair," muttered Matilda, throwing

a cushion at the cat. "Why should I have to wait until my birthday to get the necklace? That's not for five whole days!"

"That is not the worst part," said her grandmother. "We are to be stuck with Miss Pocket for five *whole* days." She looked at me hopefully. "Unless you have somewhere else to be?"

"Heavens no," I said. "I'm soon to come into a fortune. Until then, I'm free as a bird."

Rebecca picked up my carpetbag and said, "Ivy must be exhausted, and I'm sure she wishes to freshen up. I'll show her up to the guest bedroom."

Which was thrilling.

"Certainly not!" cried old Walnut Head in outrage. "Put her in the attic. Miss Pocket may be our guest, but she is not one of *us*. She is a maid, and maids do not sleep in guest bedrooms."

And with that, she turned her back and returned to her chair by the window.

Beastly bag of bones!

The attic was tucked away in the east wing—up the main stairs, across a landing, down a long hallway, and up three more flights of rickety back stairs. Finally I was led into a dimly lit corridor. Frightfully narrow. A door on either side. I was informed that the narrow staircase at the far end led up to the roof.

My bedroom was plain. Wood floors. Sloping ceilings. Whitewashed walls. Jug and basin. Little window overlooking the schoolhouse. Which was a blessing. I had no tolerance for comfy chairs, pretty curtains, or comfortable beds. The room across the hall was apparently a dusty chamber used to store the costumes and props from Lady Amelia's theatricals. So I was quite alone.

I washed my face, changed my dress, and went to explore the house. But not before sewing the Clock Diamond into the pocket of my new dress. I felt it was probably best that I kept the stone with me at all times.

I stood at the banister of the first-floor landing and looked down—a maid or two hurried past, carrying brooms and mops. Then my eyes were drawn by the radiant chandelier suspended above the great hall. Could that be just the place to hide the necklace? If only I had a ladder.

Footsteps clicked rapidly down the hall to my left. I heard a door open. Being naturally curious, I tilted my head and peered down the vast corridor—just as a girl slipped into a doorway at the far end. The door shut quietly. I *thought* it was Rebecca.

Only one way to find out.

"Rebecca?" I knocked gently on the door.

Nothing.

"Anybody there?"

I heard movement on the other side. Shuffling of feet.

The door opened. Just a crack.

"Yes?" It *was* Rebecca. She looked guilty. Or scared. Or something.

"Is this your bedroom, dear?" I asked.

She nodded. It was clear she had no intention of inviting me in.

"I have a dreadful problem," I said. "As you know, I'm soon to have five hundred pounds. Which means I will need to smarten up my bedroom. And I was very much hoping you would let me see yours, dear. You know, as inspiration and whatnot."

"It's awfully messy, Ivy," she said. "Perhaps some other time."

"Oh, don't worry about the mess," I said brightly, putting my hand on the door and pushing just a little. Well, I tried to. Rebecca had her foot wedged against the other side. "If you like, I'll help you clean up. I'm an excellent duster."

Rebecca shook her head. Then she opened the door just enough to squeeze herself through and slipped out into the corridor. The door closed behind her before I could catch more than a glimpse inside. She then took a key—threaded on a ribbon around her wrist—and locked the door. Which I thought was rather excessive.

"It's such a lovely afternoon," she said. "Why don't I take you outside and show you the schoolhouse? It used to be Lady Elizabeth's summerhouse, but now it's where Matilda and I have our lessons. It's really very pretty."

Before I had a chance to protest, Rebecca led me quickly down the hallway.

We made our way along a path beside a blooming avenue of yellow tulips, which led directly to the schoolhouse. The building was white, with a thatched roof and lattice windows. Terribly fetching. Miss Frost passed us, carrying a large dictionary and hurrying towards the schoolhouse. She stopped and directed her attention to Rebecca.

"Class commences in ten minutes," she said crisply. "You have completed your book report?"

"It is *nearly* done, Miss Frost," said Rebecca rather meekly. "If you will just give me a little more time . . ."

"Oh, Rebecca," said Miss Frost with a sigh. "You have only been my pupil for a few days, and already you are behind. I am certain you are a bright girl with great potential, but I cannot think what you do all day, locked up in your room." Miss Frost's gaze softened. "Will you promise to try harder?"

"Yes, Miss Frost," came the faint reply.

"It's my fault, dear," I said, giving Miss Frost a congenial slap on the arm. "Rebecca was hunched over her report when I found her. I practically begged her to show me the gardens. I cried. Hit my head against the wall. All sorts of madness. So you see, it's really my fault, not hers."

To my surprise, Miss Frost didn't bite my head off. In fact, her freckled frown faded and she laughed lightly. "You have a way with words, Miss Pocket. I don't know that I believe any of it, but it is most entertaining."

I huffed. The nerve!

Miss Frost looked back at Rebecca. "You have eight minutes to finish your report," she said, pointing to the schoolhouse. "I suggest you hurry along."

"Yes, Miss Frost," said Rebecca, making a hasty retreat.

When we were alone, Miss Frost quickly turned her attention to more serious matters.

"I have no business saying this," she said, her eyes falling intently onto mine, "but I am worried, Miss Pocket."

"What about?" I said.

"The diamond. I read a great deal—it is rather a habit of mine—and I have learned something of the Clock Diamond's history. It is dark, indeed. Have you . . . has there been any trouble since the stone came into your care?"

"Not really," I said brightly. "The odd break-in and whatnot. A darling old lawyer in London thinks differently—he sees danger around every corner—but I have kept the necklace perfectly safe."

"I have heard there is a vault here at the house," said Miss Frost. "I am sure Lady Elizabeth would let you keep the diamond there until Matilda's birthday." She patted down her dazzling red hair. "It is just a thought."

"There's no need for that," I said. "I keep the stone with me at all times."

"That is very unwise," declared Miss Frost, her face hardening. "In the last few weeks there have been several brazen robberies in the county. Lady Francesca's daughter was hit in the head and had her gold watch stolen as she walked home from church. Furthermore, people in possession of the Clock Diamond have a habit of dying rather violently. You would do well to remember that."

I sighed. "I suppose you think the diamond is cursed?"

"There is no such thing as a curse," said Miss Frost tersely. "Where the Clock Diamond originated, no one knows. Few people have even laid eyes on it. But I have read that once they do, they find the stone *very* hard to resist." She looked awfully grim! "Do you agree, Miss Pocket?"

"Not at all, dear. The necklace didn't tempt me for a

moment. And as for someone stealing it, fear not—I will take your advice and find a suitable hiding spot."

"I am glad to hear it." Funny, though, she didn't looked terribly pleased—and I knew why. This wasn't about some silly diamond.

"Forgive me," I said, taking Miss Frost's hand in mine, "but I can see from the pinched look upon your face that you have a heavy heart."

She looked startled. Just for a moment. Then it passed, and Miss Frost smiled as if she hadn't a care in the world. "Do I?"

"You mustn't be embarrassed," I told her. "Spinsterhood is no great crime."

She frowned, pulled her hand away. "I *beg* your pardon?"

"Spinsterhood." I said it slowly so she would understand my meaning. "You find yourself without prospects—heartbreakingly grim and monstrously unattached. This sort of thing is terribly common among book-loving, sour-faced governesses, so you are *not* alone. Do not give up hope! I feel certain there is a humpbacked footman or a toothless blacksmith just waiting to sweep you off your feet."

Miss Frost looked as if she had been sucking on a particularly sour grapefruit. Which was thrilling. Then she tucked the dictionary under her arm and stalked off towards the summerhhouse. She may have muttered something about washing my mouth out with soap.

But I can't be sure.

Filled with the warm glow that comes when you have helped a fellow traveler in need, I set off to find the perfect hiding spot for the Clock Diamond.

7

I had dinner in my room that first night, then retired to bed. Rebecca insisted that I should dine with the family downstairs. Lady Elizabeth insisted that I shouldn't. I didn't press the point. After all, I was dead tired. Or so I thought. But instead I just lay there. Looking up at the moonlight playing upon the eaves. Trying not to think about anything remotely troubling.

Normally I'm an excellent sleeper. But not tonight. For as much as I didn't want to admit it, Miss Frost had unnerved me. I'd spent all afternoon roaming about the great house, looking for a suitable hiding place for the stone. There were so many rooms. So many nooks and crannies. In the end, none felt right. So the stone was now tucked under my pillow. But my bedroom door had no lock. Anyone could come in. See me sleeping like some sort of heavenly angel. Slip their devious hand under the pillow. And take the stone.

Eventually I drifted off to sleep. I must have. After all, you have to be asleep to wake up. And that's what happened. I awoke. Suddenly. Flew up in my bed. Wide awake.

Something had startled me.

The room was thick with silvery shadows. All was still. Silent, save for the snapping and creaking of the old house. I looked about in the darkness. Nothing. Nothing . . . but *something*. I didn't feel alone. Which was foolish. Of *course* I was alone. And yet . . . it wouldn't hurt just to make sure. I felt around on the side table for a match and lit a tallow candle.

The flame bloomed inside the dark room like a bubble of honey-colored light.

"Pull yourself together, Ivy," I said, leaning over to blow out the candle. "There's no one here."

"Look closer, child."

I screamed. Jumped. Grabbed the candle. Thrust it forward; its flickering light swallowed the darkness. The tattered armchair in the corner of the room was still shrouded in shadow. But I heard something move. Or wheeze. I crawled to the end of the bed, the candle trembling in my hand.

"Who's there?" I hissed.

"Don't you know?" A blue glow bloomed in the corner. And there she was. The Duchess of Trinity. Her body spilling over the armchair like an enormous mollusk. Her face ashen. Blood drenched the front of her nightdress. She was just how I remembered her. Only dead.

"What do you want?"

"The truth," she said softly.

I backed away. Creeping up the bed until my arm hit the wall.

"I know why you're here," I whispered.

She seemed to find this amusing. "Do tell . . ."

"It's about the necklace," I said. "You're upset because I tried it on."

The Duchess of Trinity smiled darkly. "You broke your promise, child."

"It was only for a moment. I just wanted to see what it felt like. And no harm was done."

She seemed to find that amusing. "Are you sure?"

"Perfectly sure. And it wasn't pleasant at all—in fact, I fainted—and I won't be doing that again. So you see, there's really no need for you to haunt me. In fact, I'd be terribly grateful if you'd shuffle off."

She closed her eyes. Perhaps she was taking a nap.

"A great deal has happened since last we met," said the Duchess slowly. "I would hate for you to be distracted from your task. No matter what, the Clock Diamond *must* be given to Matilda Butterfield at her birthday ball. You won't disappoint me, will you?"

"Of course not." I sighed disagreeably. "Though I can't think *why* you'd want her to have it. She's violently unpleasant."

"Lady Elizabeth adores her." The Duchess seemed to purr. "Every hope and dream she has for the future of this great house is wrapped up in that girl."

"If you say so."

"The view from here is marvelous," said the Duchess playfully. "I can see *everything*. When the stone was around your neck, you looked into it. What did you see?"

"Nothing," I said quickly. "Nothing at all."

She shook her head, and as she did, starlight seemed to fall from her white curls. "What did you see, child? The *truth*."

She was rather stubborn for a dead woman.

"I *may* have seen a girl," I said.

"Who was she?"

I shrugged. "I don't remember."

"Lies," she spat. "The girl was plain. Friendless. Alone in the world. Sound familiar?"

I huffed. I may have rolled my eyes. It was perfectly clear what the Duchess of Ghostville was getting at. "She looked a *little* like me, I suppose."

"The stone has much to show you," sang the Duchess, "but it will bring you no joy. Only suffering. Do not be tempted. Leave it alone, child—for your own good."

"Really, dear, you've picked the wrong girl for this sort

of thing. I don't scare easily, and to be frank, you are giving off a revolting odor. Now if you don't mind, I'd like to get back to sleep."

All at once, the distance between us fell away. I can't say if I flew to her or her to me. All I know is, I lifted from the bed. I moved rapidly. My nightdress billowing. Legs kicking. There wasn't time to scream. Then a buzzing sound. Loud and urgent. Right in my ear. I looked up. Her face loomed before me. Her whole body seemed to vibrate and the radiant blue of her skin was blinding.

"Remember your promise, child," she hissed. "Do not disappoint me."

Then I fell. In a tangle. Landed on the bed. The candle went out and dropped from my hand. Darkness and pale moonlight filled the attic. I groped around the bedsheets. Found the candle. Struck another match. I searched the room. She was gone. I jumped up and began walking about madly. My mind a jumble of ghostly thoughts.

Finally, exhausted, I returned to bed. Pulled up the sheets.

But I didn't blow out the candle. I didn't dare.

Pancakes. Pancakes and sweet tea. Perhaps an omelet. A raw potato or three. That was what I needed. A hearty breakfast. I smoothed the creases of my white muslin dress and gazed at my reflection in the mirror. I didn't look tired. My skin was glowing. Outside, the morning with all its promise seemed a million miles away from last night. A nightmare. That's all it had been. Murdered duchesses didn't come back from the dead. Maybe that happened in books. But not real life. Not to me.

I heard noises. A fluttering sound. Like something moving. Then silence. Then more fluttering. The blubbery ghost was back! That was my first thought. The blood ran cold in my veins.

With bone-shattering courage, I opened my door and crossed the narrow hall. The room across from mine, the storeroom for the costumes and backdrops from Lady Amelia's theatricals, was filled with crates, boxes, trunks, spears, shields, and swords.

I stepped inside. Two swallows glided between the rafters.

Soft light sliced through the beams of wood, illuminating the creatures' arched wings and casting majestic shadows upon the sloping ceiling. The birds landed with ease on a high beam.

It was really rather wondrous. So wondrous that I stayed in that dusty room for the longest time. Wandering about, looking in trunks full of faded costumes, wooden swords, and drooping hats and chests full of rusted tiaras and worthless costume jewelry all tangled in a cluster. I had never seen so much rubbish in all of my life. Which is when it hit me. The most brilliant idea.

"Of course!" I said. For now I knew *exactly* where to hide the Clock Diamond.

Just at that moment, I heard footsteps approaching in the hallway. No doubt a maid coming to tidy up my bedroom. I closed the lid of the trunk and hurried from the room.

My first breakfast at Butterfield Park was heartbreaking. Not a pancake or potato in sight. Lady Elizabeth suggested I would be more comfortable eating in the kitchen with the help. I told her I was completely comfortable eating in the dining room with the aristocrats. She nearly choked on her boiled egg.

The morning passed swiftly. I received a letter from Miss Always. Terribly depressing. While her mother was feeling better, her family's cottage was small and crowded. It was impossible for her to get any writing done. And the changes to her manuscript were due at the publisher in less than a month. Her most cherished dream was of was a quiet country house where she could write in peace. But alas, she hadn't the money to let one. *Oh, Ivy,* she wrote, *whatever will I do?*

Poor, wretched Miss Always!

I went out for a walk in the meadow. Tried my best to think happy thoughts. Only four days until Matilda's birthday ball. Soon I would begin my new life. I wasn't about to let a silly nightmare spoil my sunny future. And that was all it had been. Just a dream. I felt guilty for wearing the necklace and breaking my promise to the Duchess, so I had conjured her up in my sleep. Put a lot of gibberish about the stone in her mouth. That I mustn't be tempted by what it had to show me. That it would bring me suffering. Stuff and nonsense!

I wandered back towards the house and found Rebecca sitting in the conservatory, working on her book report. She glanced up when I entered, a curious look in her eyes. "Did she scare you?" she asked.

I gasped. How did she know about the ghost?

"I'm sure I don't know what you mean," I said brightly.

Rebecca closed her book. "I don't believe you," she said. "I heard Miss Frost warning you about the diamond."

Oh, Miss Frost. The gloomy governess. I felt a wave of relief. "Well, yes," I said, "perhaps she did bother me a little. She seemed rather fixated on it."

"I don't think she likes you," said Rebecca.

"Miss Frost is a terrible governess," I said, in my most

disapproving voice. "Why would Lady Amelia employ an American? Strict, humorless, fat, lonely, and British. *That's* what a governess should be!"

"Our last governess was from Wales," said Rebecca softly. "Miss Rochester. She was lovely."

"What a coincidence," I said, falling into an armchair. "My last governess was also a Miss Rochester. Jolly good sport, she was. Only one arm, but a gifted knitter."

Rebecca looked baffled. "Is that true, Ivy?"

"I certainly hope so. But back to *your* Miss Rochester— where did she go? Did she marry? The good ones always do."

Rebecca shook her head. "She vanished."

"Vanished?" Suddenly I was very interested. "What do you mean, dear?"

"We woke up last Friday, and she was gone," said Rebecca, her voice ripe with sadness. "No note. No forwarding address. No explanation."

"Goodness," I said. "How deliciously mysterious! My godfather vanished once. In a puff of smoke. Didn't reappear until the following spring."

Rebecca was silent. Her fingers knotted together. Her gaze far away.

"And you have heard nothing from Miss Rochester since?" I asked.

"Not a word," she said. "She lived with us for two years. That's more than seven hundred days. Seventeen thousand five hundred and twenty hours. Then she was gone." She looked at me. "People do that, don't they?"

"Vanish?" I asked.

"Run out of time," she whispered.

The poor girl was positively bonkers. Who could keep track of all those silly numbers? I did my best to get back to the matter at hand. There was a puzzle here. I could feel it. "So Miss Rochester vanished last Friday?"

Rebecca nodded somberly.

I frowned. "How on earth did you find a new governess so quickly?"

"Aunt Amelia met Miss Frost on a train the very day Miss Rochester vanished," answered Rebecca. "Turns out Miss Frost had come all the way from America to take up a position with a family in London. But they had to sail for Australia all of a sudden. Miss Frost was reading Aunt Amelia's novel—that's what got them talking."

"Lady Amelia wrote a novel?" I said.

"*Summer Tempest.* Nobody bought it—well, apart from Miss Frost. Anyway, they started talking, and by the time the train reached London, Aunt Amelia had hired Miss Frost to be our new governess."

"How lucky for Miss Frost," I said, my mind spinning with dark thoughts about the vanished Miss Rochester. "It must have been the hand of fate."

Rebecca shook her head. "I'm not so sure."

After lunch that same day, I decided to spend a few hours in the library reading Lady Amelia's book. I was on my way there when a maid came rushing out of the morning room carrying a bowl of water, a damp cloth, and a grimace—she looked on the verge of tears. The tormented creature explained that Lady Elizabeth was having one of her headaches. As such, she was making everybody's life a misery.

Naturally, I knew just what to do. I picked up a basket from the kitchen and set off toward the garden.

With my supplies gathered, I found Lady Elizabeth in the morning room, resplendent in a black silk gown. She was lying on a sofa with the cat. Her withered head was propped up by a pillow. She was muttering about her life of suffering.

"You look terrible," I said brightly, setting the basket on the table. "Do you get headaches often?"

"Constantly," she snapped. "My suffering is monstrous. The future weighs heavily upon me. Thank heavens for Matilda. Without her, I would give in to complete despair."

"What about Rebecca?" I said firmly. "She is your granddaughter too."

Lady Elizabeth huffed. "That girl is as deluded as she is bumbling! No, Matilda is the future of Butterfield Park." The old bat thrust a bony finger into the air. "She will be my legacy!"

"I think you should worry less about your legacy and more about your nose." I wiped Lady Elizabeth's dripping nose with my handkerchief. "Big blow, dear—get it all out."

The old woman slapped my hand away and gasped. "How dare you!"

I looked into her fierce eyes and suddenly felt a wave of pity for her. It must be monstrous, being so old and so unhappy. "Lady Elizabeth, there is no great crime in being a dried-up bag of wrinkles. Although it may be kinder to drag you outside and shoot you."

Walnut Head gasped, and the cat leaped from her lap. "Help! Somebody help!"

"But I believe it is the headaches that are making you such a miserable old bat." I climbed onto the sofa, kneeling beside the old woman. "Luckily, I have an excellent remedy. I have a gift for such things."

I dipped my handkerchief into a cup of beef tea and began blotting Lady Elizabeth's forehead with it.

"What are you doing?" she barked.

"Be a dear and shut your cake hole." I took an onion sliced in two from the basket. "Now for best results, I normally require a butter knife and a corkscrew—but we will make do with what we have." I held out the halved onion. "Take half in each hand."

"What for?" she barked. "Get off this sofa!"

"For once in your life, do as you're told."

With a huff, she took them. I grabbed her hands, pressing the flesh of the onion against her skin. "This will ease pain in the temples."

"Claptrap!"

I picked a stalk of lavender from the basket, broke off the flower, cut it into two pieces, then wedged them into the old woman's nostrils. Then I began to massage Lady Elizabeth's forehead with small circular motions. At regular intervals, I told her to breathe the lavender in deeply. And from time to time, I blew gently on her face.

In a minute or two, five at the most, Walnut Head was quiet. Her breathing slow and even. I pulled the sprigs of lavender from her nose and took the halved onion from her hands.

"Job well done," I said.

"Claptrap," she said faintly.

Then Walnut Head drifted off to sleep.

Summer Tempest was a terrible book. Frightfully bad. Full of breathless maidens trapped by dark secrets and hideous villains obsessed with revenge. In short, I loved it!

The library at Butterfield Park was a two-story wonderland—just the place to spend the hour before afternoon tea. I had come to find Lady Amelia's book, which took pride of place in a glass cabinet by the spiral staircase. Then I settled down in Lady Elizabeth's chair by the window. The view of the rose garden—shimmering in the soft light— was so splendid, I was torn between reading Lady Amelia's book and admiring the tapestry of red and white flowers outside.

A warm glow washed over me. I wasn't tired. I *never* got tired. I have the energy of a large rabbit. Or at the very least, a field mouse. But I hadn't slept at all well last night. That silly dream. I didn't drift off to sleep. Just dozed.

The murmur of voices roused me. Whispers. Echoing through the vaulted library. I opened my eyes. Peered around the side of the chair. Miss Frost and Rebecca were standing up on the library's first-floor landing. They were deep in conversation. Voices low. Rebecca looked distressed. It seemed as if Miss Frost was doing all of the talking. Remarkably, I could hear practically every word. It was as if I could hear a pin drop.

"I don't believe you!" Rebecca's voice shattered the quiet.

"Shhh!" was Miss Frost's reply.

What on earth were they discussing? Miss Frost slipped something into Rebecca's hand. A book. It was red. Small. Rebecca didn't want it. Shook her head. Miss Frost pushed it at her. Her manner was most insistent.

"Read it," she ordered. "It will explain a great deal."

"What you're saying isn't true," said Rebecca. "It *can't* be!"

"And yet it is." Miss Frost sounded tired. "I will endeavor to bring you more proof, but there isn't much time. The matter is urgent. Believe me, I wouldn't involve you if I didn't have to. She must be watched, and I cannot keep an eye on her day and night. As such, I need your help. I need it and I will have it."

Rebecca began to cry. "How . . . how could she not know? It's *impossible*."

"Tears will not alter the facts." Miss Frost grabbed Rebecca's chin. Her voice was cold. "Read the book. Do as I ask. If you don't, this house will see a great deal of suffering. I promise you that."

Rebecca's head dropped in apparent surrender. She took

the book, then rushed down the spiral stairs and fled. Poor creature!

Miss Frost seemed to struggle for breath. She shuddered. Reached out and grabbed the iron railing. Then she straightened herself up. Patted her red hair. Came quickly down the spiral stairs. She was clearly in a hurry and was almost at the threshold of the library when she stopped and looked back, her eyes hungry. I edged behind the chair. Held my breath.

"Hello?" Miss Frost's voice was urgent. "Is someone there?"

How slowly the seconds passed! I could no longer see her. Had no idea if she was roaming the library or standing still. I prayed. Yes, *prayed*. I don't know why I feared Miss Frost so completely at that moment. But I did.

All was quiet. Then, the rustling of a skirt. Then silence again. I dared to peek around the side of the chair.

The doorway was empty.

Miss Frost had gone.

8

"You really liked it?"

"Liked it? Loved it, dear. *Summer Tempest* should be required reading in every finishing school. Young ladies must be warned about the dangers of accidentally marrying a villainous cheese maker. I still have a few chapters to go, but so far it's a triumph. A monstrous triumph!"

Lady Amelia clapped her hands (not unlike a seal). "Oh, Ivy, I *am* pleased!"

After the curious incident in the library, I had searched the house for Rebecca but found no sign of her. I had hoped she would be at afternoon tea in the rose garden. She was not. But the delicate sandwiches, fresh pastries, and vanilla cheesecake were delicious. Old Walnut Head was seated in the arbor, the cat curled up on her lap. Fortunately, she was asleep.

"The critics were rather unkind," said Lady Amelia meekly. "I fear they didn't appreciate my little tale."

"Writing a book is a fine achievement," I said, taking another slice of cheesecake. "Who cares if it is terrifically bad?"

Lady Amelia paled slightly. Indigestion, I expect. Fortunately, Matilda was on hand to take her mind off it. She spent the next half hour complaining that she had to wait four whole days until her birthday ball. She felt it a grave injustice. I pointed out that there were children in the world who had never had a birthday party in their lives and that she was a hideous ingrate. Matilda responded by suggesting I drown myself in a bucket. Which was most unhelpful.

"Luckily, I have enjoyed some wondrous birthdays," I said, taking a sip of tea. "One year my parents rented a theater in New York and had a troupe of Romanian puppeteers reenact the most thrilling episodes from my life—my heart-stopping dual with a double-crossing juggler was a high point. Another year, we traveled across India in a hot air balloon. Took hours. We landed on a mountain somewhere southeast of whatsit. Delightful village— populated entirely by panda bears. Wonderfully friendly, but *terrible* cooks."

The whole family was staring at me (except for Lady Elizabeth, who was still fast asleep). "Nothing you say is true, Pocket," sneered Matilda, "not one word of it. You're even crazier than Rebecca."

"I do love a birthday ball," said Lady Amelia dreamily. "Although masquerade balls are my favorite. I wanted Matilda to have one, but she says her face is far too pretty to hide behind a mask. Ivy, I hope our little party compares well to some of the others you have been to."

"She's not invited!" barked Matilda.

"I know you two are not great friends," said Lady Amelia, looking hopefully at her daughter. "But as Ivy will be there to present your special gift, she simply *must* come as your guest."

Adorable creature!

Matilda looked violently unhappy. Which was delightful. It seemed the perfect time to gloat shamelessly. And I would have, but for two things. The first was that Lady Elizabeth woke up with a start. The second was that Miss Frost came across the lawn from the schoolhouse to collect Matilda for her French lesson.

"If I could have a brief word, Lady Amelia," said Miss Frost. "It is about the birthday ball. I assume Matilda is to give a speech?"

"Only if she wishes to," said Lady Amelia. "Matilda isn't terribly fond of—"

"Of course she will give a speech," said Lady Elizabeth, interrupting gruffly. "It is a Butterfield tradition."

Miss Frost frowned. "The trouble is . . ."

Lady Elizabeth slapped her bony hand on her knee. "What is the trouble? Matilda, is there a problem I should know about?"

Matilda stole a glance at her grandmother, but said nothing.

"Only this, Lady Elizabeth," said Miss Frost. "I have assisted as much as I can. Matilda needs help. Professional help."

"To write a birthday speech?" huffed Lady Elizabeth. "Bunkum!"

"Oh, dear," said Lady Amelia. "Perhaps *I* could help her. After all, my book—"

"I've read shopping lists with more flare than your ghastly book!" snapped Lady Elizabeth.

Poor Lady Amelia looked crestfallen!

"Matilda doesn't want to disappoint anyone," said Miss Frost with a sigh. "She is a Butterfield, after all, and the whole county will be at the ball." She sighed again, rather loudly. "If *only* there was someone who could help."

Then it hit me. The most wonderful idea!

"I think I may have just the answer," I announced.

"Heaven help us!" barked Lady Elizabeth.

"My dear friend, Miss Geraldine Always, is in desperate need of a quiet place to work on her new book, and she would be a great help to Matilda," I said, smiling winningly. "I shall write to her this very morning and invite her to stay. It's a perfect solution, don't you agree?'

Lady Elizabeth glared at me. "You think it is your place

to invite guests to *my* home?"

I nodded. "Just the one, dear."

"Miss Pocket, the fact that *you* are a guest at Butterfield Park gives me constant heartburn. If you think I would welcome another ghastly interloper, you are even more deluded than I thought."

Which wasn't very nice. I put this down to the fact that Lady Elizabeth was shockingly old. And slightly evil. Amazingly, Miss Frost saved the day.

"I think it is an excellent idea," she declared.

"Miss Always is terribly plain, but *very* gifted, Lady Elizabeth," I said. "She could help Matilda craft a brilliant speech—thrilling, funny, moving. One that would have the whole county talking." I took a large bite of cheesecake (I felt I had earned it). "And in her spare time, Miss Always could work on her book."

"Not the *worst* idea I ever heard," muttered the old woman. "A compelling speech would honor the Butterfield name." She nodded her shriveled head. "Yes, I like it."

Lady Amelia looked thrilled. "Well done, Ivy!"

"The ball is in four days," said Miss Frost. "We haven't much time."

"Time enough," I declared. "I will write to Miss Always at once—the letter should reach her by nightfall. I will explain everything and beg Miss Always to come immediately."

And with that, the matter was settled.

With the letter written and sent, I wandered down to the schoolhouse, looking for Rebecca. I wanted to lure her away and speak with her about Miss Frost before dinner. Their whispered conversation in the library would not leave my mind. *Something* was afoot. I found the schoolhouse empty— apparently Miss Frost had dragged her pupils out to the orchard to teach them about insects. I looked about. The blackboard was covered in Miss Frost's ornate handwriting. Some nonsense about the cycles of the moon.

I sat down at one of the desks and drummed my fingers in a dainty fashion. Matilda's sketchbook was open before me, containing a woeful drawing of a bower bird. Waiting is a nasty business. Glancing out the window, I spotted an old man—a gardener, no doubt—bending over a rosebush with a pair of clippers in his hand. He had white hair. A tatty straw hat. Whiskers that went on for miles. I picked up a pencil and begin to draw him. Surely I could surpass Matilda's pitiful effort! I became so engrossed in the sketch that I didn't even hear Miss Frost return to the schoolhouse.

"I am surprised to find you here, Miss Pocket," she said crisply.

"Can't think why," I said. "I'm terrifically studious."

"Tell me, have you had any formal education?"

"Certainly. My father is a professor of pirate history. My mother teaches Latin and armed combat."

Miss Frost retrieved a magnifying glass from the bookcase and turned back to me. I glanced at the blackboard. Just for a moment. But it was enough to catch Miss Frost's attention. "Do you know much about astronomy, Miss Pocket?" she asked.

"Only what I learned at Cambridge, dear."

She laughed. Which was unhelpful. "The moon's cycles are rather fascinating, don't you agree?" she said.

I shrugged. "Not really. Of course, I have a soft spot for the full moon—murderous rampages, werewolves, and whatnot."

"Superstitious nonsense," she declared. Miss Frost walked to the front of the room and pointed to the blackboard as if she were teaching a class. "The *real* power lies in the first half-moon When it is both revealed and hidden all at once—half there, half not. Great things are possible at such a time." She let out a sharp breath. Smiled a little. "Matilda's birthday ball falls on the half-moon. I feel it will make for a most *interesting* evening."

I sighed and went back to my drawing. "If you say so."

Miss Frost sniffed and shook her head as if I were a nitwit. "What are you drawing, Miss Pocket?"

I pointed out the window to the ancient gardener. "Him."

"Him?" Miss Frost looked at my sketch. Then out the window. Then back at my sketch. Clearly it was better than I thought. "How fascinating," she muttered.

I put down the pencil and admired my picture. The roses weren't a great success. But it was a good enough likeliness of the old man.

"Miss Pocket, may I have this drawing?"

I shrugged. "If you wish."

Miss Frost took the sketch, walked to her desk, and placed it in a drawer. She locked the drawer with a key. No doubt she planned to have it framed. People do that with marvelous drawings. Then she hurried from the schoolhouse without another word.

Nightfall. It had been a day of brilliant ideas. First, inviting Miss Always to stay. Second, finding the perfect hiding place for the Clock Diamond. I had known right away that it was just the spot to conceal the stone. So I had waited until the household was fast asleep; then I grabbed a candle and made my move.

After all, I didn't want any prying eyes.

The room across from mine in the attic contained all the relics from Lady Amelia's theatricals. All worthless and discarded. What better place to hide the necklace?

I sat down upon a crate. Plucked the stitching from my pocket with a small pair of scissors and pulled the Clock Diamond out. Somewhere in the back of my mind, I heard the Duchess's ghostly warning. To not be tempted by the stone. Foolish dingbat!

I held the silver chain up to my candle and looked into the diamond. Outside the attic, a blanket of stars and a near half-moon filled the sky. Inside the stone, a twinkling of stars and a crescent moon rose high above Butterfield Park.

Behind me, a bird fluttered its wings. I turned and saw it take off and glide under the rafters, landing in the shadows at the far end of the roof. When I looked back at the stone, a snowstorm was swirling within it, each flake sparkling like a gemstone. Behind this curtain of snow I could see a house. It was gray and grim. No lights flickered in the frosted windows.

Suddenly the front door of the house flew open. A woman came out. A woman carrying a sleeping child. She wore a heavy, dark coat, and a yellow bonnet obscured her face. The child was small, with long black hair. The woman hurried away, stealing backward glances at the house. The child in her arms . . . I knew her. Was it me? I know it's me. But younger.

I watched as the woman passed through a rusted gate and crossed a dirt road. Then she began to run—trudging through

a field thick with sludge and sleet. She was running away. Holding me and running away. Where to? Where from? There were no answers. Just questions.

Questions. And footprints in the snow.

A dark mist whirled madly, eating the light. The vision was gone, replaced by the stars and near half-moon of the night sky. I dropped the necklace and stood up. Began to walk in circles. My mind crowded with thoughts. My stomach in knots. Perhaps it was just a trick. A cruel trick. But then I recalled the Duchess's words about the diamond—it did not offer fantasies. Only visions of what was, what is, and what will be.

If that was true, what had I just seen? Who was that woman? My mother?

The stone. The stone had the answers. I raced back and scooped up the necklace, holding the diamond to the flickering candle. Praying it would show me more.

It did. But not a field in a snowstorm. Nor the woman in the yellow bonnet, carrying me away. Instead, I saw the schoolhouse at Butterfield Park glowing in the light of a half moon. A figure holding a lantern was moving along the garden path towards the darkened schoolhouse.

It was Miss Frost. What on earth was she doing?

If the Clock Diamond offered glimpses of events past, present, and future—which one was I seeing now? There was only one way to find out. I returned the stone to its hiding place, raced across the hallway, and ran to the small window in my bedroom. I got there just as Miss Frost, holding a lantern, vanished inside the schoolhouse. I watched as she walked to each window and drew the curtains. Minutes passed. Why I kept watching, I cannot say. All I know is that as the clock in the great hall struck midnight, another figure stole down the avenue of moonlit tulips and headed for the schoolhouse. This person was clutching something, and when she reached the schoolhouse she stopped and looked back the way she had come. Her face a ghostly white.

Rebecca Butterfield stepped inside the schoolhouse, closing the door behind her.

Early morning. The sun was yet to rise on my third day at Butterfield Park. A blanket of fog hovered above the flower beds. The gray mist parted as I hurried down the path towards the schoolhouse. I hadn't slept a wink. Well, perhaps a wink. Maybe two. In fact, I had fallen asleep at the window waiting for Miss Frost and Rebecca to emerge. When I awoke, hours had passed.

Questions bubbled and popped in my mind. About the vision in the stone. About the mysterious woman in the yellow bonnet. About Miss Frost and Rebecca. What was the stone trying to tell me?

The door was unlocked. The schoolhouse, a chamber of shadows. I struck a match, lit a candle. I searched the room thoroughly—for I have all the natural instincts of a lighthouse keeper. Arithmetic books, history books, parchment, ink, pencils: it was a symphony of disappointment. There was nothing that offered a clue as to why Rebecca and Miss Frost were conducting a secret midnight meeting.

I glanced out of the window. The sun was just breaching the woodlands behind the schoolhouse. Time to go. My stomach was grumbling, and I was in desperate need of breakfast.

I blew out the candle.

"You are making a grave mistake, child."

I didn't turn around. No need. I knew who it was. I could see her reflected in the window. "You're not real," I said softly.

"I am as real as you, and that is a fact." She was practically singing.

I turned around. The Duchess sat at the teacher's desk before the blackboard, her magnificent blubber swallowing the chair beneath her. Fingers, fat like sausages, drumming on the desk. Blood soaked the front of her nightdress. Her head was a radiant blue. She looked very pleased with herself.

"What do you want?" I said, hands on my hips.

"I cannot rest." Her fiery eyes fixed on me. Dark smoke coiled from her nose. "Since I put the Clock Diamond in your care, you have become rather attached to it. That is a mistake."

I shrugged. "You're wrong, dear. I barely even *think* of the stone."

The Duchess smiled darkly. She didn't speak. She didn't have to. Thick ribbons of dark smoke coiled from her nose, twisting into the air like serpents. The treads of billowing mist curled this way and that, and in moments had arranged themselves into a series of letters. This was what it said :

Deliver the necklace to Matilda at the birthday ball.

Collect five hundred pounds.

Begin a new life.

The ghost cackled and the message began to crumble and fall like sand, each word dropping to the desk in a pile of ash.

"Stop looking into the stone," the Duchess said. "No good can come of it. You are seeking answers to questions that will bring you nothing but suffering, child."

"You're dead," I said. "Why don't you float away or cross over or whatever it is murdered fatheads do?"

"I am waiting."

"For what?"

The Duchess smiled again. "The birthday ball."

I looked at the hideous bloodstain on her chest and asked the question that had haunted me since Paris. "Who killed you?"

"Excellent question!" she cried. "Alas, I was dozing at the time."

"Why were you killed?" I said with some urgency. "You must know why."

"*You* know why, child," she purred.

"To get the Clock Diamond?"

"Very good," hissed the ghost. "But think only of your promise to me. Forget what you have seen in the stone. You are no longer that little girl."

I felt a deep sadness reach for me like a grasping hand. Pulling me down. I shook my head. "I don't understand. Who was that woman in the yellow bonnet? Was she my mother?"

"You have no mother," said the Duchess, her hair suddenly alive with stardust. "Only *I* can offer you a new beginning. Trust no one in this house of shadows. Keep the stone safe. Watch over it. But do not look to the diamond for answers. Do not look, child!"

I was shaking. Trembling like a rabbit in a snowstorm. And I hated it. I hated *her*. I shut my eyes. "Why shouldn't I look? I want answers, you ghoulish fatso, and I will have them!" I suddenly felt rather brave. Which is why I added, "Perhaps I will keep the necklace until it tells me what I want to know. It's not like you can stop me. You're dead!"

I heard it then. The buzzing. The vibration charging the air. I wouldn't look. Wouldn't open my eyes. But the buzzing. And the fear. So I did. I looked just as the Duchess, this creature of death, lifted up. It wasn't graceful. It was a rampage. The desk toppled over. The chair shot back against the wall. And she flew at me. Glowing like a winter dawn. Her bloodstained nightdress billowing. An instrument of rage and thunder.

And I knew she would devour me in seconds.

I don't recall running. But I must have. For my hand was on the door handle and I was flinging it open. I didn't look back. I just ran. Until I hit it. Not it, *her*. We collided like trains. I screamed. She didn't. I blinked. Looked up into her face.

She looked baffled. "Good heavens, Ivy, whatever's the matter?"

I gasped. "Miss Always?"

The formal introductions happened at breakfast. Miss Always met the whole family. She was asked many questions about her travels and her books, and she answered them all admirably.

Lady Amelia wanted to know when she had arrived. Miss Always told her, making no mention of the schoolhouse. And finding me running out of it like a lunatic. Nor did she mention walking me back inside and helping me put the desk to rights and straightening the place up.

"My speech will be the highlight of the ball," Matilda interrupted. "With Miss Always's help, I'll stun those silly girls from the village. They will worship me."

"Goodness," said Miss Always rather meekly. "I shall do my best."

Rebecca didn't come to breakfast. In fact, I didn't see her at all until I was giving Miss Always a tour of the house. We were passing through the great hall, talking of our voyage from Paris and her mother's miraculous recovery, when Rebecca hurried down the stairs and into the sitting room—where I saw her exchange words with Miss Frost, who was waiting by the window.

"Ivy?"

I looked back at Miss Always. "Sorry, dear?"

"I said, are you well?"

"Never better," I answered. "As it happens, I have a great deal of time on my hands at Butterfield Park, and the books in the library are of little interest. I was thinking I might give your last book a try." I smiled as if I hadn't a care in the world. "Wasn't it about ghosts?'

Miss Always nodded. "The great ghosts of Scotland and Wales." She was looking at me rather curiously. "Ivy, you know that as my bosom friend you can ask me anything. *Anything* at all."

"You would be shocked, dear," I said.

A smile creased her thin lips. "I very much doubt that, Ivy."

Without going into all the grisly details, I briefly explained to Miss Always what had been happening with the dead Duchess.

Miss Always stared at me with great intensity. For a moment her dark eyes seemed to crackle and flare, like coals in a furnace. No doubt I had stunned the poor creature. "That is most interesting," she said softly. But she didn't look at *all* shocked. "There are very few rules with regards to ghosts, Ivy, but there are two that are most important. The first is that only earthbound ghosts can haunt the living."

I frowned. "Earthbound ghosts?"

Miss Always nodded. "Ghosts who remain tethered to this world because they have unfinished business here. Most of these ghosts are perfectly harmless—they are messengers and soothsayers. But some are very wicked indeed, and seek vengeance for past crimes."

"Can they . . . can they hurt the living?"

"Oh, yes. Dreadfully so. Rage generates great power, Ivy."

Which was rather unsettling. "What is the second rule?" I asked.

"When a person dies, his or her spirit is given a very short time to decide whether to stay earthbound or to pass into the afterlife. It is possible to make a fleeting visit to a loved one. But only for a short time. Then the spirit must depart, never to return." Miss Always clasped my hands in hers. "You can be sure the Duchess haunts you for a reason, Ivy. Can you think what it might be?"

"Her dying wish was that I give Matilda the Clock Diamond

at her birthday ball. I'm certain she will haunt me until I do as she asks."

Miss Always's cheeks seemed to color at the mention of the stone. "Matilda must have been delighted when she saw the necklace. Tell me, did she try it on?"

"Why, she hasn't seen it," I explained. "No one has."

"Very sensible," said Miss Always. She grasped my arm. "Do you still carry the diamond sewn into your pocket?"

"Heavens no," I said, as if it were the silliest thing I'd ever heard. "I have hidden it away."

The dear creature seemed delighted. "I'm sure it's somewhere utterly ingenious."

"You are right, Miss Always," I said proudly.

"Wait." She giggled shyly. "I will try to guess. You mustn't give me any hints now. Not even a little one. Oh, dear, this house is so vast it could be *anywhere*."

"You must let me tease you with a clue or two," I said playfully.

"Well, if you insist." Miss Always's smile faded. "Go on then."

"Think of a place where—"

"Excuse me, Miss Pocket." It was Miss Frost. She was striding towards us. "Forgive me for interrupting, but I wanted to give Miss Always directions to the schoolhouse. If she is agreeable, we can begin work on Matilda's speech this morning."

Miss Always regarded Miss Frost rather coldly. "No need, I know exactly where it is. I met Ivy coming out of the schoolhouse when I arrived this morning."

I very much wanted to die. Poor Miss Always had no idea she had betrayed me. I kept my eyes on my hands (they were fascinating). I could feel Miss Frost's glare upon me. But to my surprise she said, "Well then, Miss Always, you will have no trouble finding us."

As Miss Frost departed, I saw Rebecca slip out of the sitting room and steal away up the stairs. Miss Always was keen to see the library, so I pointed her in the right direction and said a hasty farewell. For I was on a mission.

Taking two steps at a time, I hurried after Rebecca.

"Wait!"

She was pulling the key from the lock—it was fixed around

her wrist by a ribbon. About to vanish into her bedroom. She looked rather startled. "Ivy," she said. "I don't mean to be rude, but I cannot stop to chat. I have some work to do before my history class."

I raced to her door. Rather puffed. Rebecca was already inside and beginning to close the door.

"Surely you can spare a moment or two," I said, catching my breath. "I fear that you are avoiding me, though I cannot think why."

"We spoke yesterday," said Rebecca faintly.

"Yes, dear, but it's not the same, is it?" I put my hand on the door. "If anything is the matter, you can tell me. I am a font of wisdom and bright ideas."

"Nothing is the matter."

"You look tired," I said.

It was then that I noticed the strange rhythmic sound coming from inside Rebecca's bedroom. I frowned. "What on earth is that noise?"

She pushed the door, trying to shut it. "I have to go, Ivy."

"I saw you in the library with Miss Frost yesterday," I said hastily, stopping the door with my foot. "You looked awfully upset. Then last night you stole into the schoolhouse under cover of darkness. We both know who you were meeting there."

Rebecca gulped. I saw it clearly. "Miss Frost has been helping me with my work," she said.

It might have made sense. If not for the fact that she and her governess had met in the dead of night. Whatever their business, it was of a secret kind.

"You can trust me, dear," I said, in my most trustworthy voice. "In the library, you seemed to doubt what Miss Frost was telling you. She said something about getting proof. Proof of what, Rebecca?"

Her gaze traveled across my face for the longest time. She looked at me as if she were seeing me for the first time. Then her eyes pooled with tears. "Miss Frost thinks that . . . she is worried. She is worried about *you*, Ivy."

"Me?" I sighed wearily. "She's not *still* fretting about the Clock Diamond, is she?"

Rebecca nodded gravely.

"Well, she needn't worry," I said brightly. "I have the stone safely hidden away."

Strangely, this did not seem to reassure Rebecca.

"You are good . . . ," she said, tears trailing down her face. "You are good, aren't you, Ivy?"

"Good? Of course I'm good. Wonderfully good. Everyone says so." I pushed on the door, but it wouldn't budge. "Let me come in, dear. We can discuss what is troubling you."

"Be careful, Ivy," Rebecca whispered. "Things are not as they seem."

Then she shut the door in my face.

I heard the key turn in the lock.

9 ✳✳

"May I speak with you?"

She came before lunch. I had only just finished checking on the Clock Diamond and was changing the sash on my dress. Without waiting to be invited, Miss Frost walked into my bedroom.

"I was hoping to have a word," she said, pausing by the window.

"How odd." I smiled brightly. "I was just thinking the exact same thing."

"Oh?"

"Yes," I said, "I thought we might talk about Rebecca."

That seemed to startle Miss Frost. Her eyes left mine, and she looked about. "What about her?"

I fixed my gaze upon the grim governess. "She said you have been speaking to her about me. She warned me to be careful. That things are not as they seem."

"She might be right," said Miss Frost. "Turn around."

She took the sash from my hand and fixed it around my waist. "Perhaps Rebecca is slightly upset at present, but it will pass," she said. "You see, I have asked her to help me with a project I am working on."

"Is that why you met her in the schoolhouse last night?"

If Miss Frost was shocked, she hid it well. "I am teaching Rebecca about the history of a faraway place. It's a hidden place, with a secret history." Her eyes clouded over. "I told her the facts as I know them. But she had doubts."

"I should think so," I declared. "Sounds bonkers."

"Fortunately, I was able to show her compelling proof," said Miss Frost crisply. "My methods may be unorthodox, Miss Pocket, but our lesson was a great success."

I was frowning with tremendous enthusiasm. "Have you spent any time in a madhouse, dear? I'm almost certain you must have."

She walked back to the window, her rusty locks flaring in the afternoon light. "Are you seeing ghosts, Miss Pocket?"

"Perhaps," I said with a shrug.

"The Duchess of Trinity?"

I gasped. "How did you know?"

She made no reply.

So I said, "She only comes because of that silly stone. I'm certain that is why I can see her—because I have the Clock Diamond."

Miss Frost shook her head. "The stone does not allow one to see ghosts, Miss Pocket."

She sounded terribly sure.

I didn't want to ask. But I simply *had* to. "Then why can I see her?"

"I haven't an answer that would satisfy you. I only know that the stone has no such power. At least, not that I have ever heard of."

"How do you know so much about the necklace?" I asked.

"I confess, the Clock Diamond intrigues me. It has a dark but fascinating history."

I sighed. "I do hope you are not going to babble on about it, dear."

"The stone was first discovered in Budatta," continued Miss Frost, as if I hadn't spoken. "It was found quite by accident. A local tribe was cutting down whipple trees to build a canoe. The stone was found embedded in one of the logs. There it was, perfectly formed, in the middle of a tree trunk. It couldn't possibly have been created there. Diamonds are not forged from wood. Its origins are a mystery. Once the local people saw its power, that it could keep time and offer visions of the past, present, and future, they took it as some sort of divine totem. But that was not all. It is rumored that the tribe discovered the stone had *another* great power. They turned the diamond into a kind of god and built a temple to display it. The diamond was stolen from Budatta a century ago. Nobody knows how or by whom. After that, its history is unknown."

"You said the stone has *another* great power," I said, sitting down on the bed. "What is it?"

"I don't know," she said quickly. "Nobody does."

I wasn't sure I believed her. In truth, I didn't like Miss Frost. Perhaps it was her freckles or her pointed nose. No, I suspect it was her manner. She was polite. But cold.

I stood up. "Well, whatever the history of the diamond, it doesn't matter to me. The day after tomorrow, it will be Matilda's problem, not mine."

Miss Frost headed towards the door. She paused before leaving and regarded me doubtfully. "If you say so, Miss Pocket."

"How nice it is to see a familiar face!"

I found Miss Always in the library. She was in the mythology section (holding a book on ancient curses)—though when she saw me coming, she closed the book and put it back on the shelf. Naturally, she was thrilled to see me.

"I am taking a break from speechwriting," she said rather wearily. She threaded her arm through mine and walked with me towards the large windows overlooking the terrace. "Miss Matilda is a *special* girl."

"She is a fathead and a tyrant."

Miss Always laughed. "I confess, Ivy, I don't know why the Duchess of Trinity wished to reward her with the Clock Diamond."

"You are right—I can't think of a girl less deserving than Matilda Butterfield."

"Ivy . . ." Miss Always looked suddenly very grave. "Matilda told me something rather shocking this morning. She said that you have no family. That you are an orphan."

I thought back on all that I had told Miss Always during the voyage from France—the stories about my mapmaking parents and my frightfully rich grandma. I was certain that now was the right moment to speak the truth. Get it all out in the open and whatnot. As such, I said, "How monstrous! Don't believe a word of it, dear!"

Miss Always smiled at me tenderly. "I quite agree. In fact, I told Matilda that she was *quite* wrong about you. For I know a member of your family *most* intimately."

I tried hard not to look stunned. "You do?"

She nodded. "I should think so. After all, we may not share blood, but are we not sisters?"

I felt a mad impulse to hug Miss Always. And so I did.

I may have even whispered, "Bless you, dear."

We sat down on a red velvet sofa, the warm sun pouring in through the windows.

"I have unearthed a thrilling legend for my new book that is sure to delight my readers," said Miss Always, grinning madly. "It is long forgotten, dating back centuries. Would you like to hear it, Ivy?"

"Heavens no. Hearing about holy grails and Greek gods bores me silly."

Miss Always took off her spectacles. Gave them a polish. "But this one is different, Ivy. It has tragedy and hope. Death and salvation. And the hero is a girl about your age." She popped her glasses back on. "It is called the Legend of the Dual."

I realized the excitable creature was going to inflict her tale upon me whether I liked it or not. So, being a bosom friend, I said, "Get on with it, dear."

"It concerns a land cursed by a plague," said Miss Always eagerly. "They called the disease the Shadow because when people became infected, their skin would change color, as if a shadow was passing over them. Death was always swift. Millions died. The Queen and her entire family were wiped out in a single year."

"Sounds beastly," I said. "Was there no cure?"

"None," said Miss Always. "The entire kingdom was filled with despair. Then a story began to circulate through the villages and towns. It was said that on his deathbed, the Queen's mystic, who had a gift for prophecy, whispered to his son: "There will come a girl child. She is not from our world, but she will come. A child who is ignorant of the power she possesses and walks the earth unnoticed. She is the Dual—a girl who can pass freely between our two worlds. Only she can heal the plague cursing our land. Only she can save us."

I couldn't deny that the story had me intrigued. "Did they find her?"

"Not yet," said Miss Always. She blinked and shook her head. "What I mean is, as far as the legend goes, the Dual was never found. A few were chosen to leave the kingdom and search for the child. But it was like looking for a needle in a haystack. The plague continued to kill many across the land. The legend goes that if the Dual is ever found, she will bring healing to this cursed world and ascend the throne." Miss Always blushed slightly. "In the interest of my book, I am filling this particular legend with a great deal of murder and treachery. Much of it my own invention. Is that terribly dishonest of me?"

"It's shameful, dear, but perfectly reasonable. These stories are nonsense, after all."

Miss Always smiled. "Ivy, are you happy here at Butterfield Park?"

I nodded but said nothing. Part of me wished to confide in my bosom friend. About Rebecca and Miss Frost. About the vision in the stone. And I might have, if Matilda hadn't stormed into the library waving around a sheet of paper.

"The speech is awful!" she spat. "This will not astound my guests or make them laugh or move them to tears! Where is the excitement, Miss Always? Where is the humor? Stop loafing about and fix it!"

"Oh, dear," said poor Miss Always. "Well . . . perhaps we could include a thrilling episode from Butterfield family history. Something sure to excite your guests."

"Impossible," I said with certainly. "Nothing interesting or thrilling *ever* happens to aristocrats. It's scientifically proven."

"What would you know, Pocket?" snapped Matilda. "There's plenty of scandal in my family. You would be shocked."

I was hoping she'd reveal something about Rebecca's troubles. So I said, "I doubt that, dear. But if you think you can shock me, go ahead."

Matilda laughed. It was the first time I had ever seen her do it. "Grandmother would *kill* me for telling you this," she said. She frowned, but her eyes were dancing. "She was married before. He was a local man and worked in the village as a clerk. I think he was engaged to someone else, but Grandmother *had* to have him."

"Oh, dear . . ." Miss Always looked flustered. "That's not really what I had in mind, Matilda. Come now, let us go to the schoolhouse and work on something more appropriate." Miss Always began to hurry Matilda from the library.

"Wait!" I said, calling after them. "Your grandmother and the clerk—how did it end?"

"They married," she said. "He was struck by lightning and dropped dead. Grandmother *never* talks about him." She grinned wickedly at me. "Is your little heart stunned, Pocket?"

"Not at all," I said casually. "My first governess was struck by lightning. Nothing left of her but a pile of ash, poor dear."

"You had a governess?" asked Matilda doubtfully.

"I certainly hope so," I said.

Miss Always practically dragged Matilda from the library. As they hurried off, bound for the schoolhouse, a frightfully handsome footman arrived, carrying a silver tray. He walked up to me silently and presented it. The tray contained an envelope with my name scrawled upon it. I tore it open. It was from Mr. Banks.

Dear Miss Pocket,

I write to you on a most urgent matter. It concerns the gift you are set to deliver at the ball. Some information has come to light that is most troubling and makes me fear for your safety. If my letter alarms you, I am glad of it. Be alarmed, Miss Pocket, and be on your guard. The Clock Diamond is not what

it seems. I believe you are ensnared in a wicked scheme. Keep your nerve and trust
no one. I will come to Suffolk the day after tomorrow on the morning train, and I
will explain myself then. I have the money owed to you and more besides. There
is a way out of this mess.

  Hold tight, help is at hand.
Your friend,
Horatio Banks

What could it mean? Only this—Mr. Banks was deluded!
The poor man had been full of dark thoughts when I was in
London and now . . . now his imagination had run away on him.

What proof did he offer? None. Yes, it was true, ever since I had taken possession of the Clock Diamond, strange events seemed to shadow me. But I was perfectly safe. After all, I was among friends here at Butterfield Park. No harm could come to me.

Yet as I slipped the letter in my pocket and left the library, I could no longer deny one simple truth.

I had doubts.

By lunchtime it was raining heavily. Storm clouds gathered over Butterfield Park, low and menacing. Inside, the house seemed to surrender to the gloom. Candles were lit in all the public rooms and thunder shook the sky. I had taken Horatio Banks's note up to my room and hidden it in the pages of Lady Amelia's novel. I didn't want anyone reading it by accident. There was sure to be a fuss when he turned up at the house in two days—Mr. Banks was a stubborn old goat—but for now I would act as if nothing was afoot.

How did things get so terribly muddled? It was such a simple task—deliver a diamond for a miserable brat's twelfth birthday and collect five hundred pounds. Where was the harm in that? What could go wrong? Nothing. Or a very great deal. Perhaps it was the house's fault. It was big and old and full of gloom. Or maybe it was my mind. Which was big and young and full of ghosts.

I headed down the narrow back stairs and walked along the dim corridor, past Matilda's and Rebecca's chambers. When I got to the landing, I saw Miss Always crossing the hall below with a lamp, probably on her way to the library. I thought of calling to her. Telling her about the letter. It might help to speak of it. But Miss Always was a writer and therefore prone to hysteria. Horatio Banks's warning would be fuel to the fire. No, I would say nothing.

I stood at the top of the stairs and listened. Rain thundered down on the roof of the great hall. The storm clouds outside had bled daylight from the vast room—it was a patchwork of gloomy shadows, more night than day. I closed my eyes, just for a moment.

I felt someone approaching on the landing behind me. I heard no footsteps. Perhaps they were drowned out by the rumbling sky. But someone was there. I could feel it.

"Ivy?" called a voice from the bottom of the stairs.

I looked down.

There was no one there. Then I remembered—behind me. Someone coming up behind me. I started to turn around. . . .

But my feet were no longer beneath me. I was lurching forward. Stumbling. A bird without wings. Flying? No. Dropping . . . tumbling . . . thumping.

Screams, but not my own. Then light. Bright light. Everywhere.

The floor rushed to meet me.

10

There was no pain. That was the first thing. I wasn't dead. That was the second. I can't say exactly what position I landed in. All I know is that when Rebecca and Miss Frost found me at the foot of the stairs, my arm was twisted behind my back. I remember Miss Frost gently rolling me on my side and pulling my arm free.

"Are you hurt?" she asked.

"Terribly," was my reply. But when I was finally alert enough to take a moment and *feel*—I was amazed. Despite the fact that I had apparently tumbled down an enormous staircase, I wasn't hurting at all. Well, apart from a slight headache. Nor was I bleeding. As Rebecca helped me sit up, my mind flew back. Back to when I was standing at the top of the stairs. Back to my name being called. Back to feeling someone come up behind me. Back to falling.

Had I been pushed? Surely not! Yet I couldn't deny that *someone* had been up there.

"How is your arm?" asked Rebecca urgently. "And your head, Ivy, how is your head? Oh, Miss Frost, it's too awful!"

I saw Miss Frost's face harden. "Yes, it is," she said coldly. "Awful and unnecessary. But what's done is done. Your legs, Miss Pocket—can you move them?"

"They're broken, I'm sure," I said gravely. To be honest, I was rather disappointed in myself. How can a girl tumble down a great staircase and come out of it unscathed? It was a scandal!

Miss Frost felt both my legs. Had me bend my knees. Wriggle my toes and whatnot. "You are perfectly fine," she announced.

"No injuries at all?" said Rebecca, gently pushing a strand of hair from my eyes.

"None," said Miss Frost.

"What happened, Ivy?" said Rebecca. "Can you remember?"

I shook my head. "Not completely. But I think perhaps I was pushed."

Rebecca gasped. "Surely not!"

Miss Frost scowled. "I hate to disappoint you, Miss Pocket," she said, getting to her feet, "but I was passing by when you fell, and there was no one near you on the landing. I will inform Lady Amelia and Lady Elizabeth of the incident and bring back a damp cloth for your head."

Rebecca checked me over several times while Miss Frost was gone. She was *very* preoccupied with my injuries. Or rather, my lack of injuries.

When Miss Frost returned with a flock of onlookers (including a near-hysterical Lady Amelia), Rebecca said the most remarkable thing. Or rather, she whispered it. "If they ask," she said, "say that you slipped on the last few stairs and only fell a short way."

I looked up her in confusion. "Why on earth should I say that?"

"Please, Ivy," she said, her eyes dark and anxious, "I cannot explain. Just please do this for me. It is most important."

I sighed. "Don't pop a button, dear. If it matters that much to you, I'll do as you ask."

"Oh, Ivy, are you all right?" cried Lady Amelia. "You poor, poor girl!"

"What happened?" asked Miss Always, who had come running from the library. "Ivy, are you hurt?"

Rebecca informed the gathering that I was uninjured and that I had only slipped near the bottom of the stairs. As such, no harm was done.

"You might have been killed," said Miss Always (that sweet creature!).

"Yes, dear, you are right," I said bravely. "I suppose I shall have to be pushed around in a wheelchair until I recover. Lifted into chairs and carried about the place by a footman."

"Claptrap," snapped Lady Elizabeth, waving her cane at me. "I see your ridiculous imagination has not been injured either."

"I will send for Dr. Longfellow," fretted Lady Amelia.

"There's no need," said Miss Frost. "She is perfectly unharmed."

Rebecca and Miss Always helped me to my feet. Regrettably, I didn't faint.

"The poor girl *must* be examined," said Lady Amelia.

"Pocket's neck didn't break," said Matilda coldly (she had been standing by the banister watching the proceedings). "You are worrying about nothing, Mother."

Miss Frost quickly agreed. I had tumbled down the stairs. Was apparently unhurt. And there was nothing more to it. So the matter was settled. For them. But not for me.

I was left to rest in the conservatory until supper. But I was in no mood for that. After all, I felt perfectly fine. In body, at least. My mind was another matter. As the rain had ceased, I went for a walk in the woodlands. A torrent of thoughts crashed through me. I remembered standing at the top of the stairs. I'd felt someone there. I'd heard my name called. Yet Miss Frost had seen everything. She claimed I was alone up there. But was she telling the truth? And if she wasn't, why would she lie?

I wanted to scream. So I did. Several times. There was

no harm in it. While the woodlands afford a perfect view of the schoolhouse and the wildflower meadow, they are far enough away to ensure privacy. It was a mess. All of it—a mess.

The afternoon sun filtered through the canopy of maple and oaks. It filled the forest with a rosy shimmer that was something like dawn. I took a deep breath. Steadied myself. I saw Rebecca and Matilda emerge from the schoolhouse, followed by Miss Frost. They appeared to be studying the wildflowers. Or bees. Something of that kind. Miss Frost was pointing to several blooms and talking a great deal.

"They are so different."

I turned. A woman stood behind me. She was tall. Blond hair sweeping her shoulders. Her delicate hands clutched together. She was looking at Matilda and Rebecca. And she was smiling.

"I'm sorry?" I said.

"The girls," said the woman, and her voice was like honey. "They are very different. Matilda has all the answers. Rebecca, all the questions. Who is the wiser, do you think?"

I shrugged. "If it's a contest, *I* would win. I'm monstrously wise. Everybody says so."

The lady laughed softly. There was something odd about her. And also rather wonderful.

"Do you know the Butterfields?" I said.

"Once upon a time."

I looked at her carefully. She had a pretty face. Round. Soft. Her eyes caught my attention—one was green, the other blue.

"I haven't seen you here before," she said.

"I'm just visiting," I said. "On frightfully important business."

"I see." Her eyes drifted back to the clearing where Rebecca and Matilda were now pressing something into a book—wildflowers, perhaps. "They have so much to learn."

"You know Matilda and Rebecca?" I said.

"Oh, yes. Once upon a time."

Suddenly I understood. I knew who this strange, beautiful creature was. Miss Rochester—the vanishing governess! She had come back to check on her pupils. How bone-shatteringly interesting!

I looked at Miss Rochester. Then back at the girls. "Why

don't you come and say hello?" I said, watching Matilda stomp on a cluster of daisies. "I'm sure they'd be thrilled to see you."

"Don't lose heart, Miss Pocket."

I turned. Baffled at how she knew my name.

"How did you know——?"

But Miss Rochester had disappeared.

She found me before I found her. Rebecca's face was a cloud of anguish when she spotted me walking out of the woodlands, and hurried over. "You must be terribly confused about why I asked you to lie about falling down the stairs. Ivy," she said, "there's a lot you don't——"

"I've seen her!" I declared triumphantly.

"Who?" Rebecca looked alarmed, poor dear. "Who did you see?"

"Miss Rochester," I said excitedly. "The missing governess!"

Rebecca frowned. "You have seen Miss Rochester?"

"I'm utterly positive," I said with pride. "Of course, most people wouldn't have a clue, they would just think her a passing stranger. But I knew it was your tragic governess—for I have all the natural instincts of a junior Sherlock Holmes. Trust me, Rebecca, Miss Rochester has returned!"

A faint smiled washed the frown from Rebecca's face. "Ivy, are you sure it was her?" she asked.

"Positive! At least, I *think* it was her. I can't be completely sure, since I have never laid eyes on the woman before. Have you a picture of her?"

"No," said Rebecca glumly. Then she brightened a little. "But you could tell me what she looked like."

"That is easy," I said, "for her face is fixed in my mind. Lovely blond hair. Face like a cherub. And her eyes. They were remarkable—one blue, one green. I never saw such thing."

The poor dear was trembling. In fact, she looked positively stricken. My brilliant description had floored her. Miss Rochester had returned!

"It's true," whispered Rebecca. There were tears welling in her eyes. Then she lunged at me. Hugged me like a madwoman. She pulled back. Hugged me again.

Her eyes roamed my face. "Have you told anyone else—about the lady?"

"You are the first," I said.

"It would be better if you said nothing about her to anyone else," said Rebecca. "Just for now."

"Why shouldn't we tell everyone about Miss Rochester? Her return is a good thing, isn't it?"

It was as if a great wave of grief or happiness washed over the poor dear. She sobbed. Wiped her eyes. Sobbed again. She wept like a fountain. I did my best to calm her. Patted her head two or three times. Smiled kindly.

"Please, Ivy, I know I have asked a great deal of you," she said, her words tumbling out in a flurry, "but it isn't without reason. There are things . . . things that make no sense. Yet, they are true. Impossibly true! Please, just do as I ask."

I sighed. "As you wish. But I have to say, dear, in my professional opinion—you're barking mad."

She hugged me again, kissed my cheek, then ran off towards the house.

Rebecca didn't come to dinner. And I hardly saw her at all the next morning. The great house was a hive of activity—which was no great surprise, as the ball was tomorrow night. I spent much of the morning with Miss Always in the library. She was still busy working on Matilda's speech, but she always had time for me. There was so much I wished to tell her about the events of the last few days—but I had made promises to Rebecca, and I was a girl of my word. Instead, I told Miss Always about the letter from Horatio Banks—his grim warnings and that he would be calling on me at Butterfield Park the next day.

Miss Always was terribly interested. She threw a dozen questions at me. Asked me what train Mr. Banks was coming on. Expressed a strong interest in seeing the letter.

The poor creature looked rather anxious. Jumpy, even. She explained that her nerves were still afire because of my monstrous fall. She said her heart was in her throat when she saw me sprawled on the ground. She expressed amazement that I hadn't broken my neck.

Miss Always loved me like a sister!

"It is very good news that Mr. Banks is coming," she said as we walked out into the rose garden for morning tea. "From his letter, it sounds as though he has new information about the Clock Diamond. Perhaps now we will learn its great secrets!"

We found Lady Elizabeth snoozing in the arbor, the cat on her lap. Lady Amelia was fussing over the teapot. She looked terribly agitated.

"Rebecca won't be joining us," she said gravely. "I *do* wish she wouldn't hide herself away day and night."

"I refuse to pry, it's the height of bad manners," I said, sitting down in a wicker chair, "but tell me this, Lady Amelia—what does Rebecca have hidden in that room of hers?"

The poor woman paled. "It is difficult to explain, Ivy."

"She should be locked up," said Matilda brightly. "She'll go mad one day and kill us all."

I smiled warmly at Matilda. "Not all of us, dear. I'm certain Rebecca would lose interest once she finished you off."

The dear girl unleashed a passionate response—all in French. I'm certain she was complimenting my silky hair. And possibly my chin. It's difficult to be sure.

"Have you seen Miss Frost?"

We all turned. Rebecca was coming quickly towards us,

looking like a ball of nervous excitement. "Have you seen her?" she asked again.

"No, dear," I said. "Perhaps she is in the schoolhouse."

"Miss Frost is a devil," declared Matilda. "All she ever does is *teach*. It's not normal."

"Miss Frost is good and brave and noble!" shouted Rebecca. It was quite an outburst and caught everyone's attention. Even Lady Elizabeth stirred from her nap.

"She dresses like an undertaker, and her accent hurts my ears," said Matilda, folding her arms. "And everyone knows she has the complexion and manners of an orangutan."

"You take that back, Matilda!" yelled Rebecca. "Take it back!"

"I won't!" snapped Matilda.

I had high hopes that things might get violent, but Miss Always calmed things down by alerting us to Miss Frost, who was stalking towards us across the rose garden.

I cut a slice of cheesecake and sat down again.

"Rebecca, would you join me in the schoolhouse?" said Miss Frost, stopping a short distance from our tea party. She did not offer a greeting to anyone else.

"But, Miss Frost, surely Rebecca has finished with her lessons for the morning?" protested Lady Amelia.

"It's just a small matter," said Miss Frost crisply. "It will not take long."

"I don't mind, Aunt," said Rebecca quickly. "I asked Miss Frost to help me with my penmanship."

"I should think so," barked Lady Elizabeth, opening her eyes. "You write like an infant!"

I watched Rebecca and Miss Frost walk away—they were deep in conversation almost immediately. Which was terribly interesting.

"Goodness, Grandmother," cried Matilda, peering at old Walnut Head, "how long have you been out here in the hot morning sun?"

Lady Elizabeth huffed. "No idea. One hour is much the same as the next when you get to my age."

In truth, the beastly fossil had been sleeping in the arbor since breakfast. And now her face was as red as a tomato. I crouched down and examined her face.

"The news isn't good, dear," I said gravely. "You have the complexion of a boiled lobster. Your skin is practically crying out for moisture. Fear not, I have just the remedy."

"Don't you touch me!" she bellowed, and the cat jumped from her lap into Matilda's.

Lady Elizabeth reached for her cane. I had to act quickly.

"I don't wish to alarm you, Lady Elizabeth," I said, scouring the tea table for something suitable, "but this is a skin emergency."

The old woman tried to get up (possibly to hug me), but I pushed her back down. It only took a second for me to reach across the table and pick up the cheesecake and a spoon.

"Ivy, what are you doing?" asked Lady Amelia urgently. "Are you sure you know—?"

"Very sure, dear."

"Stop her, Mother!" cried Matilda. "She's dangerous!"

"Stay away!" shrieked Lady Elizabeth.

Which was ridiculous. I scooped up a large helping of cheesecake and splattered it on the old bat's face. Then another blob. Then another. She was making strange noises—

not unlike an injured piglet—which I attributed to the soothing qualities of the cheesecake. I smeared the healing balm all over her face, leaving only her eyes clear. It took just a moment or two for her red skin to be fully covered by the dessert.

"The treatment must stay on for at least an hour, Lady Elizabeth," I said, cleaning my hands on a napkin. "You may attract flies, so I suggest you go indoors."

She cursed me with gratitude and leaped up, waving her cane!

The cane swished through the air and hit a maid on the bottom. She shrieked—which was understandable—and in the process, tipped a jug of lemonade into Matilda's lap. Matilda jumped up suddenly (crying like a madwoman) and the cat went flying into the air. Alarmingly high.

I had to think quickly. It would be necessary to break the cat's fall. I grabbed the closest thing—Lady Amelia.

"Prepare yourself, dear!" I cried, spinning her around and pushing her onto the table. Her generous bosom and wobbly stomach would make an idea landing pad.

"Prepare for what?" cried the poor creature.

The whole thing was over in no time. The cat came down right on Lady Amelia's magnificent belly. It bounced and flew across the table, landing on Lady Elizabeth. The creature flew into her lap and almost immediately began licking the cheesecake on her face. Disaster averted!

There was much carry-on, of course. Matilda questioned my sanity. Lady Amelia fainted. Old Walnut Head called for me to be dropped down a well. Or, at very least, tied to a tree and hit with sticks. I felt it best to excuse myself and retire to the house. But I must admit, I felt bitterly disappointed.

All that effort, and not even a thank you!

I went up to my room with the intention of finishing Lady Amelia's book. The house was eerily quiet. Matilda was having a final fitting for her birthday dress. Lady Amelia was on hand to tell the brat how pretty she looked. Lady Elizabeth was taking a bath to remove the cheesecake. It was a perfect moment to read and rest.

But as I sat on my bed, all I could think about was the Clock Diamond—lying there in the next room, hidden among a cluster of costume jewels. Just waiting for me to hold it and look within it. Just waiting to show me what I yearned to see. I felt a hunger so urgent and painful that it made my teeth chatter.

Which would explain why I found myself kneeling on the floor among a pile of dusty trunks, staring into the stone. I gasped when heavy snow began to churn inside the diamond. A winter forest emerged. The woman in the yellow bonnet was no longer holding me. I was walking beside her. Not walking. Being dragged along. Somehow I knew we had been trudging through that forest for hours. In the trees behind us, a dark blur passed by. It was a farmer, head bowed against the snow, pulling a horse laden with logs.

I turned. Spotted him. Pulled free from the woman's grip and was running, my legs vanishing beneath the thick blanket of snow. I was calling out—though I couldn't hear the words. The farmer stopped. Looked hard into the heavy snowfall. I called out again, but a hand flew over my mouth. The woman in the yellow bonnet pulled me back. We were cowering behind a tree. My mouth muzzled. I struggled to free myself, but her grip was too tight.

The farmer waited a moment. Then whipped his horse and moved away.

Only when he was out of sight did the woman release me. She shook the snow from her bonnet and grabbed me again. With my hand locked inside hers, she pulled me deeper into the white woods.

The snow fell harder until the diamond was a radiant white. Then a dark mist churned, swallowing the light. The vision ended. I stayed there staring at the stone for the longest time. Willing it to come back and show me more. To tell me what happened next.

But of course, it didn't.

11

It was already afternoon when I finally came down from the attic. I had just turned down the hallway that led to the landing above the main stairs—it was a vast corridor, littered with hideous urns and dull paintings of hunters and hounds. I was in rather a hurry to get to the kitchen and see if Cook could spare a few potatoes. Perhaps a cabbage or two. I was famished, having missed lunch.

But all thoughts of food flew from my mind when I glanced down that dim hallway. It stopped me cold—what I saw at the other end. A small figure in dark robes. His face was shrouded by a hood, but I felt quite certain he was staring at me.

My first instinct was to look for a weapon. But there wasn't time. For at that exact moment, Miss Always swept around the corner, and as she did, the little villain seemed to vanish. As if into the very folds of her dress. It was most remarkable!

"You look as if you have seen a ghost," said Miss Always when she reached me. She was frowning now. "Are you unwell?"

I told my bosom friend what I had just witnessed. The poor creature was stunned.

"Ivy, what a remarkable story," she said gravely. "You say this little gentleman vanished as I came around the corner? But you know such things are impossible. You *do* know that, don't you?"

"Of course I do, dear," I said, trying to sound bright. "But I tell you, he looked just like the villains who attacked me in London. And if such things are impossible, what on earth did I just see?"

Miss Always pursed her lips. Murmured every so often. Then said, "Trauma. That is the only explanation."

"Is it?"

"I believe so. It is perfectly understandable that you might imagine those awful thieves from London had followed you here to Butterfield Park. In fact, I would be shocked if you *weren't* seeing things."

It had looked so real. Was I to doubt my own eyes? Yet Miss Always sounded very sure, and what reason would she have to lie? She *must* be right. It was just trauma. From the robbery. Nothing more. Which was a great relief.

Miss Always insisted on taking me to the kitchen for a pot of strong tea. We passed Miss Frost on the main stairs. For some reason, Miss Always seemed keen to hurry me along, but when Miss Frost showed a passing interest in why I looked so pale, I informed her that I was deeply traumatized.

Miss Frost seemed less interested in my trauma and more interested in the hooded villain I had hallucinated in the hallway. Remarkably, she didn't think I had *imagined* him at all. And that wasn't the only shock.

"I should think," she declared with astounding certainty, "that Miss Always might be *just* the person to ask about such creatures."

"I'm sure I don't know what you mean," said Miss Always quickly. "Come along, Ivy, let us—"

"But are you not writing a book on myths and legends?" said Miss Frost with a faint smile. Before my friend could answer, Miss Frost continued, "I seem to recall reading about a band of tiny hooded fellows, just as Miss Pocket described. Let me think, it was *so* long ago that I studied mythology." She tapped her chin. "Ah, now I remember! They are called locks."

"Locks?" I said.

Miss Always laughed, rather too loudly. "What nonsense, I never heard of such—"

"From what I remember," interrupted Miss Frost (she seemed to be enjoying herself enormously), "locks are hooded creatures who wear dark robes. They are small, usually travel in packs, are fast and highly dangerous. I seem to recall they serve a particularly hateful mistress—a cold-blooded hag of misery and death— though I cannot remember her name. Can you, Miss Always?"

"I cannot," came the firm reply.

I gasped (it seemed the right moment). "That has to be them!"

"Ivy, what a foolish thought," scolded Miss Always. "You are much too clever to be carried away by the ravings of a second-rate governess."

Miss Frost glared at my bosom friend. "I would have thought my theory was entirely reasonable, given what has befallen Miss Pocket of late. I am shocked, Miss Always, that you haven't heard of locks." She folded her arms. "In fact, I would think it quite impossible."

"Yes, well . . ." Miss Always adjusted her glasses. "I *may* have read of such creatures—just in passing. And from what I remember, locks are not at all as you have described, Miss Frost. They are a band of merry monks. Agents of peace, not violence."

"You're wrong, dear," I declared. "They're nasty little things."

Miss Frost walked on, looking rather pleased with herself. Miss Always and I continued down the stairs and into the great hall. It would hardly be worth noting, if not for the fact that Miss Always stumbled rather suddenly and fell to the floor. Tripped, apparently. Which was odd, as there wasn't so much as a speck of dust upon the polished floor. The poor dear landed with a *thump*, and when I helped her up, I saw her wrist was beginning to swell.

"I am a clumsy fool," said Miss Always, looking at her injury.

"I'm afraid so, dear," I said helpfully.

Miss Always frowned. Said her wrist was feeling numb. Apparently that was a bad sign. As she was holding her red and swollen wrist in front of my face, I felt it only proper to reach out and gently laid my hand upon it.

"Can you feel that, dear?" I asked.

"I . . . I can indeed."

Her eyes fluttered shut. Just as quickly, they sprang open. Then she pulled her arm away, covering her wrist with the sleeve of her dress.

"I'm sure it's fine, Ivy. Nothing to worry about."

Which was most peculiar. Utterly remarkable.

"I hope you do not take Miss Frost to heart, Ivy," said Miss Always as we made our way into the kitchen for our tea. "I think it is very cruel, the way she delights in unsettling you—filling your mind with mischief and folly."

I frowned. "Is that what she's doing?"

"Well, what other explanation is there?" said Miss Always. "A smart girl like yourself would never actually *believe* that a band of mythical locks have come to Butterfield Park to steal the Clock Diamond." She poured steaming tea into a cup and pushed it towards me. "But Miss Frost hopes that you will. It would amuse her greatly."

Miss Always had just confirmed my own fears about the devious governess.

"Beastly woman!" I said, reaching for the sugar bowl.

I would have thought no more about Miss Always's injured wrist, if not for a peculiar incident on my way down to dinner that evening. I had been looking for Rebecca, keen to find out more about Miss Rochester. She was not in the garden, nor the schoolhouse, so I decided to check the conservatory. As I was hurrying past the morning room, I stopped suddenly. How could I not—when from behind the closed door, I heard Miss Always utter my name?

With all the natural instincts of a Russian spy, I pressed my ear to the door. Miss Always was speaking with some urgency. This is what I heard.

"She is different from all the rest . . . that much is clear."

Then her voice dropped, and all I could pick up were fragments. "My wrist . . . swollen . . . Ivy . . . hand upon it . . . healed . . . most interesting . . . my plan is—"

Then silence. Hurried footsteps. Before I could retreat, the door swung open and Miss Always was eyeing me with suspicion. With staggering subtlety, I peered around her. The room appeared to be unoccupied.

"Ivy, what are you doing?" asked Miss Always rather sternly.

"Just eavesdropping, dear. It seemed like the right thing to do, as I heard you mention my name. Which is rather odd, as you appear to be alone."

Her hard gaze gave way to a giggle. "You must think me unhinged!"

"The thought had occurred to me, dear."

My friend raced to a writing table by the window and grabbed her bonnet. Then, putting her arm through mine, she walked me towards the great hall.

"I was composing a letter to my mother," she explained, "and it is a habit of mine to speak the words aloud before I write them down." She blushed. "I'm afraid you heard me singing your praises, Ivy. Mummy delights in reading about the wonderful things you say and do."

That explained a great deal. But not everything.

"Forgive me, dear," I said, "but I rather thought you said something about me *healing* your wrist. After you fell and hurt yourself earlier. Now that I think of it, you did react rather strangely when I put my hand upon your injury."

Miss Always roared with laughter. Put a sisterly head on my shoulder. "Oh, Ivy, you do beat all! What I said was that you *held* my wrist. You see, I was very touched that when I was hurt you showed such loving kindness—and I wanted to share that in my letter."

Which made perfect sense. And yet . . .

"May I see it, Miss Always?"

My friend stopped in her tracks. Her brow buckled. I believe she gulped. "See it?"

"Yes, dear—your wrist."

"That seems rather unnecessary, Ivy." She smiled tightly. "But if you insist. After all, I have nothing to hide."

Slowly she pulled up the sleeve of her dress. Her wrist

looked slender and pale. There was no redness or swelling at all. In fact, it appeared to be completely healed. In a single afternoon.

I was stunned.

"It is still terribly painful, though it doesn't look it." Miss Aways was speaking rather quickly. "As for the swelling, well, the sprain was really very minor. Also, I am a remarkably fast healer, and these things always fix themselves, don't they? So it's really no great surprise." She looked at me with a mixture of pity and mild amusement. "Ivy, you don't *seriously* think—?"

"Heavens no!" I said, slapping her shoulder. "Are you mad?"

I only hoped she believed me.

When we reached the great hall, Miss Always put on her bonnet and announced she was heading out for the evening. She didn't say where she was going—just that she had an errand to run. Something that couldn't wait. And that she wouldn't be joining us for dinner.

I saw her to the door, then decided to continue my search for Rebecca before the supper gong sounded. The conservatory was deserted. As was the music room. When I tried the drawing room, I didn't find Rebecca, but I *did* find Lady Elizabeth and Lady Amelia.

They were already dressed for dinner. Lady Amelia was working on her embroidery, and the old bat was reading a book.

"You're a public menace!" she barked as I entered the room. "It took three baths to get the cheesecake from my skin!"

"No need to thank me, dear," I said humbly. "The glorious glow on your haggard face is reward enough."

"Hideous child!" she growled.

I was about to depart when Lady Amelia pricked her thumb with the needle. She cried out as it began to bleed.

Naturally, I was delighted.

"Let me have a look, dear," I said, hurrying towards her.

Lady Amelia was making the sort of idiotic noises you would expect from a simpleton of high birth. Threatening to faint at the sight of her own blood. Wondering if the doctor should be called for and whatnot.

"Bunkum!" snapped Lady Elizabeth. "You're barely bleeding, you foolish woman! I shot off a toe during a fox hunt and didn't even stop for a bandage."

I crouched down before Lady Amelia and looked at the

wound. It was a great disappointment. Barely a drop or two of blood.

"Do you think I should have it bandaged?" she asked me fretfully.

"No need, unfortunately."

Lady Elizabeth peered at me. "You sound disappointed, Miss Pocket."

"I won't lie, it *is* a great shame." Then I had a glorious idea. "Lady Amelia, would you be a dear and prick yourself again— only this time with slightly more vigor?"

"I beg your pardon?" came the stunned reply.

"What did she say?" barked Lady Elizabeth, cupping her ear with a bony hand.

"I only ask in the interests of science. You see, I am testing a theory." I was explaining myself beautifully. "But I require slightly more blood—also, a little more pain." I sighed. "I don't suppose you'd let me slam your fingers in the door? It would be a *great* help, dear."

Lady Amelia gasped and paled. "Heavens, Ivy."

"Defend yourself, Lady Amelia!" cried the old bat, thrusting her finger rather accusingly in my direction. "I *knew* you were dangerous, Miss Pocket. A bloodthirsty lunatic!"

"Calm down, you abominable windbag," I said, in my most soothing voice. "Lady Amelia has the opportunity to assist me in a most remarkable discovery. She will be famous!"

Before Lady Amelia had a chance to leap up and run away, I grabbed her hand and quickly wrapped my fingers around her bleeding thumb.

"Slap her silly!" hollered Lady Elizabeth, swinging her cane at me (but missing by a mile). The crazed fossil was squinting furiously at us. "What's she doing, Lady Amelia?"

"I have no idea," said Lady Amelia, trying to yank her hand away.

"Trust me, dear," I told her, holding on tightly, "you will be amazed. Astounded. Stupefied."

I recalled that with Miss Always, I had only touched her injured wrist for a moment. But just to be certain, I held the bleeding thumb for a full minute. I may have even closed my eyes and made the odd *mmm* sound. It seemed appropriate.

Then I slowly uncurled my fingers and, filled with hope,

looked down at Lady Amelia's thumb. It looked perfect. No sign of bleeding at all. I was about to call the entire household together and declare myself a mystical healer. And I would have. If not for the hideous sight of blood oozing up from the pinprick and pooling on Lady Amelia's skin. The wound was not even *slightly* healed. Which was frightfully inconvenient.

I got up. Patted Lady Amelia on the head like a puppy. Wished her well with her injury. And made a swift exit from the drawing room.

Lady Elizabeth may have hollered at me as I left—something about me being a dangerous fruitcake—but I was walking so quickly, I didn't hear a word of it.

To my relief, I found Rebecca in the library. She was slumped in an armchair tucked away in a far corner of the darkened room, her hand dangling from the armrest. She looked dead. Fortunately, I saw the rise and fall of her chest. Just asleep. Then I noticed something else. Well, two things, to be exact. The first was a small red book in her lap—her hand was wrapped around it, her finger acting as a kind of bookmark. And it wasn't just any book. It was *the* book. The one I had seen Miss Frost force upon her. The same book Rebecca had been clutching when she had her midnight meeting with Miss Frost. That's when I noticed the *second* thing. Something was tied on a ribbon around her wrist. The key. The key to her room.

It seemed that fate was giving me a choice. I could read the book. Or take the key. Of course, I could do both. But what if she woke up when I took the book? Then I would never get my hands on that key. In the end, my decision was an easy one. With tremendous care—for I have all the natural instincts of a safecracker—I pulled gently on the pale blue ribbon. It unfurled, and the key dropped silently into my waiting palm.

At last!

I flew up the stairs and in no time was standing outside Rebecca's bedroom door. I looked up and down the hall. Then looked again. No one was about. I slipped the key into the lock. Turned. It clicked crisply. The anticipation was delicious as I opened the door and stepped inside.

"Heavens . . ." That is what I said.

I looked about, bug-eyed, my gaze passing quickly over the wondrous chamber. What had I expected to find? Something shocking? Something sinister. Perhaps. But not *this*. Not a room crowded with, covered in, blanketed by—clocks. Clocks of every conceivable kind. Cuckoo clocks. Chiming clocks. Bracket clocks. Travel clocks. Chimney clocks. Lantern clocks. Mantel clocks. Big and small clocks. Clocks in black marble and green. Clocks in brass and silver and gold. Figurine clocks. Wooden clocks. Porcelain clocks. Gold clocks. Silver clocks. There were hundreds of them. Thousands, perhaps. Clocks covering every tabletop, every chest of drawers, every side table, every shelf. Clocks covering every part of the wall. Clocks crowding the floor. A path had been carved between them, leading from the bed to the door. With smaller trails leading to each table, desk, or cabinet.

And that was not the most shocking thing.

No. What gave me chills was that every single clock in that bedroom—each and every one—was perfectly synchronized. All ticking in unison. Practically shaking the room. *Tick. Tick. Tick.* Like a heartbeat. This was the sound I had heard coming from her room. I was certain it would drive me bonkers. Perhaps that was what had happened to Rebecca.

Suddenly her peculiar behavior made more sense. Her secret package on the train. Matilda listening to the box. It all made sense. Yet it made no sense at all.

I wandered about the room. It was a museum of time. It had a strange beauty, and I got slightly lost in it, I suppose. Which might explain why I didn't hear Rebecca slip into the room behind me. She didn't yell. Didn't throw me out. Didn't even ask how I got the key.

"It's not what you think," she said.

"And what do I think, dear?" I said.

"That I'm mad," she said. "That the clocks mean something. Something bad."

I sat down on the bed. "Wouldn't it be better for you to explain it for yourself?"

Rebecca sat down beside me. "When my mother got sick, they gave her a year. That's what all the doctors from London said. She had one year to live. When I heard the news, I decided to work out *exactly* how much time my mother had. It mattered, don't you see? If she only had a year, then every day and every hour and every minute mattered. It was all that mattered."

She looked at me, and her eyes were pleading. Asking me if I understood. I can't say that I did—not completely—but I nodded. "Go on," I whispered.

"It started with one clock," she said, looking about the room, "then two. I figured out that Mother had eight thousand seven hundred and sixty hours left. One year. That's five hundred and twenty-five thousand six hundred minutes. I suppose I thought if I knew how long, *exactly* how long, and I marked the minutes and the hours . . . I suppose I thought I could hold on to it."

"To time?"

Rebecca nodded. "If I could watch the seconds and the minutes and the hours, I could somehow master it. That I could somehow get her more. More time." She smiled sadly. "It's foolish, isn't it?"

"Monstrously stupid," I said, slipping my hand over hers. "But it's also rather beautiful. Did your mother know about the clocks?"

"No." She took a shaky breath. "You see, the doctors were wrong. They lied. She didn't have a year at all. She died on the fourth day of the ninth month. She only had two hundred and forty-six days." Rebecca looked at me, tears tracking down her face. She wasn't sad. She was furious. "You understand, don't you? We lost one hundred and nineteen days. That's two thousand, eight hundred and fifty-six hours. All stolen from us—each and every minute."

I nodded. "But the clocks, Rebecca. Why do you keep them now, after your mother has . . . now that she's gone?"

"It makes me feel close to her, I suppose." Rebecca smiled sadly. "I can't stop collecting them. I *have* tried, but I can't let them go. Do you think I'm mad?"

"Definitely," I said. "But we are all a little bonkers. And what you're doing here isn't crazy. I think I would just call it sorrow and leave it at that."

She seemed to like my diagnosis. We talked for an age.

About clocks. And days. And minutes. About her mother. When Rebecca had spoken of her on the train, her voice had been full of sadness and regret. But something had changed. Now she seemed remarkably . . . hopeful. Yes, that was it.

She gave me a tour of her collection. By the time we were finished, I would have gladly never looked at another clock again. But I am a kindhearted creature—so I pretended to find them all fascinating. Rebecca was babbling on about a silver clock she'd bought from a traveling salesman in Bristol, which she had smuggled into the house under her dress, as I wandered around the room, nodding at regular intervals. I stopped before a crowded bookcase by the window and examined its ticking treasures. There were perhaps fifty clocks upon the shelves. But something else too. Behind a walnut traveling clock and a fob watch on a rusted stand. The fact that it wasn't a clock caught my eye. It was a miniature portrait in a ghastly gold frame. I was curious. So I moved the clocks and reached for the painting.

Rebecca had stopped talking. I heard hurried footsteps. Then she was by my side, snatching the portrait from my hand. "That is nothing," she said quickly.

But it was too late. I had already seen her. Flowing blond hair. Cherub face. Even her eyes, blue and green, were captured in the miniature painting. "That is Miss Rochester!" I cried. "But you said you had no picture of her."

Rebecca looked lost. Uncertain. Her eyes shifted about, everywhere but at me. Something was wrong.

"The woman in the portrait," I said, trying to swallow the dread rising in my throat, "the one I saw in the woodlands—she is your old governess, is she not?"

Silence. No, not silence. *Tick. Tick. Tick. Tick.*

I reached for the picture, but Rebecca pulled it away.

"Rebecca, who is she?" I was shocked to hear the anger in my voice. "Tell me!"

It worked. Rebecca looked at me.

"She is my mother."

12

I could speak to the dead. I never *used* to be able to. In fact, I'd gone twelve long years without ever once chatting to a ghost. Now it was something I did a great deal. Murdered duchesses. Dead mothers. I spoke to them all.

It turns out, I'm rather good at it.

"This can't be," I said, pacing back and forth between the army of clocks in Rebecca's bedroom. "It's impossible. While it's true that as far as girls go, I'm rather extraordinary, *this* is something else."

"I've heard of such things before," said Rebecca quietly.

"There's a lady in the village who will pass on a message from the spirit world for five shillings."

"That is different," I said, turning and walking the length of the room again. "Women like that have crystal balls and warts on their noses and whatnot."

Rebecca poured me a glass of water and placed it gently in my hands. "Is it really such a bad thing, Ivy?" she said. "What you can do—it's amazing."

"It's bonkers!" I snapped.

She sat down on the bed. She didn't seem entirely surprised about my new talent—which I put down to the fact that she was barking mad herself.

"If I could talk to my mother the way you did, Ivy . . . well, I would be the happiest girl in England." Rebecca looked up. "Did she have a message for me? Did she say anything about me?"

I sighed. "Only that she watches you from afar. I have a feeling she does it quite often." If it made me feel any better to offer Rebecca some words of comfort about her dead mother, that notion quickly faded (which I put down to the fact that I was in shock and therefore slightly cold-blooded). "Your mother knew my name. How is such a thing possible?"

"I don't know," said Rebecca. "Perhaps you have always had this gift."

"Stuff and nonsense," I said.

"In time it might make more sense," said Rebecca carefully. Her words curled their way into my ear like a worm. She knew something. Something that I didn't.

"You knew, didn't you, Rebecca?" I stopped right in front of her. "You knew that the lady I met in the woodlands was your mother. Yet you let me think it was Miss Rochester."

She paled. "I didn't want to scare you, that's all."

"But why weren't *you* scared? After all, you had just learned that I'd had a lovely chat with your late mother. Now that I think of it, it was as if . . . as if you were not entirely surprised."

"Of course I was," said Rebecca, clearing her throat. "It was as much a surprise to me as it is to you."

But I didn't believe her. "Where did you go?"

Rebecca looked startled. "When?"

"Right after I told you about the lady in the woods, you ran off. In fact, you were in a terrible hurry. Where did you go?

Or should I ask, to *whom* did you run?"

"I . . . I went to my room. I was overwhelmed and—"

"It was Miss Frost, wasn't it?" I said. "You went to tell Miss Frost."

Her lips began to tremble. She didn't have to answer me.

"Why were you so keen to share the news with your governess?" I said. "Some secret business is going on between you and Miss Frost. She has caught you in her web. Made you an accomplice. What is going on, Rebecca?"

"She is trying to help!" she cried, jumping to her feet. "Miss Frost has important work to do. Horribly important. She cannot be everywhere. She cannot keep an eye on you and Miss—" She shook her head. "She needs my help, and I give it gladly."

"What sort of help? Rebecca, what is so important that she needed to meet with you under cover of darkness in the schoolhouse? I demand you tell me!"

"Miss Frost . . ." Her voice was faint, her sigh was of defeat. "She wished to show me the picture you drew—the one of the gardener tending the roses."

I recalled the picture. And I recalled Miss Frost asking to keep it. "Whatever for?"

"It was of Wickam." Rebecca said this mournfully.

"Who?"

"Don't you remember? I told you about him the day you arrived at Butterfield Park." She looked at me with something like sorrow. "Wickam died last winter."

Which was rather unsettling. But not *completely* surprising. Ghosts seemed rather fond of me. "Why did Miss Frost wish to show you that I had drawn a picture of a dead gardener?"

Rebecca looked agitated. Fidgety. "Don't you think it strange, Ivy, all that has happened since you took possession of the Clock Diamond?"

"It's slightly odd, I suppose. But a lady's maid must be prepared for a certain amount of nonsense when she's surrounded by a pack of aristocratic oddballs."

Rebecca shook her head. "These strange events *must* be connected to the stone." She was breathless now. Frowning. "You do see how everything began with that necklace … you do see that, don't you, Ivy?"

"Well, of course I do, dear. But the peculiar events that have occurred since the Duchess of Trinity entrusted me with the diamond are no great mystery. Not to me."

She looked positively puzzled. "They're not?"

"Heavens no. In Paris, the Duchess warned me that dark forces were after the Clock Diamond. It's clear I'm dealing with a band of wicked thieves. As I said, no great mystery."

"But how do you explain the ghosts and the locks who attacked you in London?"

"Who told you about the locks?" I huffed. "Let me guess. Miss Frost?"

Rebecca ignored the question. "How do you explain these strange occurrences, Ivy?"

I shrugged. "I'm sure a grim old house like Butterfield has *scores* of ghosts lurking about—I just happened to have met one or two. As for the locks, well, they are nothing more than pint-sized fortune hunters—probably from the jungles of Budatta, where the diamond was first discovered, or perhaps from a disreputable circus. But they don't frighten me. I bashed them silly!"

"But the book says—what I mean is, these locks don't sound as if they are from . . ." Her voice dropped to a whisper. "*Our* world."

I snorted. Daintily. "Our world? How many worlds do you imagine there are, dear?"

"Two," she answered with grim certainty. "I believe there might be two."

I stood up and said, "You are a cherished friend, Rebecca, so I'd normally only say this kind of thing behind your back—but as your family already thinks you're nuttier than an almond cake, I urge you not to go around talking of other worlds. It's frightfully bonkers."

"You must listen to me, Ivy," she said, her face furrowed and pale. "Miss Frost is terribly worried about the birthday ball. She believes you will be in grave danger."

"Calm yourself, dear. It's a scientific fact that hysteria causes freckles, and in that regard, you've suffered enough. As for Miss Frost, she has warped your mind with her silly stories. Leave her to me."

Rebecca fell into stony silence. Her eyes glazed and anxious. I retreated from the ticking bedroom, but Rebecca's voice stopped me in the doorway. "I'm sorry about everything, Ivy," she said. "I hope one day you will understand and forgive me."

With supper over, Cook had retired to her quarters. As such, I had slipped into the pantry and was finishing up a small snack. A few raw potatoes. Half a cabbage. My cravings were a slight concern, but I was certain there was a perfectly reasonable explanation. After all, I still loved cake. Only now I preferred to eat it by the pound. But I was still thin as a whippet, so no harm done.

When my belly was full, I was keen to vacate the pantry before the scullery maids returned with the dinner plates. I was hurrying across the cavernous kitchen when I heard raised voices coming toward me. Fearing discovery, I leaped back into the pantry. I had just taken up a crouching position behind a sack of raw sugar when Miss Frost and Miss Always strode into the kitchen. Miss Always was still wearing her bonnet and gloves. Neither one looked especially jolly.

"Do you want her to put the pieces of this puzzle together?" hissed Miss Always, stopping before the chopping block and taking off her hat. "She would tell the world."

"And you would be exposed," said Miss Frost coldly.

"*We* would be exposed."

"Do not lump us together. We are not the same."

"But we want the same thing." Miss Always stepped awfully close to Miss Frost. Which was thrilling! "If Ivy is as remarkable as I suspect, why should I ignore it?"

Miss Frost laughed harshly. "You are deluded."

"I am right!"

The hideous governess reached out and seized Miss Always's arm. "I know what you are thinking, Miss Always, and I tell you this—if you try anything tomorrow night, I will stop you."

My bosom friend hissed like a rattlesnake. "Unhand me!"

"Leave the girl in peace!"

Miss Always reached for a carving knife lying beside a bowl of peaches. She waved it rather freely before Miss Frost. Which was highly unexpected.

The grim spinsters were staring daggers at each other.

"Fortune favors the brave, Miss Frost," said Miss Always. "We shall see who wins the day."

It was entirely the wrong moment to sneeze. Yet sneeze I did. But quietly—having all the natural instincts of a stuffed bear. Miss Frost and Miss Always did not hear a thing. I was sure of it. Miss Always *did* glance towards the pantry. But only for a moment. Then Miss Frost gave a slight nod of her head. Miss Always lowered the knife—which was a heartbreaking disappointment—reached for a peach, and began to slice it.

When she spoke again, her voice was considerably louder. "It would ruin the surprise if Ivy knew I was planning a special celebration for her after the ball," she said. "The poor girl deserves it after all she has been through. I know you find such things silly, Miss Frost, but you mustn't tell Ivy what I am planning."

Miss Frost smiled. "I won't . . . for now."

Dear Miss Always! Not a nefarious, knife-wielding lunatic.

Just a dear friend planning a surprise party. I was seized by another sneezing fit. The pantry was violently dusty. I had little choice but to show myself. Miss Frost did not look terribly surprised when I stepped out. But poor Miss Always was positively stunned.

"Oh, Ivy," she said, "I *do* hope you didn't hear me talking to Miss Frost."

"About my surprise party? No, dear, not a word."

Miss Frost cleared her throat. "I have a letter to write, if you will excuse me."

A great well of anger bubbled up inside me as I watched the prim and proper Miss Frost walk from the kitchen. Which was why I said, "I hope you will stop filling Rebecca's head with any more nonsense about hidden worlds, Miss Frost. The girl is confused enough as it is."

She stopped. Turned around. "My job is to educate her."

"About things that do not exist?"

"The universe is a confounding place, Miss Pocket. Some believe there is another world sitting beside our own. A world hidden by the thinnest of veils. My job is to teach Rebecca not just what is, but what may be." Miss Frost regarded me coolly. "As a girl who frequently speaks to the dead, I should think you would be more open-minded."

I sighed. "Yes, yes, my silly drawing. Honestly, dear, is seeing the occasional dead gardener really so peculiar?"

"Actually, Miss Pocket, it is," came Miss Frost's crisp reply.

"I know of a castle in Scotland that has more than sixty different ghosts," said Miss Always. "I don't think there is anything remarkable about what Ivy has seen. Nothing at all."

I wanted to kiss the dreary bookworm! Instead, I turned to her and said, "And what is your view on hidden worlds, Miss Always?"

"Complete nonsense."

God bless Miss Always!

Miss Frost folded her arms. "We are surrounded by a universe that the naked eye cannot see—and yet it is there."

"Unlikely, dear." I shook my head. "Mrs. Crabapple, the head housekeeper at Midwinter Hall, was a keen student of the cosmology and tea leaves and whatnot. She had it on very good authority that the world is actually floating inside a frightfully large glass ball—rather like a snow globe."

"I see." I could tell by the slight flare of her nostrils that Miss Frost wasn't at all pleased. "How does your Mrs. Crabapple explain the planets one can view through a telescope?"

"Stray balloons, dear. From birthday parties and such."

Miss Frost's mouth twitched. "That is the most *ridiculous* thing I have ever heard. You cannot be this idiotic, Miss Pocket. I refuse to believe it."

She stalked from the kitchen.

Miss Always looked mightily pleased. She sat down at the table, urging me to sit beside her—which I did—then offered me a slice of peach.

"She is no match for you, Ivy," she said, grinning wildly. "What a clever girl you are!"

The ghost came just before dawn. I woke up with a start from a rather troublesome dream. She was there. At the end of the bed. Her enormous body, rippling and glowing like a lantern on a lake. Her ghostly blubber spilling over the sides of the tiny bed frame. She was smiling faintly. Smoke coiling for her mouth. I didn't gasp or tremble. Despite the fact that she had flown at me in a murderous rage the last time we met.

"They don't like each other," she sang at me.

"Who, dear?"

The Duchess of Trinity groaned. "Miss Frost and Miss Always. They do not like each other."

"Miss Frost is a horrible creature. She is full of mischief and skullduggery."

"And Miss Always?"

"She is my friend," I said. "My bosom friend."

That seemed to delight the Duchess. She laughed, and as she did, starlight leaped from her hair.

I sighed. Felt rather cross. "You're dead, so I assume you know a great deal more about what is happening in this house than I do." I lit the candle beside my bed. "These locks Miss Frost told me about—I am certain it is nonsense just as Miss Always says—but what do you think? Are these strange little creatures real?"

The Duchess of Trinity closed her eyes. "Did the attack in Belgravia feel *real* to you, child?"

"Well, of course it did, you ghoulish fatso!"

"Then you have your answer."

"What are locks? Who do they work for? And why am I seeing ghosts? Everywhere I turn there is mystery and secrets! What is happening, Duchess?"

She huffed. "I am a ghost, *not* an oracle." The light pouring from her seemed to dim. Just for a moment. "You are right about one thing, child—there are people in this house who are determined to get their hands on the Clock Diamond. Miss Frost is one of them. She will try and stop you from giving Matilda the stone. She wants it for herself."

"What should I do?"

"Be on your guard," she sang. "Do not become distracted by intrigue and shadows. Remember why you came to Butterfield Park."

"Do the locks work for Miss Frost?" I asked. "Is she—?"

"Have you forgotten your promise to me?" hissed the dead woman. "That is why you are here, *that* is all that matters. Keep the necklace well hidden until the birthday ball and then hang it around Matilda's neck. The rest is of no concern to either of us." She sat at the other end of my bed, yet her voice seemed to whisper right into my ear. "Remember the five hundred pounds, child. Your future is a bright one, so long as you do as I have asked."

Although she was dead and had recently tried to devour me, she also made a great deal of sense. All that mattered was fulfilling my mission. And collecting the reward.

And starting fresh.

"She thinks you are a menace," said the Duchess. She licked her lips, and I noticed that her tongue was black. Which was revolting. "She does not like you at all."

"Miss Frost?"

"Lady Elizabeth." The Duchess fixed her eyes—two dark pools—upon me. "You have tried so hard to win her favor—but nothing works, does it, child?"

I shrugged, but I confess the situation bothered me. "The old bat is frightfully prickly."

"I believe she would warm to you if *only* there was some way you could win her favor. It would please me to see you two becoming friends. Have you any ideas?"

"Perhaps I could read to her. Old people love that. Or I could fix her hair or file her bunions. I'm certain she has monstrous bunions."

The Duchess appeared deep in thought. "It must be something simple," she said. "Lady Elizabeth must not suspect you are trying to impress her." She sighed. "When we were girls and we would quarrel, I used to know *just* how to make amends. But no, you will think it too silly."

I tried not to appear eager. "I'm sure it's terribly stupid, but just out of interest, what was it?"

"Iced tea," she said. "Iced tea with a few drops of vanilla and a squeeze of lime. There is no surer way to Lady Elizabeth's heart. It will remind her of better days. She will be moved beyond words."

Then, without so much as a good-bye, the ghost dissolved into the bed like a morning fog. After she was gone, and I was once again alone, her voice lingered in the crisp air. "Remember, child," it sang. "Iced tea with vanilla and a squeeze of lime."

I pulled back the covers and jumped from the bed.

13 *

The day of Matilda's birthday ball had arrived. Before I ventured downstairs for breakfast, I checked the Clock Diamond. It was right where it should be, lost among a cluster of worthless costume jewelry. I held it up to the light. In truth, I wasn't looking at it simply to marvel at its mystical beauty. I was deeply curious about what the stone had shown me the last time. The girl being pulled through the snow. *Me.* But the diamond glowed like a sunrise and nothing more.

The disappointment stung. If the stone was a riddle, then I hoped it might also be the solution. With a sigh, I replaced the necklace and covered the jewelry chest with a few dusty frocks. Then I placed a sad-looking boar spear and a few homemade crossbows on top for good measure.

The great hall was a hive of activity as I came down the main stairs. Maids of all shapes and sizes scurrying about. Footmen moving furniture. Butlers polishing doorknobs.

Matilda's birthday cake was already in position. It had been baked in London by someone monstrously important and had been brought overnight by stagecoach. It stood on a round oak table in the middle of the hall, directly beneath the massive chandelier. The cake was five tiers tall. One layer yellow. The next blue. And so on. It looked utterly delicious.

The Duchess's words rang in my ears as I headed for the library. About the sinister Miss Frost. About the locks. About everything strange that had happened since I took possession of the Clock Diamond. Then I remembered Mr. Banks—what monstrous news would he bring me? I checked my watch. He was due on the morning train. It embarrassed me to admit how eager I was to see him.

"I am utterly confused!" I groaned aloud. I could have

said more—about what a horrible mess I was in and what a wonderfully plucky girl I was. But I didn't. Because by that time I had entered the library. And there he was!

Horatio Banks, in his dark suit and top hat, stood before me.

"But I thought your train would not be here for at least another hour?" I said, rushing to him.

"Well, I am here now," he said, fixing his steely green eyes upon me. "Miss Pocket, there is a great deal I needed to speak with you about."

"Goodness, this room is awfully cold."

"Miss Pocket, let us begin," said Horatio Banks. "I haven't much time. Not much time at all."

"Yes, dear, immediately," I said, offering the grim-faced lawyer a seat on the sofa, which he declined. It was then that I noticed the cut on his forehead. Just below his hat.

"Mr. Banks, you are hurt," I said, pulling out my handkerchief.

"Ah, it is nothing," he said, waving me away. "As I wrote in my letter, I have conducted a great deal of research into the Clock Diamond since last I saw you. I have a contact—a master criminal, Miss Pocket—who had business with the Duchess around the time the stone came into her possession. This *gentleman* has fallen on hard times. As such, he was willing to reveal something of the diamond's lineage for a few hundred pounds. A very great deal, in fact. I must inform you, the day after our meeting in Liverpool, the man was found with a dagger in his heart."

I gasped. "You think he was killed for talking to you?"

"I am certain of it. I believe the people who have been hunting the stone were following me." He looked off into the distance. "I led them right to the wretched man."

"This is a beastly business," I said, shaking my head. I felt the need to walk about. And talk. So I did both. "I don't mind telling you, Mr. Banks, that I feel terribly ill-used. The Duchess of Trinity made me a perfectly simple offer. Take a stupid diamond back to England and give it to Matilda Butterfield on her twelfth birthday. It was utterly straightforward. Of course I said yes. What could go wrong?" I turned back and glared at Mr. Banks. "Plenty, that's what. I've been haunted by ghosts, strapped into my bed, fallen into a fire, thrown against a wall, pushed down the stairs, seen baffling visions—and that's just in the past week!"

If my tirade shocked Mr. Banks, he gave no sign of it.

He stood utterly still. He stared at me, and for the first time I saw a kind of sorrow in his eyes. The wound on his head began to weep—a trail of blood tracking slowly down his face.

"It is all connected," he said, each word slow and thick with meaning. "Those creatures who attacked you in Belgravia and the Duchess's murder before that. *Nothing* is by chance." He shook his head slowly. "Why did you put on that necklace, Miss Pocket?"

"What do you mean, Mr. Banks? Spit it out!"

"I mean this—you may have come upon the Duchess and her diamond by chance, but I am afraid there was also something else at work." He was looking at me with such sadness! "Something like fate, Miss Pocket."

"At last we are getting somewhere," I said, trying to sound unruffled. "Now be a dear, and tell me *exactly* what you mean."

"To begin with, you must not let Matilda Butterfield have the—"

"There you are, Ivy!" It was Lady Amelia. She sounded flustered.

I turned just as she hurried towards us, waving her hands about like she was hailing a carriage. "I do hope I'm not interrupting anything important?"

"I'm afraid you are, dear. We are just in the middle of a most serious conversation."

She appeared not to hear me.

"Lady Elizabeth has a dreadful headache," she said. "And on the day of Matilda's birthday ball! There is so much to do." Lady Amelia stopped in front of me and put a hand on my shoulder. "Can you help her, Ivy?"

"Of course I can," I said. I would have said more about my many talents had I not remembered my manners. "How rude of me. Lady Amelia, allow me to introduce you to a very old friend of mine, Mr. Horatio Banks."

Lady Amelia looked baffled. She didn't offer Mr. Banks a greeting, which I thought was monstrously rude. I turned to introduce him to Lady Amelia—he at least would say hello. But he was gone. Utterly vanished. I understood immediately. He wished to keep his presence at the house a secret!

"Yes . . . well, Ivy," said Lady Amelia, "if you could come with me now and attend to Lady Elizabeth, I would be very grateful. I only ask that you limit your remedy to onions and lavender. Lady Elizabeth is afraid you will attack her with a cheesecake again."

"I saved that old bat's skin," I protested.

"Yes, of course you did. Come, Ivy, we must hurry!"

Lady Amelia practically ran from the room. I followed but paused at the library door. When I glanced back, Mr. Banks had returned. He was standing by the large windows that look over the garden.

"I'll be back in a moment," I said. "You make yourself comfortable, dear."

"I haven't much time, Miss Pocket," he said.

"Ivy?" called Lady Amelia from the hallway. "Ivy, are you coming?"

"Yes, dear, but first I must stop by the kitchen."

I waved to Mr. Banks and hurried away.

Lady Elizabeth did a great deal of groaning. And a tremendous amount of moaning. But in just a few minutes, there were two sprigs of lavender wedged in her nose and she had settled. When I offered her a glass of delicious iced tea, she looked thoroughly unimpressed. When I told her I had made it myself, she looked positively stunned.

"What's this about?" she barked.

"I thought you might like it, dear. The recipe is one that I got from—"

No point bringing up the Duchess. Better to claim all the credit myself.

"It is a Pocket family recipe," I said rather grandly.

Lady Elizabeth took the glass from my hand. "What's in it?'

"The ingredients are a closely guarded secret. But when you taste it, I am certain you'll sob like a lost child who has found its mother. Now shut your trap and drink."

With a huff, old Walnut Head did as she was instructed. She took several large gulps. Smacked her lips. Frowned. "It's not *completely* revolting."

"It's delicious and you know it," I said, feeling rather triumphant. "Drink up, dear."

"Open those doors," barked Lady Elizabeth. "It's like a furnace in here."

Which was odd, as it was really rather cold. I was so preoccupied with the French doors that I didn't even hear the glass drop. But when I turned, I saw that Lady Elizabeth was slumped on the sofa like a sack of potatoes, the glass upon the floor.

I raced across the room and knelt beside her. Her face was puffing up, inflating like a horribly wrinkled balloon. Her tongue was swollen and pushing its way out (she looked like a thirsty pack mule). Her eyes were swollen shut.

She was groaning. Her skin felt monstrously hot.

Lady Amelia had come into the room by then. I know, because I heard her scream when she saw Lady Elizabeth— who by now resembled a seal, her entire body magnificently bloated.

"What on earth happened?" cried Lady Amelia, after sending one of the maids to fetch Dr. Longfellow.

"She was perfectly fine only moments ago," I said. "Happily drinking her iced tea."

"What was in it, Ivy?"

"Just the usual ingredients, dear," I said. "Ice, tea, a few drops of vanilla."

That seemed to relieve Lady Amelia.

"And a squeeze of lime juice," I added.

She gasped. "Lady Elizabeth is allergic to lime! Oh, Ivy . . ."

Which was terribly unfortunate.

We applied wet towels to the inflated monstrosity that was Elizabeth Butterfield and waited until the doctor arrived. Dr. Longfellow was not available, so Dr. Grace from the next village came instead. He looked her over. Opened his bag and pulled out various instruments of torture. Took her pulse and whatnot. Then announced that it was a simple allergic reaction. The old bat should be fine in a few hours. Six footmen carried Lady Elizabeth up to her room to rest and deflate before the party.

I felt awful. Lady Amelia assured me it wasn't my fault. Which was true enough. I knew *exactly* where the fault lay. The

Duchess of Trinity! But I would deal with her later. For now, I was keen to get back to Mr. Banks. He had insisted that he did not have much time, so naturally I didn't want to keep him waiting (for I am devastatingly considerate).

"I cannot find Rebecca anywhere!" cried Matilda as Lady Amelia and I entered the great hall. "She is the only one who can fix my hair just how I like it." She looked about like a hungry lion. "She's hiding from me, I can tell. When I find her, I'll pinch her arm till it bleeds!"

"Don't do that, dear," I said, "or I'll have to hang you from the pot rack and pummel you with carrots. Then you wouldn't look at all fetching for your grand birthday ball."

Matilda glared at me. I'm sure she wanted to scratch my face. Or, at very least, poke out an eyeball. "Why are you still here, Pocket?" she hissed. "Today's my birthday, so hand over the diamond and get lost!"

"Never," I declared. I hadn't meant to. What I'd meant to say was "Not yet" or "Not until tonight." But instead I had acted as if the diamond was mine. All mine. And I would never part with it. Not until it showed me another vision. Of the girl in the snow. And the woman in the yellow bonnet. Not until my story had an ending.

"What did you say?" snapped Matilda.

I coughed daintily—for I have all the natural instincts of a prima ballerina. "You'll get the necklace at the ball in front of all your guests," I said. "That was the Duchess of Trinity's dying wish."

"Blast!" Matilda flicked her hair, brushed past me, and stomped away, shouting for her cousin.

I had never seen the great hall so crowded. It seemed as if every servant in Butterfield Park was gathered there, polishing and sweeping and arranging flowers. So it was a perfect moment for me to slip away. Lady Amelia was fussing over the cake, and I had nearly escaped when I heard a carriage pull up before the front door.

Hurried footsteps filled the hall. Then a voice. A young man.

"Ivy Pocket?" He stopped to catch his breath. "Is Ivy Pocket about?"

Lady Amelia pointed to me. The young man's name was Fergus Green, and he ran errands for Dr. Longfellow in the village.

"You Ivy Pocket?"

"I am. What's this about?"

He gulped. I saw him gulp. "You know a Mr. Horatio Banks of London?"

I was flooded with relief. "Of course I do. He is in the library this very moment, you foolish fathead."

Fergus Green looked at me with a most peculiar expression. Like I had just introduced myself as the Queen of England. "There's been an accident, miss," he said. "Dr. Longfellow was called to the scene."

Lady Amelia gasped. "An accident? What sort of accident?"

"The train, my lady," he said. "Went off the drawbridge and into the river. Seems someone tampered with the signal. It's an awful mess. Six dead."

"Good heavens!" Lady Amelia made the sign of the cross.

The young man reached into his pocket and pulled out a crumpled envelope. He looked down at it. Turned it over in his hand. Then he passed it to me. The envelope was smeared with blood. My name written on the front.

"Dr. Longfellow found this in Mr. Banks's coat pocket,"

said Fergus. "It's addressed to you, so we thought you should have it."

I was baffled. It was all so sad. So silly. Now I understood the wound on Mr. Banks's head—but he had made no mention of an accident. Typical!

I looked down at the envelope. "I don't think it was right for you to go rifling through Mr. Banks's coat," I said firmly. "And I won't open this letter. I will return it to Mr. Banks, and he can decide what to do with it."

Fergus took off his cap. He looked at Lady Amelia, then back at me. "He won't be needing that letter," he said. "Not where he is."

"Whatever are you talking about?" I snapped. "Mr. Banks is in the library."

"That can't be, miss," he said gravely. "The old man died in the accident."

14

"Why won't she speak?"

"It's the shock, I suppose."

"Should we send for someone?"

"Let her rest, Rebecca. Miss Pocket will come back to us in her own time."

They were all there in my room. Miss Always. Rebecca. Miss Frost. Even Matilda.

Mr. Banks had been generous. One thousand pounds. That was my bounty. It was more money than I had ever seen in my entire life. All thanks to Mr. Banks. The *late* Horatio

Banks. The envelope was addressed to me. The one found in his frock coat. The one stained with blood and now resting on my bedside table. The envelope contained money. My payment from the Duchess. One thousand pounds. But that wasn't right, was it? The sum was *five* hundred pounds. Yet Mr. Banks had put in double that amount. And I knew why. He wanted me to have enough money to get away. To escape this tangle. He was coming to rescue me.

But he never made it.

"What on earth happened?" It was Miss Always. She sounded horrified. "I heard Lady Amelia say the train plunged into the river."

"There are reports the drawbridge signal wasn't working," said Miss Frost calmly. "The driver believed the bridge was down, when in fact it was up."

A gasp. Rebecca. "How could such a thing happen?" she said.

"The signal was tampered with, I should think," was Miss Frost's reply. "You went out last night, didn't you, Miss Always? Do you recall seeing anything suspicious on your travels?"

"I went into town to speak with Reverend Moore," said Miss

Always, looking tenderly at me. "I asked him to pray for a friend of mine who is troubled. But I saw nothing untoward."

"How unfortunate," said Miss Frost.

I was surrounded by ghosts. Four, at last count. A devilish duchess. An angelic mother. An ancient gardener. A crotchety lawyer. All dead.

I had gone looking for him. After I heard about the train, I ran like a lunatic back to the library. I was sure he would be there—right where I had left him. But he wasn't. I suppose it was just as Miss Always had explained. Mr. Banks was not an earthbound ghost. He had only a short time to visit before crossing over. And he would not be back.

"Would you like a drink of water, Ivy?" said Rebecca. She was sitting on the side of the bed, stroking my hair. "Are you hungry?"

I shook my head.

"I'm awfully sorry about your friend, Ivy," said Miss Always. "I wish there was something I could do to make you feel better. When terrible accidents like this happen, we are at a loss to understand them. But you must not give in to despair."

"Mr. Banks came to see me," I said.

Rebecca gasped again. "His ghost?"

I nodded. "He was wounded. He wanted to speak with me urgently, but I was so busy talking nonsense that he hardly had the chance."

"And what did he tell you, Miss Pocket?" said Miss Frost casually.

Here was my chance. To say out loud all that I was thinking. To tell them what I'd been told. They would think I had lost my mind. Or worse. They might believe every word. "I can't remember," I said.

"Perhaps it was a dream, Ivy," said Miss Always, walking over to the little window and drawing back the curtains. "You've suffered a great trauma, so we shouldn't be surprised. Yes, just a dream. Nothing more serious than that."

"You must be joking," said Miss Frost coldly. "Did you not write a book about ghosts?"

Miss Always and Miss Frost glared at each other with shocking intensity. Was it hatred? I was sure more was being said in that silence than a thousand words could express.

"If Mr. Banks *did* make a ghostly visit," Miss Always finally said, "then perhaps he did so to let Ivy know that he was all right. That death was not the end. Yes, I am sure that's all it was."

"Pocket's disturbed," said Matilda helpfully. "What sort of girl has dead people coming to visit her? It's outrageous! If she's not throwing herself down the stairs, she's attacking poor Grandmother with cheesecake and iced tea or making up fanciful stories. I can't be the only one who thinks she's demented."

"How can you be so cruel?" said Miss Always, her voice trembling.

Matilda smiled darkly.

"Your party is in just a few hours," said Miss Frost, putting a hand behind Matilda's back and walking her toward the door. "I'm sure you have more pressing things to do than stay up here and be horrible." She glanced at me briefly. "Besides, Miss Pocket needs her rest."

"Yes, that is very true," said Miss Always, who kissed my cheek and quickly departed.

But Matilda couldn't leave without slinging one final arrow. "I'm sure my cousin will take excellent care of you, Pocket." She smiled sweetly. *"Tick tock."*

Miss Frost pulled the evil nitwit away.

"Ignore her," I told Rebecca as their footsteps faded away. "She doesn't mean half the awful things she says."

"Yes, she does," said Rebecca.

I smiled faintly. "True. But I have to believe that one day Matilda will wake up and realize what a horrible, fatheaded, nitwitted, black-hearted lump of horse poop she really is."

Rebecca smiled, but the grin soon slipped from her face. She sat down on the bed again. "I'm sorry about Mr. Banks."

"So am I," I said.

"Ivy . . . how old were you when you first went to the orphanage?"

I hadn't expected such a question. In fact, I'd never told Rebecca that I had grown up in the Harrington Home for Unwanted Children. Yet clearly she knew about it. I thought about launching into a fantastical story—but I didn't have the heart for it.

"Five," I said.

"And before that?" said Rebecca.

"I lived with my parents, of course."

But Rebecca didn't look at all convinced. "What can you remember of those years, Ivy?"

"Everything," I lied. "Wonderful memories."

"I don't believe you," she said. "Please, Ivy, can you tell me the truth? It's very important."

I sighed. I hated the truth, as a general rule. But I decided to give it a try. "I don't remember much before the orphanage."

"You have no memories of your parents at all?"

"Not really. But I was taken from them. I've always suspected as much—after all, who would give up a child as heartbreakingly adorable as me? And then I saw a vision in the Clock Diamond, and I knew it was true. I was stolen."

If Rebecca was shocked or confused by this, she didn't show it. "What did you see, Ivy?" she said.

"Someone taking me from a house and leading me through the woods. A woman wearing a long coat and a yellow bonnet. She was taking me from my parents. Stealing me away."

Rebecca started to cry. The poor dear wept buckets. "I'm sorry, Ivy."

I shrugged. "It's not your fault, dear."

"Everything that's happened," she sobbed, "Mr. Banks's train . . . and the stairs . . . it's horrible!"

"Who knows why the train crashed? Perhaps it was just an accident," I said, patting Rebecca on the head (which is always a great comfort). "And as for the stairs, well, I'm sure I was so busy daydreaming I didn't look where I was going."

Rebecca's eyes locked onto mine. "You were pushed."

I gasped. Like a damsel in distress. Which was embarrassing. "Are you *sure*?"

She nodded. Tears streaming down her face. The girl leaked like a burst pipe.

"I'm sure," she said.

"Who did it, Rebecca? Who pushed me?"

"I did," she whispered.

She wouldn't say why. That was the worst part. No, the worst part was that Rebecca Butterfield—my dear *friend*—had confessed to pushing me down the stairs. Trying to kill me, one would assume. As news went, it was grim. Deliciously shocking, but grim.

"You hate me," said Rebecca.

I was standing by the window now. She was sitting on the bed, looking washed out and broken. For the tenth or eleventh time I said, "I don't understand any of this."

"It's not what you think, Ivy," she said faintly. "It's not . . ."

"Were you angry at me? Did I *do* something?"

"No, nothing." She looked up at me, and her eyes were pleading that I might understand.

"Help me, Rebecca," I said, "because right at this moment the voice in my head is shouting that you're a murderous maniac."

"I didn't want to hurt you," she sobbed.

"Well, I have news for you, dear," I said. "If you didn't want to hurt me, you shouldn't have pushed me down a gigantic flight of stairs. Over my short career as a maid, a great many people have threatened to kill me, but none have actually tried."

"No," said Rebecca, "it's not that. It's the opposite."

I glared at her as if she were bonkers. "The opposite of what?"

Rebecca stood up. Rushed towards me. Naturally I thought she might push me out the window. So I backed up. Which made her cry. Again.

"Oh, Ivy, there are things you don't know."

"Then tell me!"

She was shaking her head. "Miss Frost says I mustn't."

"Why not?" I asked. It seemed a reasonable question.

But Rebecca wouldn't say anything more. Apart from repeating that she had never meant to hurt me. Which was ridiculous.

"You pushed me down the stairs for her?" I said. "For Miss Frost?"

"No. Not really. What I mean is . . . I did it because . . . oh, what's the use, Ivy? You wouldn't believe me anyway, and I don't blame you."

A knock at the door.

"Excuse me, Miss Rebecca." It was one of the maids. "Miss Matilda would like you to come and attend to her hair."

"I'm sorry, Ivy," whispered Rebecca.

"Yes, you've said that already."

Then I turned my back and stared out the window.

"Come this instant, you wicked windbag. You blubbery beast!"

I put my hands on my hips (which felt enormously satisfying) and bellowed into thin air. Waiting impatiently for the Duchess of Trinity to appear before me. She didn't.

But I wasn't going to give up without a fight.

"Show yourself, Duchess, or our deal is off!" I declared this with heartbreaking conviction. "You can have your money back and I will bury the Clock Diamond in the woodlands—Matilda will never get to wear it!"

She came from the water pitcher. Which was slightly unusual. I heard a clanking sound, and when I looked over, the pitcher atop the dresser had lifted from its basin and was rising into the air. The pitcher stopped, hovering before me. Then it tilted, and water poured from the spout. A great deal of water. And instead of pooling on the floor in a giant puddle, it molded itself into the shape of the dead Duchess.

She looked rather beautiful, a great tower of rippling water.

Then her luminous flesh began to absorb the liquid—like a sponge. In just moments, the Duchess of Trinity was a familiar glowing nightmare, hovering above the ground in her bloodied nightdress.

The pitcher seemed content to float above her head.

"You are upset, child," she purred.

"You tricked me," I snapped. "You tricked me into giving Lady Elizabeth the iced tea with lime juice. That old bat is allergic! Monstrously allergic!"

The Duchess gasped. "I do hope she wasn't hurt?"

"Hurt? The poor cow puffed up like a balloon! Her tongue swelled like a pork sausage!" I narrowed my gaze. "Why would you want to hurt Lady Elizabeth if you sent me here to make peace with her? What is going on, Duchess?"

I don't know how I thought she would react. But what I hadn't expected was that she would begin to cry. Nor did I imagine that her tears would be an inky black. But they were and she did. Sobbing into her fat hands. A valley of tears streaking darkly down her glowing face.

"Death, child," she cried, "it scrambles the brain. Muddles the mind. Instead of telling you Lady Elizabeth's favorite refreshment, my frazzled memory offered up the one drink in the world that would injure my old friend. I'll never forgive myself. My shame will be eternal."

Which was rather surprising. She looked awfully sorry.

"Can you forgive a lonely old ghost?" she sobbed.

I shrugged. "Unlikely, dear. I have a talent for grudges. I once carried one for an entire winter. The back pain was monstrous."

She growled faintly and said, "You won't break our agreement, I trust? You will deliver the Clock Diamond as promised?"

"I suppose so." I sighed. "Everywhere I turn, there is mystery and calamity, Duchess. Mr. Banks is dead—I suppose you know that already?"

The Duchess nodded.

"He came to visit me, just as you do. Only with less growling and overturned furniture. Have you seen him? Because I'd very much like to pass on a message."

She huffed. "Mr. Banks was my lawyer, not my friend. What reason would he have to seek me out?" The Duchess cackled. "Besides, I am not an easy ghost to find."

"Duchess . . . do you know why Rebecca pushed me down the stairs?"

She did not answer. Instead, she reminded me again of our bargain. Urged me to ignore the darkness swirling around me and focus on delivering the necklace to Matilda. And beginning my new life. Somewhere far away from Butterfield Park.

It was a lovely thought.

Then she began to bleed. Not blood—water. It trickled from her, a thousand little drops, until her whole ghostly being was lost to a tide of rippling liquid. This column of water rose as if through a blowhole and poured back into the pitcher hovering above her. When she was gone, every last drop, the pitcher flew quickly through the air and settled in the basin with a faint splash.

Once again, I was alone.

Lady Elizabeth wouldn't see me. Said she wasn't foolish enough to invite an assassin into her bedroom chamber. Perfectly understandable. I waited until her maid had departed and slipped in anyway. The old bat was propped up in bed. She looked far less bloated than when I had last seen her.

Before she could scream for help, I made a groveling apology. Said I was a fool, although my intentions were pure. Offered to file her bunions. Rub her temples. Trim her whiskers. Reminded her that I would be gone from Butterfield Park tomorrow, so there was really no need to have me arrested. Mentioned the one-of-a-kind diamond I would be presenting to her precious Matilda at the ball tonight.

She said nothing in reply. But she did throw a clock at my head.

Which was enormously encouraging.

"See you at the party, dear," I said, rushing out of the room just as a vase of tulips shattered against the door behind me. "We will laugh about this little mishap in years to come!"

Despite what I had told the dead Duchess, I'm terrible at grudges. Forgiveness is in my nature—for I have all the natural instincts of a Buddhist monk. That's why I decided to find Rebecca and make peace with her. It's not that I understood why she had tried to kill me. But I knew two things for certain. One, Rebecca had a good heart. Two, she knew more about what was happening in this house than I did.

And I had to find out what she knew.

Rebecca had hugged me. Rather savagely. Said we needed

to talk. Which was encouraging. Then she ran off to finish up Matilda's hair for the ball, promising to be back in no time at all. Which was why I was standing in her bedroom. Amid her collection of clocks.

I heard footsteps approaching and turned, expecting to find that Rebecca had come back. Instead, I found Miss Frost.

"Rebecca isn't here," I said.

"I can see that." She didn't attempt to come in. "You had a great shock this morning. Are you feeling any better?"

"I'm stronger than I look, dear. Prettier too."

Miss Frost smiled faintly.

"I know Rebecca pushed me down the stairs," I said.

Miss Frost didn't flinch. Which was infuriating!

"And I know you told her to do it," I added.

"I did no such thing," said Miss Frost calmly.

"But you were involved," I snapped. "Somehow you were involved."

Miss Frost merely glared at me.

"Tell me, Miss Frost, why would Rebecca do such a thing?"

"Perhaps she was testing you."

"What for?" I fumed. "To see if I would *bounce*?"

Miss Frost offered no reply. She seemed to like awkward silences.

"Shame on you for filling Rebecca's head with such horrors," I said boldly. Then I narrowed my eyes. "You seem to find me awfully fascinating—surely I have a right to know why."

Miss Frost put her hands behind her back. "You are one of a kind, Miss Pocket."

Which was very true—but what on earth did she mean? Miss Frost was silent as the grave. And I had a murderous desire to push the hideous woman into a shark tank. Or, at very least, a bathtub full of electric eels. But instead I decided to do a little fishing. "What happened this morning with Mr. Banks's train?" I said. "Was it an accident?"

"I very much doubt it."

"Was it done on purpose, to stop Mr. Banks from telling me what he had learned about the Clock Diamond?"

"Possibly. Probably."

"Was it you?"

Miss Frost sighed. "You will have your answers tonight, Miss

Pocket," she said. "I pray you are ready."

"For what? I insist you tell me!"

Miss Frost took a deep breath. "You are ensnared in something rather diabolical, Miss Pocket. It is not your fault, but there it is. If you are smart, you will give me the stone and leave Butterfield Park before nightfall. I will take care of the rest."

Did she really think I would simply hand over the Clock Diamond? After *all* that had happened? I shook my head. "I don't think so, dear."

Remarkably, Miss Frost did not look at all upset. "As you wish," she said.

I stared at her for the longest time. Finally I said, "You're no ordinary governess, are you, Miss Frost?"

She smiled darkly. "And you are no ordinary maid, Miss Pocket."

15

Miss Always had a plan. It was breathtakingly simple and utterly perfect. And it had all started with my hair. Miss Always had come to fix it for the ball. I thought it looked perfectly lovely already—having all the natural silkiness of a prized stallion. Or, at very least, a well-bred donkey.

"It won't do for such a grand party," said Miss Always, holding a lock of my hair.

I looked at my friend—in her dull brown dress, her pale face scrubbed clean, her brown hair pulled back from her face. Was *this* dreary creature going to transform me? Apparently so.

She sat me down in the middle of the tiny bedroom and got to work. With a few clips, some cleverly placed combs, and a blue ribbon, she had my hair looking glorious in no time.

"We should go," she declared with breathtaking simplicity.

"Go?" I glanced up at her reflection in the mirror. "Go where, dear?"

"Away from this place," said Miss Always, pulling a chair from against the wall and setting it down in front of me. "Now that you have the payment from Mr. Banks, why should we stay here a moment longer?"

I was stunned. And terribly excited. "You would go with me?"

"Are we not bosom friends?" said Miss Always, as if the idea of abandoning me was an impossibility. "We could head south and visit my mother. Her cottage is small, but we would make do. I know she would be delighted to have you."

I blushed with embarrassment. It seemed like the right thing to do. "Are you sure, dear?"

"Of course I'm sure!" She was grinning eagerly. "I have thought about nothing else for the last few days. This house isn't good for you, Ivy. What with your bad dreams and poor Mr. Banks's accident and your mishap on the stairs. I'm sure it's all a terrible coincidence . . . but I cannot help but think it would be safer for you to get away from here tonight."

I gasped. "Tonight?"

"Why not?" said Miss Always. "I have finished working on Matilda's birthday speech, and you owe them nothing beyond the Clock Diamond. Naturally, you will have to hand it over before we leave—but why should you wait until the ball?"

The thought of doing just as Miss Always suggested thrilled me and terrified me in equal measure. Which struck me as odd. The stone wasn't mine. I was merely the delivery girl. Better to give Matilda the diamond now and escape Butterfield Park.

"I agree, Miss Always," I said. "How soon can we leave?"

My friend clapped with delight. "No time like the present! We just need to pack our things." She got up, looking intently at me. "Then we can retrieve the Clock Diamond from its hiding place and give it to Matilda. Perhaps we should go and fetch it now. After all, it's getting late, and

CALEB KRISP

we will have to hurry to catch the last train."

I felt elated. Thrilled. Above all, hopeful. I could just leave everything behind. The ghosts. The clock-obsessed girl trying to kill me. The sinister governess. Which was why I said, "Excellent idea. I will go next door and—"

I stopped. Never finished the sentence. It would have been easy to say, but I had learned that the Clock Diamond had a strange effect upon me. Better for me to retrieve the stone by myself once I had packed my carpetbag.

I said as much to Miss Always.

She frowned, putting her hand on mine. "Is there something you're not telling me, Ivy?"

"A great many things, dear. My head is positively bursting with *somethings*. The terrible part is, the more I learn, the less I understand."

"Which is why we are going," said Miss Always, her smile returning. "I have great plans for you, Ivy. There is a fine school in my mother's village. You will get a proper education, and I will finish my book. We will be awfully content."

I didn't cry. I wasn't the type. But I wanted to. For Miss

Always had just seen into my soul. Naturally I couldn't say it aloud, so I simply hugged my friend and said, "Thank you, dear."

We had a plan. One hour. Then we would leave Butterfield Park forever.

My bag was packed in no time. As I waited for Miss Always, I wandered aimlessly around the little bedroom. Which was how I arrived at the window. I looked out. Saw Rebecca and Miss Frost coming out of the schoolhouse. Rebecca was wearing a pretty lavender gown (no doubt dressed for the ball), but Miss Frost was typically grim in her black frock. They walked along the garden path. Talking eagerly the whole time. How dearly I would have loved to eavesdrop on that conversation!

I was so busy spying that I didn't hear it. Not right away. The piano. Each wretched note ringing through the attic, all at once close by and far away. The tune was unmistakable. "Row, Row, Row Your Boat." I knew she would be there before I turned around.

And I knew why she had come.

The Duchess of Trinity's enormous bed blocked the door. Her fabulous blubber spilling out on all sides, swelling beneath her blood-soaked nightdress. Her skin still glowed like winter—a frosted blue—and the dark smoke still puffed from her nostrils.

"Going somewhere?" she sang at me.

I didn't bother to explain. Probably because I knew that she knew. "You're here about the necklace," I said. "Well, fear not, I'm giving the stone to Matilda before I leave."

"At the birthday ball," she purred. "That was our agreement, child."

"What does it matter?" I snapped. "You wanted Matilda to have the stone on her birthday, and I will make sure she gets it. Whether it's now or tonight, what difference does it make?"

She shook her head. "The ball, child. You will give it to her at the ball."

"Why? Why must it be at the ball?"

"Because that is what I wish." Her smile was ravenous.

"I know it's not a nice thing to say, but you're a beastly old bat." I took two tallow candles from the bedside table and packed them in my carpetbag. "And don't think of following me where

I am going. I'm starting a new life. A wonderful life. And *you're* not invited."

"You really think it is that simple?" said the Duchess with a ghoulish cackle. "You think you can simply *go*? That you can betray me like this and not suffer? Child, there is no way out. Besides, if you leave now, you'll miss the best part."

"I am going," I declared, pointing in triumph at my bag, "and you can't stop me!"

"You looked into the stone, and what did you see?" she sang. "Little Ivy carried from a grim house. Little Ivy dragged through the woods. But you have not seen how the story ends." She smiled wickedly. "I know you want to."

"You are wrong," I lied.

My plan was rather simple. I would turn my back on her and look out the window until she vanished. And I would have done it too. If not for the snow. The snow falling in the attic like a winter frost. It didn't start with a few flakes drifting gently down from the rafters. No, it began all at once. A great deluge of snow, billowing and churning around the tiny room, covering everything in a blanket of frost and sleet.

I could no longer see the Duchess. I looked down and saw footprints crunching into the frost—they formed a terrifying and unmistakable path from the ghost's bed to me. Snow blanketed the ground, covering my shoes and ankles.

The Duchess was nowhere.

Until she was.

She came up out of the frost like a phoenix rising from the ice. Her skin crisp and slippery and frozen. I tried to move, but my feet were fixed in the snow.

"You will never be free of me," she whispered. Her plump finger uncurled, creaking and snapping like an icicle, and stroked my cheek. "I will haunt you to the grave, child. To the grave and beyond. Do you really want such a fate? Stay for the ball and deliver the stone just as you promised. Do as I have asked, and I will leave you in peace. You have my word." The Duchess pressed close to me, her frosted lips brushing my ear. "And one more thing, child. Miss Always has plans for you. Be on your guard."

She collapsed like an avalanche. Fell suddenly into a large pile of snow and icicles at my feet. Just like that.

"Ivy?"

Miss Always was standing at the door, bag in hand. She had her traveling bonnet on. Her smile was full of warmth and sisterly love. Did that beastly ghost *really* think I would doubt my bosom friend? Of course Miss Always had plans for me. To begin a new life together. There was nothing sinister about it.

"Ivy, you look so pale!" said Miss Always. She put down her bag and stepped into the bedroom. Surprisingly, she did not trip over the six inches of snow. Because it was gone.

"I had a slight headache," I managed to say, "but happily it has passed."

"I have been thinking, Ivy," said Miss Always. "It would be better for me to be there when you give Matilda the Clock Diamond. For legal reasons, you understand. What do you think?"

"About what, dear?"

"About the diamond," she said. "I suggest we go and get it immediately. Your wonderfully clever hiding place need no longer be a secret. Let's fetch it right now and then be on our way."

"I have changed my mind, dear." I tried to look bright.

"The Duchess wished me to give the stone to Matilda in front of her guests, so it's only proper that I should. I'm a girl of my word and whatnot."

"Oh. I see." Miss Always walked to the window and looked out at the creeping dusk. "Tonight is the half-moon," she said. "Did you know that, Ivy?"

I recalled Miss Frost telling me the very same thing in the schoolhouse. "Yes, dear."

"Such a moon has a special kind of beauty, don't you agree?" Miss Always turned to face me, and her eyes sparkled like gemstones. "Shall we go and take a closer look, Ivy? I believe the stairs out in the hall lead up to the roof. You could fetch the necklace—to save time later on—and we could sneak up and stargaze before the ball. We would be like two astronomers! Wouldn't that be glorious?"

"Gazing at the moon? Sounds frightful." I opened the wardrobe and pulled out my favorite blue dress. "Besides, now that we are staying, I have to get dressed for the party."

Miss Always nodded, her hands knotted tightly together. "As you wish, Ivy."

The ball was stupendously glorious. The great hall glowed like a freshly cut orange under the dazzling chandelier. A grand collection of ladies in shimmering gowns milled about, wearing bucketloads of rubies, sapphires, diamonds, pearls, and tiaras. There were furs and cloaks as far as the eye could see. Men in top hats and tails. Girls in silk dresses and gloves, with flowers or precious stones threaded in their hair. Servants in their best livery, carrying silver trays laden with mouthwatering food and sparkling wines. A string quartet played softly at the back.

Usually at such a fine ball, I would be carrying food from the kitchen. Or collecting coats. But now I was one of *them*. A genuine guest at a genuine ball.

The cake looked like a five-story monolith beneath the radiant chandelier. It was at the center of the great hall. The star attraction. Well, apart from the birthday girl.

Matilda stood by the fireplace, holding court. A gaggle of girls seemed to hang on her every word. Even I had to admit she looked very fetching in her dress of white embroidered silk with a yellow velvet trim, her dark hair piled up atop her head like a crown. I spotted Rebecca. She was standing by the grand staircase, looking about nervously.

Miss Always was nowhere to be seen. I hadn't laid eyes on her since we had agreed to delay our departure. No doubt she was busy preparing my surprise party. I did spot Miss Frost, hurrying up the main stairs. Instinctively I looked for Rebecca. She was gone.

"Do not imagine you are fooling any of my granddaughter's guests, Miss Pocket. A maid cannot pass for a princess, despite what you read in novels."

Lady Elizabeth was leaning on her cane, resplendent in a glittering black gown. Her face was still slightly bloated, which was a blessing. She eyed me with suspicion. "Why are you smiling at me? Stop it this instant!"

For some reason I thought of Matilda's story about her grandmother's first husband. And I couldn't resist. "I was just trying to picture you as a young woman," I said brightly. "I'm sure you were pretty, in an uninteresting kind of way. Did you have a great love? Something tells me you did. But his heart belonged to another. Didn't end well, I shouldn't think. Nothing says heartbreak like a bolt of lightning. Or so they say."

It was cruel. But then, so was she.

Lady Elizabeth looked at me as a vulture does its prey. "Who told you?" she hissed.

I smiled innocently. "Told me what, dear?"

"The Clock Diamond has given you a lot of power, hasn't it, Miss Pocket?" The old crow's withered face bristled with rage. "You have enjoyed living above your station, keeping my granddaughter waiting these past five days. But your time is at an end. The cake is soon to be cut, and Matilda will be giving her speech. Have the diamond ready to present to her."

I patted her head (it seemed the right moment). "Excellent idea."

I climbed the stairs, leaving the hum of voices and the sweet melody of the string quartet behind. I passed across the first-floor landing and turned down the hallway, my head full with thoughts of parting with the stone. The time *had* come. There would be no more visions. I would never learn the end of my story. And that filled me with crushing sorrow.

By the time I climbed the rickety back stairs up to the

attic, I felt as if I might burst into tears. Which was shameful! I hurried down the narrow corridor and opened the door to my right. Soft moonlight pressed through the narrow gaps in the sloping roof. I didn't bother lighting a candle. No need. I would only be there a moment. I stopped before the trunk. Moved the boar spear and crossbows from the top. Opened it. And dove down to the cluster of worthless jewels below. The cleverness of my hiding place still thrilled me. I pulled apart the tangled mess of imitation necklaces, searching for the Clock Diamond. Even in the half-light, it didn't take long for the truth to dawn. Great strings of costume necklaces were webbed between my fingers. I checked. Checked again.

The horror hit me like a punch.

The diamond was gone.

I struck a match. Lit the candle. Churned to the very bottom of the trunk, hoping against hope that the diamond had somehow come loose and slipped beneath a hat or a bonnet. It hadn't. My heart thumped madly.

I closed the trunk. Sat on the lid. Took a deep breath. The

Duchess would *kill* me!

Who had stolen it? Miss Frost? Yes, that devious governess was just the type to steal the Clock Diamond! Was she not unnaturally preoccupied by it? Had she not demanded I hand it over just hours ago? Miss Frost was the thief. She must hang for the crime!

I would hunt her down. Expose her as a villain! And I would have, too. If not for the creak of the floorboards. From a darkened corner of the room. Ever so faint, but undeniable. I stopped dead. Listened. *Snap.* This time from the other end of the attic. The faint shuffle of feet.

"Hello?" I said boldly. "Miss Frost? Show yourself, you nefarious nitwit!" I picked up the boar spear. "I have a weapon, and I shall use it with deadly force!"

The candle trembled in my other hand. I set it down on the trunk and stepped into the center of the room. Footsteps. Rapid footsteps. They moved in unison—emerging from the shadows like ghouls. Four hooded locks. One from each corner. I thrust the boar spear out in front of me and turned in a clockwise direction. "Give yourselves up and hand back the stone!" I shouted. "Because let me be very clear, I am a fierce sort of girl and won't hesitate to skewer the lot of you!"

The locks moved in unison. At great speed. Rushing to the center of the room. Swarming me in mere seconds. I felt icy talons grip my arms and snake around my ankles. I saw the Clock Diamond sparkle in the candlelight, twisted around one of their bony fingers. Then the spear flew out of my hand. Next I was spinning. Then my feet were swept from under me. I hit the ground with an almighty *thump*. Groaned. Managed to pull myself up. Looked about.

I was alone.

My attackers had fled with the stone.

I ran like the wind. Tore down the rickety back stairs. Barreled along the hallway towards the landing. I saw a flash of dark cloak at the far end of the corridor. My chest burned, but I didn't stop. I charged on like a bull. Willing my feet to move faster. To catch those hideous little villains! Then another glimpse. A lock rushed into the mouth of the hallway. He turned sharply and vanished through a door. The door to Rebecca's bedroom.

Fear flared inside me.

"Rebecca!" I shouted.

I gave chase, skidding to a stop before her bedroom. The

door was open. I raced in at full speed, knocking a dozen clocks to the floor. Frantically, I looked around. No sign of the thieving blackguards. I checked under the bed. Nothing. The closet. Empty. Without warning, the door slammed shut. I ran over and tried the handle. It was locked.

"Blast!" I thundered, pounding on the door.

"Ivy?"

I gave a startled cry. Spun around. Miss Always was standing in the corner. Her dark brown dress seemed to meld with the shadows. Had she been there all along? She walked towards me, carefully navigating the clocks.

"Miss Always," I said, catching my breath, "you startled me."

"I'm sorry," she said. "You burst into the room in such a hurry, I suppose I was struck dumb. Whatever's the matter?"

"The diamond," I said, "it's been taken. I was chasing the locks who stole it!"

Miss Always stopped in front of a small table. A teapot lay upon it. Two cups. A single spoon. A bowl of sugar. "You are not yourself, Ivy," she said slowly. "The fall. The shock of your friend Mr. Banks. Miss Frost's silly stories. It has taken a terrible toll on your nerves."

With great care, my friend poured a cup of tea. A cloud of steam curled up into the air. She put the cup on a saucer and held it out to me. She said, "Drink this. It will make you feel better."

"Miss Always, now is not the time for a cup of tea," I declared. "If I am making this up, who locked the door? Was *that* my nerves?" Then a new thought troubled me. "What are you doing in Rebecca's bedroom, anyway?"

"I thought I heard a noise," said Miss Always.

"Then you *must* believe me!" I said. "What you heard was those nefarious locks."

Miss Always smiled thinly. "But you can see there is no one here but you and I."

"Look, dear, I haven't the time to convince you that I am telling the truth," I said, trying again to open the door. "They are getting away. We are running out of time!"

The heavy *tick tick tick* of Rebecca's clocks was like a hammer pounding in my head. In heart-stopping moments of crisis, my most brilliant ideas are born—for I have all the natural instincts of a trapped miner.

Without hesitation, I leaped over the clocks. Jumped onto the bed. Stepped across to the window ledge. Pulled up the window. It would take great skill, but I was confident I could crawl along the ledge and get to the window next door, which was Lady Amelia's bedroom. The risks were huge. But nothing else mattered. I must get that stone back! It was as if my very life depended upon it.

"I will return for you, dear!" I yelled.

I was halfway out of the window when I felt a hand grip my arm, trying to yank me back inside. Those villainous locks had returned. I twisted my head, trying to pull my arm free. But I did not see a villainous lock. Instead, there was Miss Always with the strength of Hercules, yanking me through the window.

"Ivy, don't do it," she cried. "You will fall to your death!"

"Stuff and nonsense!" I barked, pulling away. Miss Always's grip slipped—slightly. I put one foot on the ledge and steadied myself. "I know what I'm doing, dear! Let me go!"

I gave a final heroic yank. Pulled my hand free. Miss Always stumbled back. I steadied my footing. Then I heard her cry out like some sort of monstrous crow. I stopped. Looked through the window. Miss Always was glaring at me. Her face ghostly white. Her eyes fierce. The room seemed to tremble. The window shook. Clocks rattled and fell. From behind her, almost from the folds of her dress—they came. A dozen hooded locks. They flew out like a pack of rabid wolves. Two at a time. From either side of her. Cloaks billowing. Arms outstretched.

I was stunned. Horrified. The hideous little scoundrels moved as one. Their bony fingers grasped my arms. Then my ankles. Pulled me as if I were a rag doll. I flew back through the open window and tumbled to the floor of the bedroom.

Miss Always cried out in horror. "It can't be real!"

One of them hovered over me. I looked up. Glimpsed its face. Bronzed skin. Eyes like two dark moons. Pale lips. And something else. This creature's chest was heaving, but I heard no breaths. Instead, there was an unmistakable ticking sound! I kicked the nasty beast as hard as I could. He flew back and crashed to the ground. Miss Always shrieked and fell on the bed. "Ivy, be careful!" she yelled.

The remaining locks—five or so—were edging steadily towards me. Closing in like a noose. What I needed was a weapon. I looked about. There was nothing. Nothing but clocks.

That was it!

I spun around and picked up two large clocks. One gold. One silver. I took aim and threw the first. It struck the lock square in the face. Then the second, which landed perfectly in another's chest. The little monsters stumbled. Hissed. Then dropped to the floor. The remaining villains rushed at me. But I was fast. I kicked one in the stomach, then grabbed two more clocks. Repeated my assault—thumped a pair of them on their heads. They fell in a heap. Only one remained. He lunged at me, his hood flying back. It was a beastly sight. No hair. Teeth like glass. Eyes black as ink. Skin flaring like a lantern. Talons reaching for my throat. I picked up a marble clock in both hands and brought it down upon the villain's skull.

The hissing fathead dropped like a brick. As he fell, the Clock Diamond tumbled from inside his cloak. I lunged. Scooped it up. Raced to the open window. Climbed out. I slipped the stone into my pocket and jumped out onto the ledge. Carefully, but quickly, I edged along the side of the great house. Beneath me, the torches lit for the arriving carriages illuminated the two-story drop in gloomy detail. I was terrified. But also terribly brave. Stupendously anxious. But heartbreakingly intrepid.

Miss Always stuck her head out the window.

"Ivy, come back!" she shouted. "You will kill yourself!"

I prayed she was wrong.

16

I didn't look down. I barely breathed. The window. All that mattered was the window of Lady Amelia's bedroom chamber. I moved swiftly, taking small sideways steps. My hands dug into the grooves of the stonework. I no longer heard Miss Always. It felt as if I traversed the narrow ledge for days, until I reached out and felt the cold glass of the window against my hand. I had made it!

"Please be unlocked," I said.

I took a breath and then pulled on the window. It opened! With one hand on the casement, I climbed into

Lady Amelia's bedroom. A lamp was lit on a table by her bed. The room was silent. Empty, as far as I could tell. The Clock Diamond. I felt for it inside my pocket. Thank heavens it had not fallen out.

I ran towards the bedroom door—but never reached it. For I heard the unmistakable squeak of the handle being turned. Someone was coming in! In a flash—for I have all the nimble quickness of a startled rabbit—I threw open the lid of a trunk at the foot of Lady Amelia's bed and jumped inside. As I silently closed the lid, I saw the bedroom door swing open. Then heard the shuffle of feet. It was them.

I heard doors opening and closing. Drawers being pulled out. Windows being raised. I managed to pull a blanket over me. I was in utter darkness. It felt like a coffin. The locks made little sound. Just the ticking from deep within their hideous little bodies. I held my breath. Prayed they wouldn't find me.

Next, I heard one of them walking close by. Then stopping. I closed my eyes tightly. Said a prayer. Then heard movement again. Then the rapid shuffle of little feet. Fading away.

They were leaving!

I didn't dare open the lid. Not yet. Not until I was sure it wasn't some kind of trick. But at least I felt calm enough to open my eyes. To my surprise, the darkness inside the trunk had given way to a kind of half-light. Not strong, but enough to illuminate the wooden box. It was the Clock Diamond. Shimmering like moonlight in my pocket. I pulled it out.

A wave of pure delight washed over me.

I might have even squealed, had it not been for the snow. It began to fall inside the stone, just as before. Snow. Then a forest. A track of footprints. Two people. A woman in a yellow bonnet and a girl. A girl who was me.

The woman and I had been walking all day. I simply knew that we had. And as we trudged along, the scene began to shift. The woods melted away, sinking into the snow. In their place, buildings began to rise up from the ice. Town houses and factories. Banks and bakeries. Cobblestones sleek with frost. Streets and lanes. Horses, carriages, and burrows.

London. We were in London.

The woman pulled me through the crowded streets, her

face still concealed by the yellow bonnet. She dragged me by the hand until we came to a stop before a red-bricked building. It was narrow and high. White windows. Blue door. A faded brass plaque was fixed below the doorbell. I didn't need to read it. For I already knew *exactly* where we were. THE HARRINGTON HOME FOR UNWANTED CHILDREN. The door swung open.

The wind howled and churned. I pulled from the woman's grasp and ran down the steps. But not far. My feet slipped on the icy cobblestones, and I fell. The woman was upon me in moments. She reached down to yank me to my feet. Just then, a gust of wind howled around us—blowing the yellow bonnet from her head. The woman's red hair flared like a torch in the snowstorm. Miss Frost.

The woman was Miss Frost!

She pulled me to my feet and dragged me back up the steps to the orphanage. We vanished inside, the door slamming shut behind us. "No, not yet!" I wanted to cry out. A dark mist whirled inside the stone, devouring the light. The vision was over.

It was her. That wicked creature! She took me from my parents. Ripped me from the life I had before. The life I couldn't remember. It was Miss Frost. It was *all* Miss Frost. But why would she have stolen me away? And why had she come to Butterfield Park? And why was Rebecca helping her?

I needed answers, and I would get them. The truth about this whole wicked business. I pushed open the trunk and climbed out. My heart hammered as before. But no longer in fear. It was rage that coursed through my veins. Rage that propelled me as I ran from Lady Amelia's bedroom. Rage that glistened in my dark eyes. I was going to end this, once and for all.

I was going to find that evil governess.

The hallway was empty. But Miss Frost had to be close by. I had seen her climbing the stairs earlier. And it made sense that she was overseeing the work of those beastly locks.

I took off towards the back stairs, breaking into a spirited run. I bolted like a stallion. The hallway flew by in a blur. Which is why I didn't see the two locks hiding in the doorways on either side of me. They shot out like arrows. Before I even felt them latch on to my arms, I was off my feet, flying backward.

Their grip was deathlike. I landed on my back with a thunderous crack.

But I recovered quickly and kicked the nearest one in the stomach. The vile ghoul landed in a tangle halfway down the corridor. I jumped to my feet as the second one came at me. He was awfully quick. I was thrown against the wall. His talons flew to my neck, thrusting my head against the wall. I could feel the air being squeezed out of me. My vision began to blur. My throat was afire. The lock's grip tightened. He was going to kill me.

In a flash I sank my teeth into the villain's arm, biting with gusto. I have tremendous teeth. Slightly large. Not in a camel kind of way. But big. Useful. The lock hissed. His black eyes rippled. His grip slackened. On a stand nearby was a ghastly gold-and-purple urn. I hooked the lip of it with my finger. Brought it crashing down on his hideous little head. It smashed brilliantly. The lock fell to the floor in a heap. His arm was wonderfully red and full of teeth marks. A clear liquid oozed from the wounds. If it was blood, it was unlike any I had seen before.

Then I remembered. Miss Frost. I thundered back down the hallway. They came around the corner. Four of them. Charging towards me at great speed. Their robes fluttering around them like capes. Was there an endless supply of these wretched creatures? I skidded to a stop. Turned and took off the way I had come.

I sprinted onto the landing that overlooked the great hall. To my left were the main stairs. And standing guard there—two locks. They didn't lunge at me. Just stood there, blocking my escape. I charged across the landing towards the west wing. I was nearly there when they came. A dozen of them. Swarming out of the hallway like a pack of hungry jackals.

I pulled up. Looked back. The locks chasing me had stopped. I was surrounded on all sides. There was no escape. One of them lifted a clawed hand towards me, his talons unfurling. The others followed in unison. They never spoke. Perhaps they couldn't. But I knew perfectly well what they were saying. *Hand over the Clock Diamond. Do it, or die.*

As one, they began to move. Like a caged animal, I looked

desperately about. There was no way out. Well, apart from jumping over the banister. Which would break my neck. Or at the very least, a leg or two. The locks were nearly on me. Which might explain why I started running. Right at the banister. It's certainly why I leaped into the air. My feet hit the top of the banister. I pushed off. Jumped higher. I didn't look down at the great hall below. I just flew through the air towards salvation. I would either reach it . . . or die trying.

The chandelier rushed at me. My arms flailed about. I could feel myself beginning to drop. In desperation, I stretched out my fingers. Hooked an iron branch between the glowing candles. I grunted. My arms strained. My knuckles white as they gripped the branch. The chandelier swayed violently. A scattering of crystals fell from the branches, dropping to the great hall below, hitting an elderly couple in the head. Naturally they looked up. As did others around them.

That's when the screaming began.

"Good lord, what is that?" cried one silly woman.

"A child!" screamed another. "It's a child!"

"Help her. Somebody help her!" hollered a girl.

"I'm perfectly fine!" I shouted. "Please, go on with the ball! Pretend I'm not here!"

But I wasn't fine at all. My fingers were slipping. I was dropping before I knew it. Heard thunderous screams. Shut my eyes. Waited for the crunch of my bones on the hard floor.

Instead, I hit with a splatter.

As if I had landed in mud.

Or a five-story birthday cake.

Great chunks of cream and frosting and vanilla cake arched through the air like a water fountain—a mighty shower of deliciousness raining upon the aristocrats of Suffolk, hitting foreheads and hats and eyeballs and gowns with thrilling accuracy. My eyes flew open. I was wedged in Matilda's cake. My back hurt. But nothing appeared to be broken. Two of the servants rushed to lift me from the landing site. Dismounting from the cake proved rather humiliating. The entire room was gathered around. I felt an explanation was in order.

"It's actually a *very* funny story," I said, wiping large chunks of vanilla cake from my dress. "It involves a slippery floor, a jar of marmalade, and my tragic past as a frightfully unreliable trapeze artist."

"You've ruined my cake!"

It was Matilda. Naturally.

"I never wanted you at my party! I never wanted you in my house! What a spectacle you have made of yourself, hanging from the ceiling like a monkey. Are you really so desperate for attention? I almost feel bad for you, Pocket. It's no wonder you're an orphan. Your parents probably died of shame." She looked over at her friends. "Don't feel bad for the little maid. She does this sort of thing all the time. Where is the diamond, Pocket? Give it to me and get out of this house!"

My mind was elsewhere. Miss Frost. The locks. I didn't have time for this. Well, perhaps just a moment or two.

I smiled at Matilda. "You seem upset, dear. Have some cake."

My hand was behind her head in a flash. Her face flew towards the battered birthday cake and landed with a glorious splutter. A large piece of cream sailed through the air and planted on Lady Elizabeth's nose. Matilda shrieked like an angry parrot. Lady Elizabeth called for my public execution. All around, the guests were gasping and snickering in shock. I believe I even glimpsed Lady Amelia stifling a giggle.

But I didn't stay around to enjoy the moment. For I had spotted Miss Frost racing at great speed across the landing above. A look of thunder upon her face. I licked a blob of frosting from my finger and bounded up the stairs after her.

Miss Frost had vanished into the east wing, though I wasn't at all sure why—why had she not come after me? I charged down the hallway, eagerly glancing into each open door. No sign of Miss Frost. Or her devilish locks. Even the door to Rebecca's room was now wide open—I was relieved that Miss Always had managed to escape. At the end of the corridor, I turned left and mounted the narrow back stairs up to the attic. My bedroom was silent and still. But there was a great racket coming from the room where I had hidden the necklace.

I raced into my bedroom and grabbed the poker from the hearth. Then hurried out into the corridor and threw open the storeroom door, fully prepared for battle.

Here is what I saw—Miss Frost clutching a sword. She was panting rapidly. Around her were a dozen hooded robes in piles upon the bare floor. White smoke rose from the garments, as if from the embers of a dying fire.

Miss Frost fixed her eyes upon me. She lowered her sword. "Miss Pocket, I have been searching for you all evening."

I lifted the poker and pointed it at her. "I know everything!" I shouted.

"Lower your weapon," said Miss Frost coolly.

"I won't!" I thundered, stepping towards her.

Miss Frost lifted her sword, and we began to circle each other.

"Where is the Clock Diamond?" said Miss Frost.

"Where you can't find it, you villain!"

"Calm yourself, Miss Pocket. I am sure you are full of questions. But right now I am trying my best to keep you safe. Miss Always believes that her time has come, and she will do whatever it takes to—"

"Stop blaming Miss Always!" I hissed. "I know you took me! I saw it in the stone. You stole me from my home. From my family. You dragged me to that beastly orphanage!"

Anger boiled within me. It felt like a tempest in my chest. I lunged, thrusting the poker at her. With ease she used her sword to sweep it aside.

Miss Frost sighed. "Hunting for the Clock Diamond has led me to many dark places, Miss Pocket," she said. "It was in such a place that I found you."

Hearing the truth at last was rather shocking. I had so many thoughts and questions, I didn't know which one to grab first. "The house I saw in the stone," I said finally. "The one you took me from—did I grow up there?"

Miss Frost shook her head. "The house was full of vagrants, criminals, and other undesirables. It was a forsaken place, Miss Pocket. A place of last resort."

"A poorhouse?"

"I was there following a lead concerning the Clock Diamond. I found you and your mother in a back room. You were sleeping in her lap—curled up like a kitten."

I squealed. A wave of joy rushed through me. My mother!

But Miss Frost was frowning. "She was dead, Miss Pocket. Quite dead."

Miss Frost stepped towards me, but I backed away.

"You were sound asleep, and so I took you. What else was I supposed to do? Leave you there? Yes, you tried to run away, and yes, I stopped you." Miss Frost cleared her throat. "For reasons of my own, I didn't wish to be seen, so I left on foot, cutting across the woods. You woke up, told me your name, and . . . and asked for your mother. When we got to the orphanage, you threw a fit. Hit your head on a desk. I came the next day and you didn't recognize me. The doctor said you had no memory of the previous day. Or of your mother. I was relieved."

"Who was she?" I said next. "Who was my mother?"

Miss Frost's eyes shifted about. Just for a moment. She said, "I do not know. Your mother had no possessions. Her clothes were threadbare. She wore no jewelry. Perhaps her family had turned her out on the street. Who can say?"

"But what about my father?" My voice rang with bitterness. "I must have one, mustn't I? Why didn't you try and find him? Anything would have been better than sending me to that awful place."

"Miss Pocket, judging from where I found you, I suspect your father is either dead or unaware you exist." She bowed her head to meet my gaze. "Life had abandoned you both, Miss Pocket. Your mother wore no wedding ring. Do you understand?"

Of course I did.

"You've been lying to me this whole time. Lying and plotting and scheming behind my back," I said.

A shadow passed across Miss Frost's face, though she made no reply.

"Does Rebecca know?" I demanded. "Is that what you two have been conspiring about in the shadows? Is that the big secret? Tell me, Miss Frost—I have a right to know!"

"This isn't the time."

She was wrong. Now was *exactly* the time. I wanted answers, and I would have them. "Did you come to Butterfield Park for the Clock Diamond or for me?" I shouted.

"The simple answer is—both."

"I suppose you killed Rebecca's old governess to take her place?"

Miss Frost gave me a disapproving glare. "I paid Miss Rochester two hundred pounds to leave Suffolk and spend the summer in Italy."

Which was hugely disappointing.

"The stone, Miss Pocket," she said with icy calm. "Where is it?"

I lunged for her a second time. Miss Frost stepped back and, with a flick of her wrist, pressed her sword to my chest.

I looked at her, the hatred crackling in my eyes. "You are a bad person, Miss Frost."

"Perhaps."

A scream broke the spell. It came from the hall outside. It was unmistakably Rebecca. I turned towards the door.

"Rebecca?" I shouted. "What have you done to her, Miss Frost?"

Silence.

When I turned back, Miss Frost had vanished.

I charged down the rickety back stairs. Tore around the corner and into the hallway. Rebecca was at the far end. Being set upon by a gaggle of locks. They had her in their grasp and were dragging her away. Not if I could help it!

"I'm coming, dear!" I cried.

Gripping the poker tightly in my sweaty hand, I took off at speed. Rebecca was being pulled into a doorway near the landing. She clung to the sides of the doorframe, trying desperately to hold on. As I raced past Matilda's bedroom, a lock flew at me. I didn't even stop. Just swung the poker, knocking the fathead right in the stomach. He doubled over and dropped.

"Hurry, Ivy!" shrieked Rebecca.

I was upon them now. Two of them rushed at me, claws out. I thumped one in the head. The other seized my wrist and began to squeeze it like a vise. In a flash I was burying my teeth in his hand.

Inspired by my brilliant fighting skills—for I have all the natural instincts of a warlord—Rebecca stomped on another lock's foot. She followed up valiantly with a kick to the shins, but slipped and fell (for she lacked my gift for combat). Still, the evil pygmy fled like a startled rabbit. I went to work on the other two, bashing one on the head and the other in the chest. I was marvelous! I scanned the corridor, expecting to see a fresh supply of the tiny monsters charging towards us. But there were none . . . at least for now. I grabbed Rebecca by the hand and pulled her up.

A wasteland of locks lay upon the floor around us.

"Are you hurt?" I asked Rebecca.

The poor dear tried to catch her breath. She held out her arm. Three scars were seared across her wrist. "I'll be fine," she said. "Ivy—"

Hurried footsteps echoed in the hallway behind us. And screams. Bloodcurdling screams. I twisted around. Miss Always flew past. Followed swiftly by three locks. Then I heard an awful *thump*. Next, Miss Always's wretched cry. What I saw next, passing at the end of the hall, chilled my blood. The villains, dragging Miss Always along the ground like she was a bag of grain. Her legs kicking, her nails clawing at the floor in a useless attempt to stop them. Then she was pulled from view towards the back stairs.

"Fear not, Miss Always, I will save you!" I shouted.

"Ivy, it is a trick!" said Rebecca, grabbing my arm. "Miss

Always is not the great friend you think she is. She has been using you terribly. Promise me you will not follow her up onto the roof!"

The roof? So that is where Miss Frost was conducting her wicked scheme!

"You poor, deluded halfwit," I said gently. "If Miss Always wanted the stone, she could have grabbed it on the boat. But she did not wish to even *look* at it."

"That is only because she thinks you might be of some use to her," came the beastly reply. She tightened her grip on my arm. "You told Miss Always that you had tried on the Clock Diamond, didn't you, Ivy?"

What did *that* have to do with anything? "Yes, I suppose I did."

Rebecca nodded her head and muttered, "She believed that it was proof."

"Proof of what?"

"Everything." Her voice was trembling. "Oh, Ivy, Miss Always has a black heart."

"And Miss Frost is a saint?" I snapped. "She took me, Rebecca. She dragged me to the orphanage and left me there to rot."

"What if she had no choice?"

I was stunned. Rebecca *knew* about Miss Frost's treachery? And still she defended her? There was only one explanation. "You are suffering a brain fever, dear," I said. "Stick your head in the nearest bowl of fruit punch—it is an excellent remedy."

I hurried away, bound for the roof.

"Ivy, let me help you!" shouted Rebecca.

"No need," I said, not looking back. "I will see to Miss Frost."

"But, Ivy, you don't understand! Please don't go up on the roof. It is a trick!"

She continued to call after me, talking a great deal, but her words quickly died away.

For I was already gone.

17

The trapdoor was open. I glimpsed a twinkling of stars in the sky above. I could hear the clashing of metal against metal. Grunts and gasps. I put my foot on the first step of the rickety little staircase. Stopped. The Clock Diamond. Something told me it would be a grave mistake to bring it up onto the roof. So I hurried into my bedroom. Looked about for a suitable hiding spot.

Only took a moment.

I raced to the dresser, pulled the stone from my pocket, and dropped it into the water pitcher. It landed with a satisfying *plop* and quickly sank to the bottom. Perfect!

I crawled through the trapdoor and stepped onto the roof (which wasn't easy while carrying a large fire poker). The house had a pitched roof over the east and west wings and a flat one capping the great hall. Which is where I stood. The sharp clash of metal hitting metal charged the air. There, in the distance—Miss Always and Miss Frost. Around them were piles of smoldering cloaks. Miss Frost and Miss Always stood not three feet apart. There was a dagger on the ground at Miss Always's feet. And a sword at her throat.

My first instinct was to cry out. To yell something devastatingly useful, like "Don't do it!" or "Lower your sword, you diabolical fathead!" But I did neither. Instead, I sneaked up on them. Miss Frost had her back to me. Miss Always was remarkably brave. Her eyes were not pierced with terror. In fact, she didn't look frightened at all. I crept along, stepping carefully over the joists in the slate roof. I noticed Miss Always glancing my way. But just for a flash. She was a smart one, Miss Always. She knew I had come to rescue her, but she didn't give the game away.

"Why are you doing this, Miss Frost?" she cried suddenly. "I do not understand!"

This seemed to confuse Miss Frost. She said, "What game are you playing now?"

"I do not have the Clock Diamond," said Miss Always frantically. "I cannot give you what I do not have. Please don't kill me!"

"Kill you I must," came the cold reply. "Though why you are acting like a damsel in distress, I cannot imagine."

I was upon them now. Poised to strike. Just at that moment, Miss Frost seemed to sense my presence. She swung around. But too late. I brought the poker down upon her hand. The sword dropped to the ground. In a flash, brave Miss Always had scooped up the dagger at her feet and was bearing down on Miss Frost.

"Well done, Ivy!" she said.

Miss Frost raised her arms in surrender and began to back away.

"Don't be a fool, Miss Pocket," she said. "See what is right in front of your face. Your friend is not what she seems."

"Watch her, Ivy," said Miss Always, waving the dagger at Miss Frost. "She is a cunning beast. An assassin who wants the Clock Diamond for herself. She will do anything, kill anyone, to get it."

"Miss Always is twisting the truth," said Miss Frost. "It is she who would do anything to get the stone. I wish to guard it. She wishes to control it."

Miss Frost took careful steps back, retreating from the dagger until she hit the stone parapet that ran around the edge of the roof. Miss Always lunged at her, pressing the blade into Miss Frost's pale neck.

I fell in beside Miss Always and pointed my poker at Miss Frost. "Those hideous locks work for *her*, don't they?"

Miss Always didn't answer. But Miss Frost did.

"The locks do the bidding of the gatekeeper."

"Is . . . is that what you are?" I asked.

She shook her head. "That is what Miss Always is."

"Lies!" hissed Miss Always. "There is only one way to end her reign of terror, and that is death."

I gasped. "You . . . you want to kill her?"

"It must be done," said Miss Always.

"After she kills me, she has plans for you, Miss Pocket," said the governess. "Horrid plans."

My head was spinning. What was I to believe? Naturally, I trusted Miss Always. But I had never seen her like this. The woman I knew would faint at the sight of a wasp. Now she was eager to cut Miss Frost's throat? It was baffling. Yet how could I trust Miss Frost? She was a villain.

"All these years, I thought it was my mother who put me in that awful place," I said faintly. "But it was *you*, Miss Frost. You put me there."

"The orphanage was clean and reputable," said Miss Frost crisply. "I knew you would not be beaten or starved. That you would have shelter and food in your stomach."

"It was beastly," I whispered.

"It was an orphanage, Miss Pocket. I kept something of an eye on you over the years—always from a distance—paid for your clothes and certain privileges. I tried to ensure you got on in the world. Why do you suppose the Midwinters took you on as a maid?"

I gasped. "That was your doing?"

"I felt such a position would give you a decent future. I never imagined that you would find your way to Paris and end up with the Clock Diamond. If I could have stopped it, I would have—but by the time I traced the stone to France, the Duchess was dead and you were sailing for England."

"What a remarkable coincidence," said Miss Always with a mocking grin. "You *happened* upon Ivy and her mother while hunting the stone. Then Ivy *happened* upon the diamond in Paris. It would make a thrilling work of sensation fiction, though I doubt anyone would believe it."

"It does sound rather unlikely," I said to Miss Frost.

"And yet it is the truth," she replied coolly.

"I believe your mother is alive, Ivy," declared Miss Always. I was stunned! "She is probably still looking for you. We can find her together, you and I. We will travel all over England if we have to and leave no stone unturned. Do not be fooled by Miss Frost. She is a kidnapper and a killer. Who do you think tampered with the drawbridge signal, killing Mr. Banks? And who do you think plunged a dagger into the

Duchess of Trinity's heart? It was all *her*."

Now, normally I am brilliant in a crisis. But I confess to a certain amount of confusion. Fortunately, a thought occurred to me. I turned to my friend. "How do you know so much about my mother?"

She didn't answer. Not right away. At last she said, "I have been conducting some research into Miss Frost and her evil deeds . . . the information I gathered has been most shocking . . . this woman is from a faraway place . . . I didn't want to tell you about it until I was sure, Ivy."

"Her research is very hands-on," said Miss Frost with a dry laugh. "She commits the crimes, then blames them on me."

I needed to think. But there wasn't time. For Miss Frost made her move. She pushed the dagger from her throat and ripped the poker from me in an instant. She spun around, swiping Miss Always's hand, clipping the dagger. It twirled through the air. Now it was Miss Always who had her back to the wall.

I was about to charge at Miss Frost (it seemed like the heroic thing to do), but she looked at me and said, "*Think,*

Miss Pocket. If all I wanted was the Clock Diamond, why would I encourage you to hide it? Would it not have been easier for me to overpower you and steal it days ago? Tracking the Clock Diamond is my job; murder is not."

"She tore you from a loving home, Ivy," said Miss Always, her eyes moving between Miss Frost's weapon and me. "She destroyed your one chance at happiness. Haven't I cared for you and tried to keep you safe? Ivy, can you really trust the word of a kidnapper over your bosom friend?"

It was suddenly so clear.

I thought about all that had happened since I had first met Miss Always. All that we had shared. All that we had spoken of. And for the first time, I saw the whole picture. All the pieces that I had been unwilling to put together. And it was monstrous. I looked at my friend and said, "Now that I think of it, you were fixated by the Clock Diamond from the very first. You were always asking me about it on the ship. And when we docked, you where *terribly* interested in where I would be staying in London. Well, the only person who knew where I would be, at the house in Belgravia, was *you*, Miss

Always. And the night of the break-in, there was a woman in the shadows."

"Miss Frost!" she shouted at me. "It was Miss Frost!"

I shook my head. "I saw you on the ship—your publisher never had a long-lost son, did he? You were conspiring with one of your locks. And tonight I saw those hideous creatures emerge from your dress. As such, I have no choice but to assume you are a diabolical, diamond-hunting, lock-loving lunatic. Which is violently disappointing."

"Well done, Miss Pocket," said Miss Frost, her eyes fierce with pride. "It took some time, but you got there in the end."

Miss Always didn't take it at all well. In fact, she was rather upset. She threw back her head and let out a murderous cry. The skin on her face began to ripple. Her eyes turned an inky black. Her neck puffed out like a lizard's. Then a dozen villainous locks flew out from the folds of her dress. It was terrifying and spectacular, all at once. They swarmed around Miss Frost like a tempest. Clawing at her with icy talons. The poker flew from her hand. She fell back against the parapet. Miss Always raced across the roof and picked up her dagger.

Miss Frost began kicking and punching like a madwoman. She bent down, collected the poker, and ruthlessly drove the sharp end into the heart of each and every one of the locks. They seemed to crumble one by one before my eyes, collapsing in a pile of smoldering ash. All that remained were their cloaks.

"Ivy, watch out!" cried Miss Frost.

But too late.

Miss Always spun me around and pushed me against the parapet. A dagger pointed at my heart. "Where is the Clock Diamond, Ivy?" she said softly.

"Somewhere you'll never find it," I declared. "You were my friend, Miss Always. You said we were like sisters."

"I already have a sister," she said coldly. "Pushed her down a well when she was nine. Unfortunately, she lived."

"You killed the Duchess, didn't you?"

A mad kind of pride glistened in her dark eyes.

"How could you be so cruel?" I said. "I believed you, Miss Always. I believed *in* you."

She smiled. With one hand, she pushed the dagger against

my chest. With the other, she searched the pockets of my dress. "I apologize for lying to you, Ivy," she said brightly. "Believe it or not, I fully intended to tell you the truth right before I killed you on the ship. But then I discovered you had tried on the necklace."

"What has that to do with anything?" I snapped.

"Only *everything*." Miss Always said this with wicked delight. "You became far more interesting after that."

Miss Frost had retrieved her sword. She charged towards Miss Always, her weapon extended. But Miss Always stopped her cold. "One more step, and I will pierce her heart."

"You *can't* kill her, and you know it," said Miss Frost evenly, inching closer. "Besides, without Miss Pocket and the stone, you have nothing."

I felt the blade pierce my flesh. I didn't cry out. But I wanted to.

"It is a half-moon, Ivy," said Miss Always. "Do you know what that means?"

"Haven't a clue, dear."

"It means I can go home. And you shall come with me."

"That will not happen," declared Miss Frost fiercely. "The girl would not survive it."

"Survive what?" I asked, rather anxiously.

"Do you recall the story I told you just the other day, Ivy?" Miss Always's voice hissed like a rattlesnake. "The lost myth about the Dual?"

Yes, I remembered. Hidden world. Beastly plague. Millions dead. And a silly story about a girl who can pass freely between two worlds. A girl who would heal the plague, ascend the throne, and whatnot. I sighed. "What about it?"

She glared at me. "Can't you guess?"

"Miss Always thinks you are the Dual," said Miss Frost, her voice thick with doubt. "She is wrong, horribly wrong, but that won't stop her trying to prove it."

I looked at Miss Always. Of all the questions swirling through my head, I could only think of one. "Why would you think such a thing?"

Miss Always looked at Miss Frost and laughed. "Shall *you* tell her, or will I?"

Miss Frost was frowning. "The evidence is slight at best."

"You are still here, Ivy," said Miss Always, her eyes blazing. "That has never happened before in the entire history of the Clock Diamond. Is that not peculiar? Is it not thrilling?"

I had no idea what the halfwit was talking about!

"And it is written that the Dual will have healing powers," Miss Always continued breathlessly. "Wondrous healing powers. Ivy, you held my wrist when it was sprained. Your touch healed it in mere seconds. I believed that it would, and it did!"

"It was wishful thinking and nothing more," snapped Miss Frost.

"I'm afraid Miss Frost is right, dear," I said, looking at the deranged lunatic. "After I heard you talking in the morning room, I tested my healing powers on Lady Amelia. I'm afraid I couldn't even mend her pricked finger. So you see—I'm not even slightly miraculous."

Miss Always was smiling. Didn't look at all bothered. "The Dual has no power in this world," she said gleefully. "She is a girl just like every other. It is only my people, from *my* world, that the Dual can heal. And heal me you did." The bug-eyed fruitcake looked up at the dark sky. "We can cross tonight, Ivy. The process is easy enough. Come with me. Come and fulfill your destiny."

It was bonkers. The whole thing. And yet . . . if *any* of it were even a tiny bit true, it might be rather lovely to cure a plague and rule a kingdom and whatnot. It's not like I had anything better to do.

Miss Frost was now only a few feet from where Miss Always held me at knifepoint. She said, "You are tempted, are you not, Miss Pocket? Miss Always makes it sound rather thrilling. And why shouldn't she—after all, what has she to lose? If you *are* the Dual, she would seek to use you as an instrument for power and control. You would be her puppet. And if, as I suspect, it turns out you are *not* the Dual . . ."

"What then?" I asked.

"I would bring you back," promised Miss Always hastily. "I would bring you back to England, safe and sound."

"She couldn't, Miss Pocket," declared Miss Frost, "for there would be nothing left of you. The journey between worlds would destroy an ordinary child. You would be torn limb from limb."

Which was monstrously unpleasant.

Before I could decline Miss Always's generous offer, Miss Frost swooped. Her sword sliced the air, came down with a spark upon Miss Always's dagger. Miss Always spun around in a blur, swinging the dagger right at Miss Frost's neck. But the governess ducked. Brought down her blade. Cutting Miss Alway's hand as if it were butter.

Before the wound had even begun to bleed, Miss Frost had knocked the dagger from Miss Always's hand and had her cornered. A sword under her chin.

"You are trapped, Miss Always," she said, panting. "You cannot take the girl *and* get the stone *and* make your escape. You will die on this roof—I will see to it."

"We cannot have that, now can we?" said Miss Always. She turned towards me, eyes ablaze. "Believe it or not, I have enjoyed our time together—but we shall have to postpone our journey. For now. But not forever."

It happened quickly. Miss Always kicked Miss Frost rather expertly in the shin, pushed her aside, and leaped onto the parapet. She glanced back at me. Her smile was wicked. Then she stretched out her arms and jumped.

I screamed. Ran to the edge of the roof. Miss Frost fell in beside me. The moonlight cast the ground below in a silvery haze. I expected to see Miss Always tumble to her death. But she did not. Her skirt billowed around her. Her arms outstretched. She landed on the graveled driveway in a crouch, then rose to her feet with ease. She took off, running at speed towards a darkened carriage waiting by the wildflower meadow. The door flew open as she approached. She jumped in. The driver whipped the four horses, and they took off, vanishing into the woodlands.

Miss Frost grabbed my shoulders and held them tightly. "Miss Pocket, listen to me. Do not give Matilda the necklace. It can do great harm. Keep the stone, Miss Pocket. Keep the stone and go from this place. I will find you."

"Find me? Find me where?"

"Do you trust me, Miss Pocket?"

"Of course not," I snapped. "I have no idea what just happened. I have no idea who *any* of you really are. How did Miss Always jump from the roof and not break her neck? Where is this other world you keep talking about? What is happening?"

"The moment you put on that necklace, you entered a war, Miss Pocket. Now do as I say—take the stone and leave Butterfield Park."

She let go of me and jumped onto the parapet, concealing the sword in a sheath fixed to her waist.

"Where are you going?" I shouted.

"To kill your friend."

Then she jumped. I watched her fly through the air, graceful as a swooping eagle. Her hair came loose and fluttered in the wind like scarlet ribbons. She landed lightly and took off towards the stables. Moments later, a horse bolted out, Miss Frost atop it. She galloped into the woodlands and was quickly lost from view.

"Wait!" I hollered. "You know more than you are saying! Who was my mother? Tell me who I am!"

But my words died in the cold night air.

The guests were gone by the time I came down from the roof. All traces of the locks had vanished. I heard two maids gossiping on the stairs—apparently the ball hadn't recovered after the business with the cake. The birthday girl had run up to her bedroom and locked the door, only coming out with the promise of a new horse.

The servants were clearing the great hall as I came down the stairs. A few of the maids gave me devious looks. As if the disastrous ball was all *my* fault. Perhaps it was. I was past caring about any of it. About riddles without answers. About friends who were really enemies. About a stupid diamond that shone like the sun, glowed like the moon, and teased you with visions. My mother was dead. And if the world wouldn't give answers about who she was, then I would stop asking.

I had the Clock Diamond in my pocket and a job to do.

And I intended to finish it.

The family was gathered in the library. All except for Rebecca. Lady Elizabeth was stroking Matilda's cake-crusted hair, whispering in her ear about how one day she would be mistress of Butterfield Hall. *Then* she would have the last laugh. Lady Amelia was pacing about, looking anxious. They all glanced up when I entered the room.

"I hate you, Pocket!" hissed Matilda. "I hate you and I wish you were dead!"

"Of course you do," I said flatly. "Normally that would be a huge blow—but not tonight. I'm sorry for shoving your face in your birthday cake, Matilda."

"I should think so!" snapped Lady Elizabeth.

"Didn't I tell you, Matilda?" said Lady Amelia. "Didn't I say Miss Pocket would be terribly sorry?"

"I'm sorry I didn't do it days ago," I said. "Matilda, you're a stupendously awful girl. You treat Rebecca with monstrous contempt. You browbeat and bully your mother. You bark at the servants. The one person you treat with any regard is Lady Elizabeth, and that's only because she's going to drop dead any moment—and you want to make sure she leaves this ghastly estate to you."

"Have her flogged!" cried Matilda. "Somebody fetch me a horse whip!"

Lady Elizabeth used her cane to thump the table. Her beady eyes glowered at me. "Wicked girl! Pack your bags and get—"

"Don't worry, I'm going," I said. "But first there's something I have to do."

I reached into my dress and pulled out the Clock Diamond. It glowed in the palm of my hand—a twinkling of stars, a half-moon. Matilda eyed it greedily. Lady Amelia gasped in wonder. Lady Elizabeth licked her thin, shriveled lips.

"Someone told me tonight that I must keep the stone," I said. "That I wasn't to give it away. But as far as I can tell, it has brought me nothing but trouble."

"Give it to me, Pocket," ordered Matilda. "Hand it to me right now!"

I held out the necklace. It throbbed in my hand. Like a heartbeat.

"Take it," I said.

I had my back to the library door. So I didn't see Rebecca slip quietly into the room. She had a gift for moving about unnoticed. Which was how she managed to get so close to me. So close to the diamond.

Matilda grabbed the stone from my hand. It was a blow to be parted from it. But I did not let it show. Matilda held it up, her eyes swelling with wonder and pride.

"Oh, before I forget," I said, "the Countess of Trinity had a message that went with her gift. She wanted me to tell you that the Clock Diamond came with the kind regards of—"

Rebecca ran at Matilda, snatching the Clock Diamond from her hand. Matilda screamed. Demanded the immediate return of *her* necklace. But Rebecca wasn't listening. She raced up the spiral staircase to the balcony above.

"I have to do this," she called, her voice shaking. "I have to try it on, just once."

"What has come over you, Rebecca?" cried Lady Amelia.

"Give it back, you nutter!" hollered Matilda.

Perhaps I was still numb to what was really happening. The pieces of the puzzle were there. Yet I had not put them together.

But Lady Elizabeth was starting to. She gazed not at Rebecca, but at me. "The Duchess's message—what was it, Miss Pocket? What did she wish you to say?"

In the confusion, my mind went blank.

"Come down this instant!" shouted Matilda, stomping

her foot. "It's *my* diamond, not yours!"

"I can't," said Rebecca softly. She unclasped the silver chain, gathering each end at the back of her neck. "It's the only way, do you see?"

"The only way for what?" I said.

"The message!" cried Lady Elizabeth, thumping the table with her cane. "What was the Duchess's message, you impossible girl?"

My gaze shifted from Rebecca to old Walnut Head. The answer she was seeking was somewhere in the fog of my mind. "She told me to say the Clock Diamond came with the kind regards of . . . of . . ." Then it came to me. "*Winifred Farris.* With the kind regards of Winifred Farris."

Lady Elizabeth's gasped. "No . . . not *Farris.* Dear god!"

I looked up at Rebecca. She was looking back at me. Only at me. She said, "I have to see her again. I have to see her and be with her, just like you did, Ivy. Tell Miss Frost I'm sorry."

She let go of the necklace. It dropped and hung around her neck. The Clock Diamond glowed darkly. Then, a faint buzzing. A familiar buzzing. Charging and rippling through the air.

"Rebecca, *no*!" cried Lady Elizabeth. "It is a trick. Stop her!"

The stone's black glow was smothered by a scarlet light. A pulsing scarlet light. Then yellow. Then red again. Rebecca stumbled. Reached out for the railing.

The buzzing was like a wasp in my ear.

"What on earth is going on?" snapped Matilda. "Cousin, give me that necklace *now*."

"Take it off, Rebecca!" shrieked Lady Elizabeth. "Please, take it off!"

Now a bright mist churned and filled the stone. It was beautifully white, radiating from the diamond like a searchlight. An endless, perfect light.

Rebecca let out a piercing cry.

I was already running up the stairs by then. Calling Rebecca's name again and again. By the time I reached the balcony, she had already fallen. The library was suddenly quiet. The buzzing began to fade. I dropped to my knees. Rebecca's body had withered to a husk, as if her very life force had been pulled from her. Her face was a hollow shell. Her skin, bone dry. Her cheeks, hideously sunken. Her arms, little more than drooping flesh hanging from bones. Her eyes, a milky white. Her hair, brittle as straw. Her lips, yellow and curled into a grin.

It struck me as heartbreakingly cruel—the sound I heard in the deathly silence of that library. The ticking of the clock on the mantle. Each solemn tick counting the seconds and minutes since Rebecca Butterfield had run out of time.

18

Vengeance had come to Butterfield Park. And it had a name. Winifred Farris.

The body had been taken away. Dr. Longfellow could not explain what had happened to Rebecca. Some sort of rare blood disease, he supposed. We were still gathered in the library as the sun came up. It was as if no one had the heart to go to bed.

A few questions were asked about what had happened to Miss Frost and Miss Always. I said Miss Always had received bad news about her mother's health and had rushed to her side. As for Miss Frost, well, who could say? No one seemed terribly bothered that she had vanished.

The Clock Diamond had been removed from around Rebecca's neck. It lay upon the table, shining pink like the dawn. Now wasn't the time for questions. Yet I had so many.

Lady Elizabeth sat in her favorite chair before the window. Her back to us all. She was the first to speak. "When I heard the Duchess of Trinity's message—'from Winifred Farris,' the name the Duchess longed to have . . . I knew the necklace was not a peace offering, but revenge," she said.

The story was simple and rather sad.

"When we were girls, the Duchess always won—no matter what it was, she won. Luck of the angels, they used to say. I suppose I resented it. She was engaged to Nathaniel Farris, the handsomest young man in the county. Everyone believed they would live happily ever after." The old bat smiled bitterly. "But he broke it off and married me instead. Then, like a fool, he changed his mind. He said I was cold and wicked and that I only married him so Winifred couldn't have him."

"Was he right?" I asked.

She huffed. "I suppose. He ran to her house in the dead of

night, begging for forgiveness. God smiled on me and sent a bolt of lightning. Winifred saw the whole thing from her bedroom window. She lost her mind after that. Fled England, never to return."

"I don't understand any of it," said Lady Amelia, her face a track of tears and sorrow. "What happened to poor Rebecca?"

"She put on that wretched necklace," said Lady Elizabeth.

"You think that is what killed her?" asked Lady Amelia.

"I know it," barked the old woman. "That diamond is cursed. It must be!"

And of course it made sense. Rebecca had put on the necklace and dropped dead. And yet . . .

"Forgive me, Lady Elizabeth," I said, "but while I was on the ship coming from France, *I* put on the necklace. I promised I wouldn't, but I did. And, well, it didn't kill me."

"I wish that it had!" hissed Lady Elizabeth. She rose from her seat, and her eyes blazed with life and fire and hatred. She pointed her cane at me. "You did this! You visited this curse upon us. I won't forget, Miss Pocket. Take that wretched stone. Take it and go!"

Matilda's eyes fixed upon the Clock Diamond. "But, Grandmother, the stone is much too valuable to give away to a *maid*. I wouldn't wear it, of course, but it would be a wonderful addition to my collection."

Lady Elizabeth regarded her granddaughter with a mixture of admiration and disgust. "I sometimes wonder if you have a heart, Matilda," she said.

Matilda said nothing but gazed darkly at the stone.

Lady Elizabeth used her cane to hook the necklace and lift it from the table. It dangled there, right in front of my face. "You and this instrument of suffering deserve each other, Miss Pocket. Take it, pack your bag, and get out of this house. You are not welcome here."

"Of course, Lady Elizabeth," I said. "I'll go."

And so I did.

Before I left Butterfield Park I passed by Rebecca's door on my way downstairs. Her room looked as if a tempest had swept through it. The floor was a battlefield of scattered clocks. They no longer ticked as one. The room had lost its heartbeat. I wondered what

they would do with all of those clocks now that she was gone. Bury them. Or throw them away. So I took one. It was small. Silver. Badly dented and scratched. With a brass top. I slipped it into my carpetbag and walked out of the great house for the very last time.

It is possible I heard the Duchess of Trinity's ghostly cackle as I closed the front door. It is possible she sounded thoroughly pleased with herself. But if I *did* hear it, I certainly did not show it. My days of talking with vengeful ghouls were behind me.

The rising sun dappled the tulips and roses, causing the petals to sparkle. I would take the train back to London. I would start over. I had one thousand pounds in my pocket. But what of my one thousand questions? They nipped at me like termites upon a log. Yes, I had *some* answers. I now understood the Duchess's role in this dark mystery. She had used me from the very beginning, to get revenge upon Lady Elizabeth. All that mattered to her was killing the old bat's pride and joy—Matilda. But instead, Rebecca had been the victim.

And my mother, dead and forsaken. Who was she? And how did we come to be in that awful house? And what did Miss Frost know that she wasn't telling me? And what of Miss Always and

her belief that I was the Dual she had been searching for?

Yes, I had answers. But not enough of them. Not nearly

enough.

19

I had a ticket to London in my hand. The train wasn't due for thirty minutes, so I sat down and waited. It seemed like a perfectly sensible thing to do.

"I trust you have the stone?"

Miss Frost was at the end of the platform. A dark horse stood grazing beyond the station gate. She walked across the platform and sat down beside me. "The Clock Diamond, Miss Pocket—do you have it?"

I nodded my head. "It killed Rebecca. She shriveled up like some sort of monstrous raisin."

"That is what it does," said Miss Frost crisply. If she was sorry to learn of Rebecca's death, her face betrayed nothing. But then she said, "Foolish girl! I *told* her not to put it on."

"I wore the diamond," I said. "I put it on, just like Rebecca."

"I know," said Miss Frost.

"Then why am I alive and she is dead?"

Miss Frost lifted the hem of her dress and pulled a small knife from her left boot. She grabbed my arm. Pushed up the sleeve of my dress. The knife hovered above my flesh. Naturally, I tried to pull away. But Miss Frost had an iron grip on me.

"What on earth are you doing, you mad cow?" I snapped.

Miss Frost pressed the sharp blade into my skin, slicing a straight line across my forearm. The cut wasn't terribly long. But it was most effective. I stared at the wound, but I didn't cry out. Not when the cut drew no blood. Not even when, in its place, gray mist coiled up from the wound like smoke from a tiny chimney. In moments the smoke faded. Then the wound healed over as if it was never there to begin with.

I simply said, "Am I dead?"

"When the Clock Diamond is worn, it is fatal," said Miss

Frost calmly. "No one has ever survived it before. That is what makes you of such interest, Miss Pocket."

So I was dead. Or something like it. It was a most peculiar feeling.

"Rebecca pushed you down the stairs to prove that you *could* be hurt," explained Miss Frost. "To prove that what I had told her about you wasn't true."

My mind was seething with slippery questions. *Could* I die? Would I get any older or be forever twelve (which would be violently inconvenient)? Would I continue to see ghosts? Would I always be so hungry? Would I develop a ghostly glow like the Duchess of Trinity?

Miss Frost seemed to read my mind. "For some reason,

you have survived the stone. Why, I cannot say. Perhaps we will never know."

"If Rebecca knew what the Clock Diamond could do, why did she put it on?" I asked.

"Rebecca believed the stone would lead her to the one person who really mattered—her mother. I tried to make her understand that your case was most unusual. That you only saw ghosts because you are, at least in part, a ghost yourself—but she would not listen."

A cloud passed over the sun, casting us in a kind of mournful shroud—more shadow than light. "Is Rebecca inside the stone?" I asked. "Is she trapped in there?"

"The Clock Diamond isn't a destination. It is a door."

"A door to where?"

"My home—and Miss Always's too. And before you ask, no, I will not discuss where I am from. The less you know, the safer you will be."

"Hideous creature!" I declared.

Miss Frost smiled faintly.

"If the stone is a door, why does it kill people?" I asked. "There must be a *reason*."

"The Shadow," said Miss Frost.

I frowned. "That silly plague Miss Always told me about?"

"It haunts my homeland, killing all but the lucky few who are immune. Once infection sets in, nothing can be done. There is no treatment. Nothing . . . except for one thing."

"Nothing except for *what*, you monstrous woman?" I was baffled. Befuddled. Dumbstruck. What on earth was she talking about?

"A very great woman by the name of Professor Peggotty Spring found a way to cross from my world into yours using the Clock Diamond," explained Miss Frost. "She planned to bring back medicine to help our people."

"And did she?"

"Yes." Miss Frost closed her eyes. "But it did little good. The story is long and rather gruesome, but in the end the professor settled in England and began experimenting . . . finally discovering that the very vehicle which allowed her to cross over—the Clock Diamond—was the answer to her prayers. If worn by a person from this world, his or her life force would pass through the stone, creating a powerful healing force in mine. It is terribly complicated, but the facts are not—the one thing that could ease great suffering in my world, would cause great suffering in yours."

I gasped and jumped up. "So Rebecca is there! Can you bring her back?"

Miss Frost looked rather uncomfortable. Just for a moment. Then she said, "She is dead, Miss Pocket—you saw that for yourself. Each time a soul is captured, it enters my world as a powerful healing energy. As you might imagine, this makes the stone very valuable indeed."

"It's a nasty business, this stealing of souls. Utterly fiendish!"

"You are right," said Miss Frost with a frown.

"How on earth did the stone end up with the Duchess of Trinity?"

"The truth is, I do not know. Over the decades, the necklace has been rather difficult to keep track of. Somehow the Duchess managed to acquire the stone and . . . well, I do not need to tell you what she wanted it for."

"Did you kill her?" I said, sitting down again. "Miss Always, I mean."

"Unfortunately not." Miss Frost stared off into the distance. "My sources tell me she returned home just hours after fleeing Butterfield Park." She was frowning again. "Under normal circumstance, the gatekeeper would *never* leave England without the stone—not without a very good reason."

Now it was my turn to frown. "You encouraged me to invite Miss Always to Butterfield Park. Didn't you know who she was?"

"Of course, Miss Pocket. Once I learned that you had tried on the stone and lived, I knew Miss Always would get foolish ideas about you. I suspected she would attempt to drag you away on the night of the birthday ball. As such, I wanted her within my reach."

"Miss Always believes that I am the Dual." I said this casually. "I'm sure it's all nonsense. But it *does* make me wonder why the stone didn't kill me, like it does everyone else."

"It is curious, I admit." Then Miss Frost arched her left eyebrow and glared at me doubtfully. "You have a great many talents, Miss Pocket—self-delusion, bad manners, general insufferability—but as for you being the savior of an entire kingdom? I think not. Besides, the legend goes that the Dual will be a girl of high birth. Which rather excludes a common maid, don't you think?"

I huffed. "Hideous woman!"

Then my mind flew to yet another confounding question.

"So if Miss Always is a gatekeeper, what are you?"

"I am Mistress of the Clock," she said, smoothing down the folds of her dress. "My vocation is to chronicle the Clock Diamond's history, monitor its use, and ensure its survival."

Which was awfully troubling. "If you wish to ensure the stone's survival, and you know that it kills the innocent," I said, "how are you any different from Miss Always?"

Miss Frost bristled. She may have even fumed. "I seek to use the stone *ethically*. Miss Always cares little who the necklace kills—young or old, healthy or ill. And she seeks to possess the diamond as a way of controlling fate. We are *nothing* alike, Miss Pocket!"

"Don't burst your girdle, dear," I said with heartbreaking good taste. "It was just a question."

Miss Frost stood up. "Hand me the Clock Diamond."

I wanted to protest (it was awfully tempting), but I didn't.

She took the necklace from me and hung it around my neck. "Right now it seems you are the only person in the world this stone cannot hurt." She slipped the diamond under the collar of my dress. "Tell no one about it. Let no one see it. Understand, Miss Pocket?"

I nodded.

Then Miss Frost pulled an envelope from her pocket and handed it to me. "Go to this address the moment you arrive in London."

I pursed my lips. "And what will I find there?"

"What you have always wanted. A home. A family."

I gasped. My mouth dropped open. "A family? Who? Who are they?"

"Good people." Miss Frost saw the curious look upon my face and sighed. "They have always wanted a child, and as it happens, I have one to spare."

I gulped. Such a thing did not seem *possible*. "You have told them all about me?"

Miss Frost frowned. "Not everything."

"This is terribly unexpected," I said rather meekly.

"Perhaps they should meet me first . . . what I mean is, I am *certain* they will adore me—how could they not?—but perhaps they should at least see me before—"

"Just be yourself, Miss Pocket," said Miss Frost. "The rest will take care of itself. Think of it as a new beginning. A fresh start." Her eyes softened. "Be happy, Miss Pocket."

I nodded. Didn't speak. Couldn't, really.

Miss Frost lifted her gaze, her eyes cool and sharp once more. "When Miss Always returns, she will think I have spirited you far away. The last place she will think to look for you is in London—the daughter of a thoroughly respectably businessman and his charming wife."

The word "daughter" thrilled me so.

"What is their business?" I asked, rather excitedly. "They build railways, don't they? Or perhaps they own hotels or banks or gold mines. Oh, it is sure to be gloriously important!"

Miss Frost allowed a small grin. "They make coffins, Miss Pocket."

The train rolled into the station, great puffs of steam billowing around our feet. Miss Frost picked up my bag and placed it in my hand. "You must not miss this train."

I decided the time had come to ask the only question that really mattered.

"Miss Frost, who was my mother? I suspect you know more than you are saying."

She did not hesitate. "Your mother is dead," she said. "Beyond that, I cannot help you." She pointed at the train. "Do hurry. It is about to depart."

I walked solemnly to the first-class carriage, where the stationmaster took my ticket. The carriage door was shutting behind me when I heard Miss Frost call my name.

She put a hand upon the window and said, "You will not see me, but I will be about."

I nodded. "Yes, I thought you might."

Then the whistle blew, and the train moved out of the station. I quickly found my seat and looked out the window. Miss Frost had not waited to see the train roll away. She was already on her horse, galloping to destinations unknown. And as shocking as it may seem, I missed her already.

Epilogue

Lulled by the train's jolting rhythm, my mind wandered to lost friends. Mr. Banks. Rebecca. And in a strange way, Miss Always. For I had lost her too. And, of course, my mother. For so long I had harbored a fantasy that she would come and take me home. But that wasn't to be. It was foolish to pretend it didn't hurt. But if these new sorrows settled inside me like a morning fog, shrouding my hopes and making happiness difficult to find—well, I felt certain it would not last. Misery did not suit me. I wasn't the type. And while I still had questions about the Clock Diamond and why it hadn't killed me, I refused to fret over them. I was bound for London. A new life. A family of my very own. There were sure to be wonderful parties. And glorious dresses. And a great deal of cake (not to mention raw potatoes). I won't deny a few nerves as I thought about all that was to come. But despite my fears and my sorrows, one thing was perfectly clear—I would be the most adored (slightly) dead girl in all of London. Perhaps even England.

Which was really no great surprise—for I have all the natural instincts of a coffin maker's daughter.

THE END

Acknowledgments

Thank-yous are a revolting business. One is expected to gush and praise wildly. Make heartfelt declarations of appreciation and whatnot. It's monstrous! Why on earth must I acknowledge people, simply because their efforts were instrumental in getting this book into print? Yet, if I don't offer undying gratitude to the small army of people who helped bring Ivy Pocket lovingly to life, there will be hell to pay. As such, I will be brief. Madeleine Milburn is utterly dedicated, hugely effective, and awfully loyal. As far as literary agents go, I suspect she is one of the very best. She is ably assisted by Cara Lee Simpson. Cara is smart and astute and thoroughly pleasant.

On the publishing side there is Virginia Duncan, who did a brilliant job knocking Ivy into shape. Sylvie Le Floch's art direction is rather wonderful—with great care and artistry, Sylvie has pulled all the pieces together and created a truly beautiful book. Barbara Cantini is an illustrator of whimsy and wonder. She has somehow managed to capture the Ivy Pocket of my imagination—which I put down to great talent. Or witchcraft. At Greenwillow/HarperCollins and many other publishers around the world, there are teams of people who have done terrifically important work bringing this book to market. If *Anyone But Ivy Pocket* roars into the bestseller lists, I offer you all my heartfelt thanks and a thousand good thoughts. But if Miss Pocket finds herself in the discount bin six months from now, then I wish each and every one of you a lifetime of disappointment and regret. Which is rather harsh, but there you are.

Closer to home, there are parents. Mine are above average and I thank them. Paul printed whatever needed printing. Carol urged me to stop waffling and write the damn book. Various nephews and nieces feigned interest from time to time—especially Shannon and Kaelin. While others urged me to prepare myself for literary failure—thank you, Dylan. Which brings this torturous groveling to a close. And if you happen to still be reading this, and you know what books can do—how they are a door to another world, how they are a refuge and a wonderland, how they thrill and comfort, how they break hearts and kindle hope—well, then there is no need for me to thank you as well. For you already know that life is simply better with books. And with that in mind, I would urge you to go out this instant and choose your next adventure.

Ivy Pocket

A PREVIEW OF SORTS

My task here, dear reader, is really very simple—I wish to tease and tempt you with a tantalizing glimpse of what befalls our heroine in the next part of her remarkable adventure. I am going to assume that you have only just finished reading *Anyone but Ivy Pocket*—I will also assume that you are now so devoted to Ivy that the thought of waiting until the publication of the next book fills you with unspeakable misery and a strong desire to tear out your hair. Which is not nearly as much fun as it sounds. Much better to tear out somebody else's hair.

Or, better yet, to read what follows—

I am about to reveal a great deal about the events chronicled in *Somebody Stop Ivy Pocket*. I shall describe in glorious and captivating detail exactly what befalls Ivy when she reaches London and begins a new life with the Snagsbys.

Get comfortable. Have a glass of lemonade at hand. Perhaps a cupcake. The odd bowl of popcorn. Your best pair of slippers and whatnot.

For I am about to begin. . . .

Oh, but *where* to begin? *Somebody Stop Ivy Pocket* is positively bursting with mystery and adventure. With danger and treachery. I could describe how Ivy befriends a gorilla with a peg leg and a tragic secret. Giving you a heart-stopping account of how they collect driftwood, bed sheets, and abandoned puppies and use them to defeat an evil, fire-breathing milkmaid. Or I could make your blood run cold, as I offer you a terrifying glimpse of the moment Ivy falls into a shallow puddle and isn't seen again for seven chapters.

The trouble is, none of these things actually happen. What *does* happen is monstrously unexpected and rather thrilling. And I would tell you all about it, if I wasn't so busy writing the infernal thing!

What I can say is that Ivy will find that her new life is not exactly as she imagined. The past casts a long shadow. London is a rather dangerous place. And friends are hard to find.

To say any more would spoil things, don't you think? I am almost certain that it will be worth the wait. I advise you to put down this book and wait quietly on a park bench until the next part of Ivy's great adventure is ready.

Until then, farewell.

a prized stallion

a junior Sherlock Holmes

a prima ballerina

a Buddhist monk

"For I have all the instincts of . . ."

a writer of penny dreadfuls

a princess in a tower

a stockbroker

an assistant librarian

a five-star general

a coffin maker's daughter

a physician

a sedated cow

a caterpillar

a postmaster's daughter

a highland hermit

a secret agent

a startled rabbit

a lion

a trapped miner

a cheese-maker's niece

a startled rabbit

a lion

an assistant librarian

a five-star general

"For I have
all the instincts of . . ."

a Buddhist monk

a junior Sherlock Holmes

a highland hermit

a cheese-maker's niece

a sedated cow

a prized stallion